Sometimes I Don't Love My Mother

N.N. CANALES

ISBN: 0996544798
ISBN 13: 9780996544795

FOR LOWE

PREFACE

I could have been a dancer. But my mother never put me in dance class, and it never occurred to me to ask her to until it was too late. She's the reason for why I will never be a lot of things: a loving daughter for one, a kind-hearted soul for two. And she's also the reason for why I am so many other things: unforgiving, bitter, angry, shrewd.

Blame. Yeah, I blame her. After all, she brought me into this world, and she was in charge of how I grew up to face it. There were so many things she could have done differently with me. Why didn't she? Who knows? Maybe it could have been conveniently explained with her being properly diagnosed. Well, maybe not exactly, but at times, when I would catch her talking to herself, I would wonder if she was all there.

And I've saved plenty of blame for myself. I blame myself for what my life ultimately turned out to be. But the fact still remains that I wouldn't have done any of it, not one single thing, without having her for a mother.

1

When I was four, my mother was pregnant, and I wanted the unborn baby to have the name of one of the Brady Bunch kids.

"If it is a boy, can we name it Greg, Peter or Bobby? And if it's a girl, can we name it Marsha, Jan or Cindy?" I asked my mother, who had been sitting in a recliner, as I knelt at her feet.

"Uh-huh," she said, not really listening to me.

"Mommy," I began, yanking on the tip of her gown, "how did you get the baby in your stomach?"

"By Daddy," she said.

"I know, but how?"

"By Daddy," she repeated, as if to end the conversation.

"Mommy, how? Please tell me," I said.

"Syd, not now," she said, not looking at me, staring at the TV but not really watching it. I felt smaller than I already was. I knew there was more she could have said. She could have made up something cute, like the stork story, or anything at all to let me know she was listening.

When Chance was finally born, I had aged a little bit, had grown thicker skin. I had been ignored before he had been born, so I didn't know that I should be jealous at all the attention he received. When it was time to pick up my mother and the new bundle of joy from the hospital, I rode with a friend of my mother's, Sally, to the hospital.

Sally was a typical '70s white woman: Patty Hurst-looking, extra long, thin blonde hair, with unassuming features. She was married to a black man and had four half-black children. All girls. I played with the youngest periodically.

While I sat in the hospital lobby with Sally, as my mother filled out some last-minute paperwork, she told me, "You know, your brother is a lot cuter than you were when you were born."

I'm going to tell my mother you said that, I thought. But I didn't. I just learned how to hold my first grudge. My mother never said a word to me during the drive home, but I didn't hold that against her.

It seemed as if there was a secret she knew about me that she was keeping from me but had told everyone else, so I felt as if I didn't really know her. That evening before Chance was born, I had sat at her feet until the Brady Bunch ended, saying nothing. There was no point. There was nothing I could do to win her attention.

I didn't know what to make of my mother, so the feeling of love I had for her was like believing in God, a relationship based primarily on something you could not see. And it was something I could not feel. I remember being on the street, or in a market or at the park, watching other little girls being embraced, their hair being stroked or kissed by their mothers. I would look on, trying to feel the stroke, imagining how it would feel against my skin, envying the affection and closeness from a mother that I did not have. I began to wonder why it was that my mother never touched me, because I'd seen other mothers showing affection towards their daughters, giving it naturally and with ease. She didn't ever hold me close to her bosom the way a loving mother would, squeezing me tight as if to keep me from being swept away from her by a raging current. She made me feel as if I had somehow floated away from her long ago, and if she knew how to pull me back, she wasn't willing to make the effort.

Still, she was like the Virgin Mary to me: perfect, pure, saintly. She was as beautiful as any woman needed to be. She was petite, with eyes the color of beach sand. Her skin was almost light enough that she could slip into the white world and pass. I used to think she actually was white when I was a child, but I didn't dare ask her, because I didn't ask her anything anymore. She had become like a museum piece I looked at from a distance. Yet somehow the distance I felt from her made me idolize her. She became like an expensive vase placed in the living room that I was forbidden to touch, and so I didn't. I was in awe of her.

I was sitting on the floor of our sprawling den, playing with my dolls when my mother casually blurted out that she had never wanted me. And when she discovered she was pregnant with me, she began taking hot baths in an attempt to get her period so she wouldn't be pregnant anymore. She said from the very beginning my father had been the one who truly wanted me to be born. He begged her to keep me, saying I would bring them luck.

I wondered how she could tell me something so utterly pointless and vile, and at that moment there was a part of me that wanted to cry. Instead, I stoically went back to playing with my dolls. My mother was no longer a saint in my mind. But knowing my father had always wanted me drew me even closer to him, and I fed off of that knowledge as if it was the only thing keeping me alive.

My father, Seneca, was the color of a Hershey Bar, handsome and lean, standing six-feet tall. His eyes were cocoa brown, medium-sized, and he had thick eyelashes that curled at the ends. When he was in a good mood and smiling, I would get carried away gazing at him and liked to pretend he was my prince. My father was my world, and he was the person without whom I would have been lost. He was the one thing I couldn't live without. Later in life, when my life wasn't much of one, I looked into his eyes and nothing mattered except that I was there with him. He had all the answers and always assured me I'd be all right. I was born to him, of his blood. He had always wanted me.

He was the ideal parent, easy to love and easy to believe in. There was nothing mysterious or vague about him, So I would grow up defining who I was by the relationship I had with him. It was at the core of my existence, and I put an extreme amount of faith in it, way more than I should have, because there was no way my father could ever realistically live up to my expectations. It would require him to give up on too many other things and too many other people; this was something that would take years for me to finally see.

The first time my love for my father was tested was when I found a stray dog in the street, in front of my house. The dog was small, mangy and dirty, just the kind I liked. I fed the black-and-white dog. Well, actually what should have been white was brown from dirt, and I basically thought of him as belonging to me. My parents decided to humor me for awhile by letting him stay for a few days, until about the third day, when suddenly my father sternly told me to pick up the dog and get in the car. I can still remember the sound the engine made from inside the truck, can feel myself bounce from the rough ride, and smell the motor oil on my father's hands.

I dream about that warm autumn day in slow motion, with burned leaves falling softly through the air to the ground. The wind smelled like dust that day in Sunny Beach, where I grew up under power lines. I was in the middle of the street, barefoot, feeling the newly paved asphalt sizzle my feet. I stood outside of myself, looking on as the breeze cradled my face. I remember my eyes narrowing with worry as I asked my father why I needed to get in the car. "Because we need to take the dog for a ride," he said. I got in the car, because in those days I didn't argue or resist, not even a little. I reluctantly did exactly what he said.

I rode in the car with my head turned away from my father, my eyes peering out of the window. I didn't want to look at him, so I have no memory of what the emotion was on his face as we drove off. I didn't want to know. I didn't want to see how he could hurt me and not care. I wanted to still be able to forgive him and love him after it all was over. I watched middle-class houses go by, all so quaint, with loving families inside; and I imagined how many minutes I had left with my dog, the dog I had grown to love in such a short time.

I imagined telling my dad how much I loved the dog, and that I really wanted to keep him, needed to keep him; that the dog gave me a sense of purpose, because I was a lonely child in a house with an older sister, an older brother and younger brother, all with whom I felt no bond. We shared only a roof and parents; we had no ties that would bind, as far as I could tell. The ties that should have bound us strangled me. As much as I was detached from my mother, I was from them.

I told my father that I knew what he was planning and resented him for it, but my mouth said nothing, my brain did all the talking. My body ached and quivered. I wondered how my father could not know that what he was about to do was not going to offend me, make me cry, make me want to hate him.

I was about to feel pain and anguish for the first time in my life, and I never learned how to let go of it, to befriend it, because it was like a family member that was always around and not going anywhere. It was a chronic disease that crept up on me when I least expected or wanted it to. Pain came when it felt like it, whether it was already raining or not, whether you had had enough already, whether you begged it not to.

My father stopped the truck, took the dog out of my hand, walked from the street to the sidewalk, and placed the dog over a short fence, into another family's yard as if the dog were their problem now. I did something I knew I would always regret; I looked back as we drove off. I watched my dog leap out of the yard and chase our truck down the street. I looked on as he went from the sidewalk into the street, running for dear life after me, after the hope I had given him of a warm box and food. I didn't turn away until I felt the tears well up in my eyes, and I let myself cry. I also made myself look at my father. I wanted to look at him now, wanted to see his face so I could allow myself to be angry with him.

That was the first and last day I felt real hate and anger at my father. After that, all the other times and reasons I had to be angry with him weren't as easy. I would forgive him for anything, even pretending he didn't deserve my anger, pretending it wasn't his fault; that my mother had something to do with it, or I genuinely deserved it. I couldn't willingly make myself a mental orphan.

At that time, I felt like an only child who just happened to have siblings. And I believed things would be better for me if I really were an only child, so I'd pray at night that they would be dropped off in another yard, the way my stray dog had been.

"You're so ugly, and you look like a boy," Lachlan, my older brother, said.

"Shut up, darky," I said in response, knowing that I would be striking the sharper blow. Lachlan hated to be called darky, because he was dark. His color, compared to mine, was like comparing a Mounds to an Almond Joy. I was the Almond Joy. He was obsessed with his skin color and his hair. He couldn't find a balance, or justification, or make sense of it. Our mother was so fair-skinned, and his father was a warm chestnut color. I was happy with my milk-chocolate brown color, and I found his unhappiness with his color to be something bordering on ludicrous.

I had the most contact with him out of my other siblings up to that point. He let me know he did not appreciate my existence, but he never really did anything to give me lasting hurt. He played practical jokes on me, like turning the hour hand on our clock to make me think my nap time had arrived, when it was still two hours away. And he liked annoying me by calling me names and hitting me in the back of my head as he swiftly passed by.

He was fun to watch, though. He was always doing something to make sure my parents didn't forget they had a son named Lachlan; whether it was mouthing off to the nuns at school, which meant my parents had to leave work to pick him up, or having my parents waste money on a tutor for him that he really didn't need. And there was the time he told the school he was being abused by my father. If he hadn't had a reputation at school for being a real piece of work, a problem, my father probably would have been locked up.

Lachlan was an active boy. He was in the Boy Scouts, loved riding dirt bikes, and he had a plethora of friends of all races and nationalities. He also had two dads. I envied him for that. I just had my bike and a cousin I adored, Minnow.

Lachlan enjoyed putting my parents through hell. When they were upset and fighting with each other over him, he was at his happiest. He had a different father than Chance and I, but my father treated us all the same. Lachlan just didn't want to be treated the same. Although my father had been around since Lachlan was in diapers, Lachlan never accepted the situation. He was like an illegal alien having the audacity to want to be here but refusing to assimilate. I pitied him, but not as much as I pitied my older sister, Casey, who shared the same father with Lachlan.

Casey was like a shadow passing by in my peripheral vision. She spent a lot of time in her room on the phone, even when she was supposed to be babysitting Chance and me. When I would eavesdrop through her door, while she was on the phone talking with her friends, I thought I was finding out what the sick world of being a teenager was like.

Casey was not popular, but she had a small following of friends. She did not meet society's typical standards of beauty, but she was very dateable because she was skinny and had a loose, fun personality. Her life was full of drama, thought of as pretty pathetic to my young mind. I was not a part of her world, which was fine. Her life even then teetered on destruction, and I was happy just to be a spectator, a spot on the ceiling she would never see.

I always assumed Casey would have a hard life, something that she would create all on her own. She and Lachlan had the same father, but she never visited him on the weekends as did Lachlan. Lachlan shoved himself down his real father's throat by making sure his father picked him up every other weekend, per the custody order. But my sister acknowledged that she wasn't wanted and decided to stay away.

As a child, I can recall no instances of real conversation with her, but I watched her, and I listened. Through her, I learned what not to do, what to look for, who to stay away from and what to become; anything but another version of Casey.

When she was sixteen, she smashed some guy's car she was driving before s+he actually knew how to drive. The car was packed with teenagers, and she allowed herself to be talked into getting behind the wheel. Seconds later, she plowed into a parked car. It was assumed I was sleeping in my bed when she came home crying uncontrollably, the kind of crying where you can't understand what the person is saying through all of the hiccupping and snot. She came in the house and went directly to my parents' bedroom, where they normally took care of business that had to do with Lachlan and Casey getting into trouble, especially since it usually occurred after the sun went down.

This worked out great for me because my room was right next to theirs, and from there I heard it all. I heard all the fights, the screaming and yelling, the cussing and things being shattered, spirits and hearts being broken. All I could think of was how sorry I felt for my father, for what he had married into, for the stress he must be enduring, and for what would be left of him for me.

So my parents would fix the problem of my sister smashing two cars, like they always fixed everything she did. I rode with my father on the day he went to pay for the damage. I remember thinking what an idiot she was when I saw the two mangled wrecks. Which is more mangled, I wondered, these tangled pieces of metal or my sister's brain? It was as if my parents knew they had created a broken child and kept a fix-it kit close by, always ready to make repairs. That day my father made Casey feel like they could solve anything, and after they were done with yelling and being upset they'd still love her.

To this day, my favorite kind of endings are not the happy ones but the bittersweet ones, the ones where someone has greatly won and someone has miserably lost. I revel in the endings that leave someone devastated, broken to the point of disrepair and leave someone triumphant but not so much so that there is no regret. I always wanted some of the devastation she caused to remain like a place where a bomb had just gone off, where you could see debris spread around for miles. But she was always all right, until the next time when she came home pregnant.

My mother had found a letter that Casey had written to a friend, where Casey had admitted to having sex with a boy from her high school, and Casey now feared she may be pregnant. When Casey got home that night, my mother confronted her. But that particular night, Casey was not going to be confronted; she was a woman now, and the other woman in the room, my mother, was not going to tell her what to do, intruding into her world.

"So who is this boy that you've been having sex with?" my mother demanded. "Didn't you know you could get pregnant?" Casey, at five-eight, towered over my mother, and to gain even more leverage, she moved her hands that had been dangling carelessly at her sides to her hips.

"Yeah, I found this letter in your room," my mother continued.

"And I guess this means you've been going through my things," Casey retorted.

"Why didn't you tell me this was going on? What is wrong with you?" my mother said, throwing the letter at my sister that she had balled up in anger. "Where have you been sleeping with this boy, and who is he?"

This was going to be a good one, and I couldn't wait for it to begin. Casey was going to get it now, but I knew I would have to lay as still as a statue in my bed if I didn't want my door to be shut. I was a part of it, as much a part of it as if I were standing in the lit room with the fireworks coming out.

"Cheryl's house while her parents have been on vacation," Casey said standing her ground.

"I asked you who the boy was."

"Well, why should I have to tell you? I don't ask you who you screw," my sister fired back, turning to go out of my mother's room, making the decision for everyone involved that the conversation was now over.

My young heart stopped, and I braced for the bomb about to go off. When Casey said that, she may as well have slugged my mother in the stomach. Somehow having sex had given my sister some confidence, that or just turning seventeen had, and she thought she could take my mother on that night. Did she really think she'd get all of that out of her mouth and still make it easily back to her room? I was impressed by my sister's newfound boldness, but I knew she was about to pay for it. I would pay in a similar way one day, only I wouldn't be nearly as deserving.

My mother lunged at my sister, who was half way down the hall at that point. She grabbed Casey, spun her around and pushed her through the rest of the hallway into her room, passing my bedroom. Once there, they began to really fight. I heard Casey scream as my mother punched and kicked her.

"You stupid bitch," my mother screamed.

"Mom, stop! Get off me!" Casey pleaded. My father tried as much as he could to stop my mother, but he didn't want to become a part of it, so he did little to break it up. So my mother beat the crap out of my sister, first taking the slippers she was wearing off her feet, slamming them against

Casey's face. Casey raised her arms in defense, but my mother hit those too, scraping them. My sister was chased all over the room like a dog chasing a cat, relentlessly. No matter where she went, she could not escape my mother. I heard every blow, and there were a lot of them that came with all the thumping and things breaking from hitting the floor or my sister.

"You can't control my life. I can do whatever I want," Casey whimpered from the floor.

"Then you can get the hell out of my house if you think you're grown. You've gotten yourself pregnant, and I'm not going to take care of it. You're not going to talk to me any way you want. You're so stupid. You haven't listened to anything that I've told you."

My mother and father left Casey's room with her lying bruised and swollen on the floor. My mother seemed tired, even though at the time she was only thirty-six. She didn't understand what she was doing wrong in raising my sister. My sister, on the other hand, didn't know anything about anything. She was a follower, doing things because it was what everybody else was doing, with no sense of herself.

But as always, the happy ending afterwards. My sister had an abortion and it was, "Poor Casey. How awful it must have been for her; maybe we need to give her more attention, and maybe we are too strict and have suffocated her."

The days that followed bore no traces of the ones before. Casey was Casey Angel again, and she went on with her life, having learned nothing. I remember thinking maybe she needed to be thrown out of the house and forgotten about, written off like someone doing life in prison; it's no use hoping they'll get out because you've already been told they never will. I enjoyed thinking how much better I was than Casey, luckier and smarter.

I didn't know then that I wasn't. She would be forgiven for everything until the second coming of Christ, and I would not be afforded any such luxury.

My parents had a lot less guilt to overcome when it came to me, so beginning with first grade, they had sent me to Catholic school.

2

Catholic school was like going to church all day, five days a week, year after year. We prayed when we got there, prayed before we went to recess, prayed when we got back. We prayed before lunch, and when we got back, and we prayed before we went home. We also went to church twice a week. Before long, I guess I became hardened to it. It became a chore more than a way of life and a belief.

Still, I knew I was better than the kids at the public school closer to my house that my parents said was free. The children who went there did not wear uniforms that were tailored just right, and they were not nearly as smart. When I entered Catholic school, I was six and very aware of myself; I already knew I was different, and feeling this way made me feel better about myself when I'd walk home from the bus stop and get called names by the kids attending the free school.

"Hey, black girl. Come here so I can sock you," a round-headed Mexican kid called after me. I turned to see him start to walk faster after me, so I began to walk even faster until I got a safe distance from him.

"When I catch you, I'm gonna kick your ass, cause you smell bad and you're ugly," he called to me.

"You poor thing. Too bad your parents can't afford to give you a decent education," I said to myself. "You're making fun of me because you're jealous. It makes perfect sense."

The mean Mexican boy did that to me for weeks, so I was forced into taking different streets, hoping he wouldn't be walking down one of them. I shuddered at the thought that I could run into him, and I was able to avoid him occasionally, but the times he did catch up to me, he tried his best to get me. If I were on the other side of the street, he would cross to it. I would then immediately cross back to the other side, and he would then follow. One day I got sick of it and decided to put an end to the torment I was enduring. He was interrupting my pleasant walks home.

On the days I walked home, I was in a different world. For the fifteen minutes that it took me to walk from the bus stop to my house, I was whoever I wanted to be. I pretended to be a singer, Natalie Cole, and I sang on the way home, careful not to get caught doing it. I sang, "From now on, babe, from now on, from now on, babe." I enjoyed the slight warmth of the sun on my skin as it enveloped me completely. I only escaped it if I walked underneath a tree providing shade.

But before I had been allowed to walk home by myself from the bus stop, my mother would meet me there, saying she needed to make sure no one kidnapped me. The act of her meeting me and her actually wanting to meet me at the bus stop confused me somewhat since I had grown accustomed to her indifference. I couldn't make sense of it, of her. I couldn't understand why she'd want to make sure I got home safely when she went out of her way to make me feel so completely unwanted.

She'd been laid off from her job at a paper factory, and she was a stay-at-home mom now. I was very independent at the time, mostly from being ignored and from having to comb my own unruly, kinky hair, because If I didn't, I'd end up going to school with unruly kinky hair. At that time, I even knew how to fix my own grilled-cheese. I went virtually unnoticed in my family, forced into fending for myself, so I resented my mother for meeting me at the bus stop to walk me home. One minute she couldn't be bothered with things like if I had fresh clothes to wear to school or if I even had lunch money, and the next she was trying to save me from some would-be kidnapper.

One day after the bus dropped me off, my mother was late getting to the bus stop to pick me up. She had always told me if that happened, to wait there for her. But I decided not to wait, and I walked home by myself. And not only that, I took a different street, one I knew she wouldn't be coming down. When she got to our house, pushing Chance in his stroller, I was already there, sitting smugly on the porch, because I had walked home all by myself and successfully avoided the boy who was trying to get me. I had proved to myself that day I didn't need her, something I would do for the rest of my life.

She was not amused and told me not to do that ever again because it scared her to death, and she thought someone had kidnapped me. I looked up at her, deep into her eyes, struggling to understand her fear. I so wanted to believe what she was saying was true, but feeling like she didn't love or want me was gnawing at me like I was a piece of meat. My childish mind ignored her request. I pulled the same thing on her several more times before she finally told my father, who promptly spanked me with his belt. I seethed at my mother after I came out of their bedroom rubbing the welts on my sore butt.

So there I was again, waiting at the bus stop angrily, while my mother was once again late, with the rising heat from the almost-summer sun cooking my eczema, making it hurt and burn.

"You see," I began, "this is why I wanted to walk home by myself. I don't have a long-sleeved shirt on today to cover my arms, and the sun is burning me," I cried while showing her my arms where the eczema had flared up. But she only looked on, giving Chance a cup of iced water to sip on for our walk home, practically ignoring me. I shamelessly cried as we walked the few blocks back home.

"It burns," I complained. When we got home, my body and anger were cooled by the air conditioning and my mother letting me watch the "Partridge Family" and "The Ghost and Mrs. Muir," while she began dinner. I snuck outside afterwards, though, and was beaten up by a boy named Ronny, whose birthday, he said, was on May 1. I remember this because my birthday was also in May. He had lured me down to his house that was three or four houses down from mine. He said he had wanted to play a game with me, but instead, he kicked me in the shins and told me to go home because I was ugly and stupid. I went back inside and said nothing to my mother about what happened. I felt as if I had deserved it since I had been foolish enough to fall for such a trick.

But even with having a jigsaw puzzle for a mother, the pieces strewn about in her head like jacks, the year when I was in the first grade was a great one, and I began to flourish with her at least being there with me when I got home from school. As I began to try to talk to her, attempting to tell her one of my typical kid jokes, like, "Hey, Mommy, why couldn't the skeleton cross the road?" she'd tell me to just go watch TV. And it became my favorite thing to do. I watched old TV shows like "Lassie," "Green Acres" and "Bewitched."

Unfortunately, my mother went back to work only a few months later, and she hired a family friend to pick me up from the bus stop. I resented her for that. The woman was practically obese, wore disheveled clothes on her body, and I could tell she didn't like me, just pretended to when my mother was around.

She gave me pancakes for lunch that had a strange, blue hue to them, that tasted gross. I threw them away in the garbage underneath her sink when she wasn't looking. I felt she had no business giving me pancakes for lunch every day, carelessly doused with syrup. I despised this wreck of a person named Tippy, who ended up ignoring me just like everyone else, so it didn't take long for me to decide not to wait for her at the bus stop. She immediately informed my parents, of course, and my father rewarded me by spanking me with his belt. But I had gotten to see Natalie Cole live for the first time at Tippy's house on the "Dinah Shore Show." My parents finally caved or simply decided whoever would attempt to kidnap me would surely bring me back I was such a nightmare and allowed me to finally walk alone from the bus stop to Tippy's.

"All right. I'm tired of running from you. You want to beat me up, then go ahead. Here I am," I said to my tormentor on yet another day he was out to get me. I was expecting to have to fight this Mexican boy, who lived in a house not as nice as mine and went to that inferior school.

"I was just kidding. Dang. Can't you take a joke?" he said, backing down from my challenge. I watched him cross the street and go inside a modest house with chipped paint, dying grass and a broken gate. I could tell it was much smaller than the large house I lived in, since my dad had put an addition on it, something that was a staple of the '70s. He probably has even more brothers and sisters than I do, I thought. I felt even more superior after that, and for years to come, I used the same tactic to deflate the arrogance of my enemies.

3

I'll just go ahead and admit I was a devious child. There was nothing delightful to be found about me. The nuns at the Catholic school I attended, Holy Innocence, were indifferent toward me. I know I was not well-liked. I was just some black girl who didn't get along with the other children, who frequently had to get an IOU for lunch because my mother kept forgetting to give me lunch money, the girl who really didn't shine. So I kept telling myself that one day I would.

The one bright spot of the five-and-a-half years I spent at Holy Innocence was my best friend there, Wendy. By the time we were nine, we were inseparable and everyone knew we were best friends. We ate lunch together and spent the night at each others' homes. Wendy didn't have a father and lived with only her mother. They had a small apartment in the lower income part of Sunny Beach, but my mother still allowed me to spend the night there. I felt as if she would have allowed me to spend the night with Jack the Ripper if I had asked. I remember thinking Wendy's mother was the type of mother I wished I could have because she put Ding Dongs in Wendy's lunch. I never had anything with sugar in it for lunch. In fact, my mother didn't even buy sugar. I had to eat Cornflakes, every kid's nightmare.

Wendy's relationship with God ran hot and cold. We were in church, and I was bored with the priest's sermon that I could never relate to, because at such a young age I was unable to grasp the full meaning of God and the Bible, the spirituality and goodness that went along with it. I wanted to crack jokes and laugh.

"Shhhh, be quiet, Sydney. We're in God's house," Wendy whispered. Her refusal to join in with my good time was annoying, and I resented her for it and felt betrayed. How dare she, I thought. She had showed me how to get away with stealing only a week ago. By the third grade, all the time I had spent in Catholic school must have rubbed off on me somehow, because it had never occurred to me to take something that wasn't mine. Wendy and I were on our way home and we stopped in the same corner market that we always stopped at to buy candy, only this time we didn't have any money. Wendy suggested we go in anyway.

"Take something," she said near the assorted candy rack positioned midway inside the store.

"But I don't have any money," I said, puzzled at the thought.

"So. It's easy. Watch this," she said, and she put some Mike and Ike's in her pocket and began walking towards the door. My eyes grew wide, and I marveled at what I had just witnessed, so I took something. I don't remember what, a box of Junior Mints, perhaps. I put it in my pocket and walked out.

"See how easy it is? I told you," Wendy said, as we walked back out into the sunlight that seemed brighter than it had been before. I squinted as I looked at Wendy.

"How long have you been doing this?" I said with the amazement of having just discovered something new.

"For awhile. My cousin showed me," she said shrugging her shoulders.

So that's how it started. It was passed down from dishonest person to dishonest person. I knew I was being used; I knew that if Wendy had someone else that was stealing alongside her, she would feel better about going back to God's house.

I had never felt a high like stealing something and getting away with it gave me, and it became habitual. A few weeks later, Wendy found God again and quit stealing. But it was already too late for me. I had found something new, and I liked how it felt to get away with taking something that wasn't mine. It made me feel good. Feeling good when I wasn't with Wendy was wonderful and different, so I wasn't about to give it up. In fact, I wanted to find a new recruit, a protege, to share in the dishonesty that I was engaged in. I didn't want God to see me be bad all by myself. I tried to get my cousin Minnow to steal with me, but Minnow was the quintessential goody-goody, even more naive about doing bad things than I was. He would have no part of it, so I continued stealing until I got caught and was embarrassed into stopping.

The owner of the liquor store nearest my house grabbed my shoulder one day before I could leave the store with my stolen loot.

"Hey, aren't you going to pay for that?" he said. I was thinking about how much he sounded like Captain Hook and my eyes bulged out.

"No, I don't have any money," I replied, shaking, thinking of my father's belt, not knowing what he had in mind for me next.

"Then don't come back in here unless you do have some money." Suffice it to say, that was the end of my thieving ways.

Minnow's mother was married to my father's brother, and our mothers were sisters. My mother always liked to say that that made us double cousins. We spent a lot of time together since both sides of our family were deeply connected.

Minnow had the Jackson 5 look back then in 1978, which meant that he had the typical afro but minus the fisted comb sticking out from the back of his head. He wore Wallabee shoes and cords when he wasn't wearing his Catholic school uniform. Minnow looked like a completely innocent child. All he needed was a halo to match his angelic eyes, nose and mouth. He was your basic adorable little kid, and the best part of all was he didn't realize it. It was an effortless part of his soul to be kind, and loving and good. I would have really disliked him if I had not been busy adoring him. He was even-tempered and sweet, two things that seemed to not be possible in my personality.

By my fifth-grade year, my hair was always thrashed; my socks hung loose around my ankles like two accordions, and I looked wild and untrustworthy around the eyes. The not-quite-faint scratches on my face didn't help either. I looked as if I had been in a cat fight and had miserably lost. Minnow had remained unaffected by the process of growing up; he just got taller. I, however, was just one or two more bad acts away from being miscreant of the year. I envied Minnow's ability to be fair and tolerant of people. But none of his good qualities were rubbing off on me, and I lashed out at kids whom I thought deserved my wrath.

One such kid was a girl new to our school named Carrie. She reminded me of a child lost, still living in the world of "Little House On The Prairie." Her uniform was visibly a hand-me-down. She had short, thin, strawberry-blond hair that always appeared to be tussled. Her face was freckled, and she was waif-like. She seemed out of place at my school, much unlike a city kid, and I decided within a moment of my first glimpse of her that I would not like her.

Carrie's innocent mistake was trying to befriend Wendy. One day before we were to take a test, Carrie didn't have a pencil and she asked Wendy if she could borrow one. I turned around just in time to see how nice Wendy was being to Carrie. As Wendy graciously gave the pencil to Carrie, I was appalled. That's all it took; I hated Carrie from then on, and I wanted her to know she wasn't going to come into the class all new and everything, with her I'm-so-innocent act and take my best friend away.

I waited after school outside of the bathroom where I had just seen Carrie going in. As soon as she came out, I kicked her in her shins.

"I hate you, you stupid worm," I said, waiting for her tears to fall. And they did fall, quickly, profusely, smearing the dust present on her face from being at school all day. Carrie looked so sad as she stood there crying in front of me, shocked and surprised. I could tell nothing like that had ever happened to her before. I hardened myself to it as I told her to watch it, and I walked off leaving her standing there with sore legs. I didn't care what she did after I left. I just knew I felt as if I had gotten revenge. I liked the way it felt to be bigger and stronger over her. I enjoyed what I had done to her, and I never thought about the repercussions, the consequences I would endure from her family or from the nuns.

I became a bully, though I didn't realized it then. Not only that, my ungodly behavior also had me lowering myself to where I began to take sweets from the other kids' lunches. I took a Reggie candy bar from the lunch of a boy named Shubert our lunches were stored in a closet, along with all of our other things, like backpacks and sweaters. It was quite easy. I would just pretend that I needed a pencil or something from my backpack and go into the closet and rummage through everyone else's things, until I found something sweet that I liked.

The smells of the different lunches I sifted through were so distinct. I knew how each and every child's house must have smelled when I stuck my nose in the individual bags. If the smell was poor, I'd move on. I felt no guilt since I stole only from the kids that I didn't like. Shubert had complained in front of everyone that I smelled, so he was a victim for which I felt no guilt. I can still hear Shubert's startled voice. "My Reggie. Somebody took my Reggie."

I was seated at my desk when he found out it was missing from his bag, praying I wouldn't get caught. Actually praying not to get caught for something wrong I did. And I never was caught or even suspected, but I did eventually stop. Well, I left the school, and that is probably the only reason why I stopped.

I was basically on a self-destructive path then. I didn't care about anything. I had just turned ten, despised my mother, my home, my life, myself. I was a miserable little girl. Wendy and Minnow were all I had, and I felt Wendy slipping away from me, making friends with some of the other girls in class, not paying as much attention to me anymore, or so I thought. Minnow was too busy being good and kind to get with my program, so I felt alone.

The beginning of the end of my days in Catholic school were drawing nearer. Things were about to catch up with me in the mild winter of 1980. In class, we received our report cards from our teacher, and I quickly noticed the Bs going from top to bottom. I looked over at Wendy's report card and caught a glimpse of it dotted with all As. I knew that I wasn't as smart as she was, but I knew I had worked harder than all Bs. I wondered why I couldn't have at least gotten one or two As. I've been so robbed, I thought. This is some bullshit, I reasoned. This is not right. This is crap.

It all worked to compound my downward spiral, and I hated the school and my new teacher, who was not a nun. We had started out the school year with Sister Bernadette, but she left in the middle of our school year and left being a nun altogether. The convent kept it hushed about why she wasn't going to be a nun anymore, but I made up a story in my head that it was because of a man she met someplace; he wanted to marry her, and she couldn't refuse him. She was a lot happier now.

The woman who replaced Sister Bernadette looked like a man. She had manly dark-rimmed glasses, wore manly dark-colored jeans, sported a manly haircut and no makeup. She had pale-brown hair, short, cut close next to her ears. I knew at the sight of her she would not be a pushover like Sister Bernadette. I didn't like her, so I decided I wouldn't talk to her, which was probably the reason for the Bs riddling

my report card. Needless to say, we did not get along. She was on to me, and she had seen my kind before. I thoroughly resented her lack of stupidity.

I was sitting at my desk, which had been recently rotated to the back of the classroom and within direct view of Carrie's, thinking about how since Mrs. Dean became our new teacher, the class wasn't fun anymore. I was seething, and at that moment I caught Carrie looking over at me for no apparent reason. I was instantly annoyed and directed my attention over to her, along with my anger and ill will. I raised my hand, balled it into a fist and gestured to her as I mouthed the words, "I'm going to get you after school."

Mrs. Dean was also watching, shaking her heard and looking at me like, no, you're not. I knew I would get to Carrie anyway. It hadn't been since Sister Bernadette was our teacher that I had gotten the pleasure of hurting Carrie and she was about due. The last time I had beaten Carrie up, had kicked her in the shins, she told Sister Bernadette. But I had already gotten on the bus for home, so she couldn't confront me until the next day.

"Carrie says yesterday, just outside the girls' bathroom, you kicked her in her shins. Did you do that?" Sister Bernadette asked, looking concerned, not wanting to believe that I, or anyone for that matter, was capable of doing such an overtly cruel act.

"It was an accident. Oh, did she think that was on purpose?" I suggested innocently.

"Yes, she did," Sister Bernadette said. "Tell her you're sorry the next time you see her." For a moment I wondered how long I would actually get away with tormenting Carrie, and I skipped down the playground to find Wendy.

So after school, just as I planned, I waited for Carrie to go into the girls' bathroom, like most of us did since we all had either a long walk home or a bus ride. When Carrie came out, I kicked her in her shins, where she stood in the doorway, which was partially shaded by steps leading up to our classroom.

"Stop kicking me," Carrie screamed. "It hurts. Why are you doing this to me?" Mrs. Dean, happened at the time to be coming down the steps to catch me.

"I'm going to tell the principal, and then I'm going to call your parents. You're a very mean girl. You hit her for no reason," she said with contempt I had never head before in a person's voice. She put her arm around Carrie and left me there. But my bad luck wasn't over yet. Carrie had a brother and cousin that went to our school, and on this day, I think Mrs. Dean told them what I had done and instructed them to take care of me. Brian was Carrie's dark-haired, chubby older brother, and, quite frankly, I was shocked he hadn't gotten involved sooner. Tony was her cousin, and he was taller than most of the other kids in our fifth-grade class. To me he seemed big and brawny. I had always been leery of him.

"We're tired of you beating up Carrie," they said, surrounding me. "Now, we're going to beat you up."

They both shoved me, and dust began to kick up from the black asphalt and from our shoes as we moved from side to side, with them punching and kicking me. They pounded me at the same time and roughed me up quite a bit. I could hack it, though. I knew I was getting what I deserved. It really didn't bother me; I just hoped I wouldn't bleed. I had been beaten up before, and it was no big deal this time.

Afterwards, I walked to the public bus stop with Wendy. I was glad that she had stopped at the doughnut shop down the street from our school and had missed the previous bus, so I wouldn't have to ride the bus by myself.

Wendy's bus stop came miles before mine, but I just didn't like waiting at the bus stop alone. While we had been walking to the bus stop, I discovered I needed to go to the bathroom. I hadn't gone as usual because instead I had waited for Carrie to come out, and now I was paying for it. I knew Wendy wouldn't wait with me for the next bus to come while I walked all the way back to school, so I just tried to hold it.

She seemed to not notice the missing buttons and dirt on my blouse. We walked along the busy highway as Wendy was more talkative than usual, but I couldn't converse with her. It was becoming increasingly more and more difficult for me to focus. My head was spinning, and my bladder was feeling like it was going to rupture. My mind raced between my making a run for the school bathroom and going behind a building. My palms and my forehead began to sweat. I knew I was in trouble, but I never actually thought I wouldn't be able to hold my pee. I was so wrong.

As Wendy and I approached the bench for our bus stop, Wendy was still gabbing, going on and on about school, with her words getting distorted inside my head, and I just couldn't hold it any longer. I stopped walking, while Wendy continued on, and I don't know what happened, but I just kind of slumped, or sat or even fell to the ground next to the curb with my feet stretched out in the street, and I peed. I had no choice as it came out.

My relief was short-lived, though, because some of the people on the street saw and were looking on in horror, except Wendy. She had been looking down the street, in the other direction. I got up from the ground and took my sweater from my backpack and tied it around my waist. Soon after, the bus came and we got on. I glanced back at the puddle of pee as I was boarding the bus.

As bad as my luck had been all day long, there was a pack of rowdy teenagers, mostly black, fresh from the high school, on the bus and no more available seats. I had to stand amid all the seated heads that would reach my waist and my wet and about-to-smell clothes. Wendy was lucky, she found a seat at the very first stop and she only had two more stops to go. I, on the other hand, had to take my lumps, though I was not surprised.

"Wait a minute," someone said. "Somebody stinks."

"It's her," someone else testified. "Oh, my God, did she pee on herself?" someone fretted.

Damn, I thought, this sucks. This just really sucks. I stood there, holding onto one of the poles in the middle of the bus, swaying as the bus rumbled down the street. As the teenagers on the bus laughed, I removed myself from it, trying to block it out so I wouldn't cry, not that I wanted to.

"She's not even cute," one girl accused.

"Yeah, and what kind of a skin color is that for a little girl?" another girl seated next to her commented. But I just stood, not noticing or caring whether a seat had become available with which to end my humiliation. I was not inside myself, and I would not allow myself to cry because I knew it was my fault, and crying would have been too easy, would have felt too good, would have eased the pain of my humiliation by making someone feel sorry for me. I didn't want anyone to feel sorry for me, because that would have made me seem weak, and I was anything but weak.

I walked the three blocks home from the bus stop with the sun going down in front of me, trying to think of a plan for how I was going to get out of the trouble I was in after I had been caught kicking Carrie.

4

I stood on the sidewalk in front of my house, swaying in the breeze, look-ing down, contemplating going in. The early evening wind was kicking up, making my wet clothes feel colder against my moist skin. So I walked along the narrow side of our house, passing through an old, broken wood-en gate my dad made that I used to be shorter than, that scraped across the concrete ground, reminding me of a dungeon door. I opened the screen to enter a house that should have been more of a comfort but was now beginning to feel more like my tormentor.

"Mom, that new teacher just keeps bugging me," I shouted into the open air, into nothing, unaware of my mother's exact location within the house. "She doesn't like me, and now I'm in trouble with her again."

"Come in here and pick out something you like," my mother calmly called to me. But I went to the bathroom and changed out of my wet clothing, reliving every awful moment with each tug and pull I had to go through to get free of the soggy mess. After changing into fresh play clothes, I rounded the corner of the kitchen to see my mother's brother, Bunchy, sitting at the table next to a bulging rack of clothing. I immedi-ately thought of hypodermic needles and syringes.

He was my mother's youngest brother, an off-and-on again drug addict and alcoholic for most of my life. He was six-four, skinny, light-skinned, and had an unkempt goatee and wild, curly hair that was growing at three different stages on his head. At this time, he was "off the sauce," as my mother would say as an excuse for letting him back into our home.

Today, he was selling clothes. I suspected they were stolen, and now he was selling them to family and friends at a discounted rate. The previous week my parents bought a hot TV from him, which I had been enjoying. I really didn't need to add receiving stolen property to my deviant behavior, but I was drawn like nothing before to the rack of clothes.

The story with Uncle Bunchy is the one time my mother allowed my sister and me to go with him for the day, we ended up somewhere in South Central L.A., in a dilapidated home where he was using a bong to get high with two or three of his friends. As I watched his lips turn a deep purple and his eyes shine over like a couple of glazed doughnuts, I thought to myself, and this is the person my mother chose to trust with my life today. Since I wasn't raped, which I had fully expected to be, I never told my parents what took place that day. And I'm sure, judging by the person my sister would later become, that it never entered her mind to tell them either.

A few months went by, and I hadn't seen him at all. Now, I was about to pick out a piece of stolen clothing that would help to change the course of my life forever. I stood from a distance looking at the clothes, not wanting to get close to my uncle until I absolutely had to, if I even had to. I spied a puffy, bright yellow-and-orange zip-up, hooded jacket that I loved. I moved closer to the rack and picked up the jacket, ignoring my Uncle Bunchy's presence.

"You'd better be nice and say hi to Uncle Bunchy," my mother scolded.

"Hi, Bunchy," I said succinctly, avoiding his eyes, wishing I could tell him what a real loser I thought he was. After I eased my arms in through the sleeves, I began admiring myself in the jacket. I liked the look and feel of it and envisioned myself sporting it to school. But I knew that particular jacket could not be worn to Holy Innocence, and that meant I wouldn't get to wear it very much at all. I doubted my mother would even let me have it since it couldn't be worn to my Catholic school. But I was salivating over the jacket, picturing myself wearing it, and at that point, I would do anything to have it. I marveled at the jacket, turning it from side to side, as I continued whining to my mother that I couldn't take it anymore at that school and that the teacher was unbearably mean to me, that I didn't want to go back there.

"What? You know, I'm tired of that school, too. You don't have to go back there. Maybe it's time for you to go to public school. I'll talk to your father when he gets home." And with that I had just sealed my fate. I couldn't know the consequences from leaving the comfort zone of my friends and a school that I'd been at since first grade. I figured leaving was better than taking responsibility for all that I'd been doing and especially what I'd done to Carrie.

I didn't want my parents to find out I had been a bully, a liar, a person who stole, that they really didn't know me at all. And by sacrificing my school and friends, they never would. And plus, I had that cool new jacket to start the first day of my new school in. I felt as if I was embarking upon a new beginning and everything would be great. Except payback just happens to be a bitch and karma a motherfucker.

I was going to be bussed across town to Fisk Elementary School. Until then I'd been riding all my life with senior citizens, the disabled, the mentally challenged; adults who were on the bus because they hadn't properly invested in their future, and other kids and teenagers like myself. The yellow school bus was foreign to me, something I did not understand, housing a pack of wild animals jumping around outside of their cages. But I was about to get a crash course in what to do when you find yourself abruptly immersed, riding on a bus with lower-income black kids 101.

I walked on a dirt pathway along a busy street to my new bus stop. The steps I took were heavy and long as my new reality was becoming clearer. I could see before I even got there that the corner where the bus would now be picking me up was bustling with kids. Some were playing in puddles of water, running around playing tag. There were kids dancing and listening to Walkmans. It was only a few who conducted themselves with any degree of tact and decorum.

I crossed the street and stepped on the curb to wait for the school bus with everyone else. A wave of self-consciousness splashed over me like a tossed bucket of paint, clinging to every part of me as I stood very aware of myself. I so wanted to become invisible when I heard giggles. I assumed they were laughing at the jacket I was so proud of. A boy I could see out of the corner of my eye, who was pointing and smiling in my direction, confirmed my assumption. I stood in one spot like a statue. I thought if I didn't move they would stop noticing me.

The school bus finally arrived already half full with rowdy kids and halted itself right in front of me. The doors swung back, opening to me like the entrance to a space shuttle. I stood there for a moment contemplating my next move: Talk to no one, only speak when spoken to, try to look nonchalant, act like I'm above it all, I reasoned as I ascended the steps.

I rode in a seat with no one next to me, peering out the window, cut off from everything else going on around me. I may as well have been on my way to Cambodia it was all so unfamiliar. A paper airplane whizzed by my head and Walkmans buzzed with music. The bus driver was bobbing to his own music. A football was being tossed around, as the air filled with the sounds of overly loud conversation, joke-telling and laughter. Kids were getting up and changing seats, running back and forth to quickly hit someone they were taunting. The bus driver only got annoyed when his favorite song came on and he couldn't hear it through all the noise.

"Hey, now everybody got to be quiet. This is my song," he said with one hand waving in the air. Jerome, the driver of the bus, had a Jheri curl dripping with oil and a mouth full of gold-capped teeth. "Part-Time Lover" by Stevie Wonder played on the radio, fighting to be heard over all the commotion.

I guess it didn't matter that what was going on resembled a war once his favorite song came on. I had a hard time believing I'd actually survive all this until the end of the year.

I found the location of my fifth grade class easily enough, and my teacher introduced me to the class and assigned a girl for me to sit with who would show me around. Her name was Jody. She was eager and smart, with pale, lightly freckled skin, and hair the color of midnight falling down her back. Our friendship began with a smile and blossomed over the chipped beef sandwich and rhubarb sauce we ate for lunch that day.

It took a while for me to realize that Jody was not a part of the in crowd, which should have come as no surprise since my introduction into the class had been painfully uneventful, and it was easy to see since none of the other popular, good-looking kids really talked to her or me. They just sort of didn't see us and looked through us as we passed by.

I noticed only two of the kids from my school bus were actually in my class. The rest were spread throughout the school or stayed on the bus to be dropped off at the junior high school next door. There were two different fifth grade classes to accommodate the large amount of fifth-graders, and most of the black kids ended up in the fifth-grade class that I wasn't in. I had gotten special treatment because I was transferring from a private Catholic school, which was known for producing smarter than average kids, which meant I was placed into the smarter fifth-grade class, a class with two other black kids besides myself.

I wasn't complaining, though. The morning ride in with them was all the affirmative action integration I needed. I was safe in the classroom. However, the playground was another story.

"Hey, you, come here," called a tall black girl who was large for her age and had breasts bigger than my mother's. I'd just released my hands from the monkey rings I was sailing on, falling gracefully down to the blacktop. I squinted to see who it was. Unimpressed, I turned my back to her and went to find Jody, who hadn't returned from the bathroom yet.

"You know you hear me," she called. I kept going. She grabbed a short, pig-tailed, scraggly friend of hers, and they both caught up to me and accosted me near the handball courts. The clothes they wore resembled the ones my mother took to Goodwill, having decided they were no longer nice enough for me to wear.

"What, you think you better than us?" she chided.

"No. What gave you that idea?" I said sarcastically, inspecting their clothing to see if any of it had once belonged to me.

"Well, you hanging out with that white girl."

"And?" I said with my eyebrows raised.

"What, you think you white or something?" she said. Towering over me, I could feel her hot, toasted breath blowing against the top of my forehead, displacing my hair.

"Umm, yeah, I get away with it every day. I'll be Chinese tomorrow."

"Look, bitch, we ain't playing with you."

Startled, I blinked back the shock I was now feeling and imagined myself taking two steps back. My ears had never heard a kid cuss on the playground before. I'd never been called an expletive. I knew then that I wasn't in Kansas anymore and there was no one to save me. I wasn't like these new and improved black kids born in the '70s, after the Civil Rights Movement, a byproduct of bussing. These kids were tough.

Just hours after I arrived, I'd watched them bully the white kids into submission. I hated the way they were able to strike fear into their eyes. I discovered virtually all the black kids were bussed in, and the white kids lived near the school and walked or rode their bikes home. The white children felt invaded when the bussing started years before, and the black children felt like refugees ready to take prisoners.

I was in for a brutal shock, having come from a different world, landing somewhere in the middle, after having been at a school resembling a melting pot of Asians, Hispanics and Caucasian children learning together without any racial acknowledgment. My parents never told me that there were black kids growing up in poor conditions, without fathers, without the guidance I had. I didn't know kids were cussing at school. For that you'd get the paddle at my old school. These kids were ruthless, and mean and hostile. But I wasn't going to back down or show the fear I'd seen going on around me. I was prepared to get a bloody nose and scuffed knees first.

"I don't think we like you," big boobs said.

"And I don't care," I said, continuing with my indignant attitude.

"Well, you will when we kick your ass after school today," she said. Now, the bully was being bullied. I wasn't ready for that. I would find out from Jody that the bully's name was Porsha and her scraggly friend was Cleo, and they rode on the same school bus I did.

"Good luck on the bus," Jody said, through the sound of the 3:00 school bell ringing, signaling the end of the day. I raised my eyes to the clock to be sure it was time to go. I liked Jody tremendously. I kept calling her Wendy from time to time, but she didn't mind. Jody was positive, creative, and seemed to like me back. We drew our own mazes and exchanged them. Hers were always better than mine.

"I'm not afraid of them, Jody," I said positively. Jody paused a moment in disbelief and told me good-bye and that she would bring bandages and gauze pads with her to school tomorrow to help me dress my wounds. Then she rode off confidently on her bike.

I waited near the chain-link fence that was the boundary between the school and the sidewalk, with the sky growing dark, ominous clouds appearing, the wind kicking up and blowing like rain was about to pound the earth. I searched the crowd like an eagle for Porsha and Cleo. Moments later, three different busses came barreling down the street to pick us up. Teachers were strategically positioned where they could see everything that was going on in case trouble broke out, so Porsha and Cleo were nowhere to be found. I took a seat in front, directly behind Jerome, and waited for the bus to fill.

Porsha and Cleo got on together, finding me right away. My plan to sit in front had backfired. I would have been better off trying to blend in in the back amongst the Jheri curls and backpacks. They proceeded to sit in the empty seat directly behind me, saying nothing, but I could feel Porsha's Cheeto breath blowing on my neck. Cleo whispered into my ear that they were going to beat me up when I got off the bus. I swallowed hard and froze in my seat. I began to panic and feel sweat trickle down the sides of my hairline.

I tried to imagine what they would try to do. I wasn't looking for trouble or embarrassment. I thought if I was the first off the bus, then maybe I could get a good running start. Kids frequently ran after they got off the school bus, to be the first across the street, so no one would suspect that I was running from a fight.

When the bus approached my stop, I stood up before the bus had come to a full halt and stood in front of the doors without Jerome noticing me there. The bus stopped, the bus doors swung open, and I was hit in the head by one of the doors. My head snapped back from the blunt force, and I was in a daze of confusion and seeing stars. But there was no pain. I barely felt the thud from the heavy rubber-trimmed door and hadn't yet realized I was bleeding.

Jerome jumped out of the driver's seat and sat me back down, telling me he would be calling dispatch for help. Jerome had positioned me in the seat in front of a large mirror overhead that reflected my sad image clear to the back of the bus for all the kids to see. The school bus erupted in laughter at my appearance. I had a red, inch-long gash on my forehead, with blood slowly pulsating from it. I looked disheveled. My hair was out of place. I truly wanted to disappear, never to be heard from again. Oh, that new black girl, she's gone. Nope, we don't know where to. As a million thoughts raced through my bashed head, I asked myself how could I do it? Why didn't I just wait? I sunk into feeling like an utter loser and total moron.

My father happened to be driving by and saw the bus's flashing lights with my head in a slumped position propped up against the window from the opposite side of the street. He parked his car and sprinted over to the bus. Jerome was hysterically apologizing to my dad, with spit collecting in between his gold caps, explaining that he hadn't seen me there when he opened the doors. My dad calmly took me out of the seat and drove me to the hospital. I had to get stitches, and Porsha and Cleo would have to wait to kick my ass; the day already had.

The Band-Aid above my bruised, half-closed eye now made me an uninteresting target, and they left me alone for the rest of the school year. I wondered what would have happened to me if I had just stayed at Holy Innocence. Well, I probably would have gotten the paddle when the principal, Sister Mary Agnes, found out about Carrie. My parents probably would have finally found out that I was no angel. I would have stayed at that school until the eighth grade and then gone on to the Catholic high school, Saint Anthony. Wendy and I would have applied to college together, then on to law school, where I would meet the man of my dreams, living happily ever after.

I wished more than anything that I could turn back the relentless hands of time and have things back as they were. What had I done to myself? Reality now was that a year-and-a-half later, after I finished the sixth grade at Fisk, I would continue to ride on the same yellow school bus with the same jerky black kids, going half a block farther down the street to Crawford Junior High. The worst was not over yet. Fate was not done with me.

5

My friendship with Jody lasted throughout fifth and sixth grades, spilling over into seventh. We had devolved into two of the most socially revolting seventh graders ever. We were nerds. We had gotten caught up in the elementary school time warp and couldn't get out. We still believed boys had cooties. I actually wore a baby-blue, plastic Smurf jacket, a short afro and glasses. And everything Jody carried to school was from Hello Kitty, known for its chain of stores that catered to the likes of little girls. They sold school supplies, plastic purses, stuffed animals and other miscellaneous things. Their logo was something that looked like a small, white, fluffy cat that could be found on the front of most of the merchandise, in different shades of pink. With Hello Kitty and Smurfs, we were the epitome of innocence, perfect for ridicule, and lunchtime was the perfect setting.

Passing the ninth-grade boys and dodging the birds that circled above, dropping their waste at random, was our lunchtime torture. As Jody and I made our way through the staggered lunch tables to our favorite spot, a table full of ninth-grade boys laughed at us as we went by.

"Oh, my God, here comes Smurfette," one boy said, making his voice sound like an Englishman's.

"Yeah, and her sexy sidekick Hello Kitty," another boy said using the same accent.

"Why must we go through this every day? Why can't they just leave us alone?" I asked Jody, setting my tray down, frustrated with the whole junior high lunchtime scene.

"Because they're dumb," Jody said. "And we wouldn't be in seventh grade, and this wouldn't be junior high if we weren't made fun of on a consistent basis, Sydney. There's nothing we can do about it except to just realize it's a part of our junior high experience."

Jody was not doing a good job at convincing me to take on her pragmatic approach, and I could still hear their laughter behind us. Now I felt I was fighting an additional war to go along with the one I was already fighting at home. I'd been called enough bad things while getting my public school education that by then my responses were normally over the top. I turned and looked at the table of boys seated behind us.

"Shut up, you dirty bastards," I screamed. A boy who'd been left back a grade more than once, resembling Fat Albert, and growing facial hair prematurely, stood up immediately, flinging his hands up in the air.

"What, you want some trouble? You want some of this?" he said. "You want a piece of me, little bitch?"

I turned back around to face my food, having no choice but to back down from his challenge, while a clump of swirled, black-and-white bird poop, the size of an apricot, was falling like a bomb through the sky in my direction. It continued through the air, gaining momentum as it entered my airspace, landing in my mashed potatoes and gravy, splattering my nose and mouth. I couldn't leave the area fast enough. What was it about junior high that brought the worst things out in kids? Trying to solve that question was right up there with what really happened to JFK and Marilyn Monroe.

I sat in fifth period math class, not paying attention to the lesson, mutilating my pink eraser with my Number 2 pencil, angry about my empty stomach, hoping the school bus ride home would not be any more painful than usual.

I had become somewhat of a cult figure on the school bus, the freak who was almost murdered by the school bus driver after he deliberately flung open the school bus doors in an attempt to get rid of me because he was so annoyed by my existence. Jerome had been fired, forever taking with him the story of what really happened, so the truth remained distorted. I became a pariah. No one cared to sit next to me or get to know me; they were probably afraid of the shiny, half-moon shaped scar left over from the stitches on my forehead. I hadn't done anything to deserve that treatment. Or had I?

I couldn't understand why the kids, particularly the black kids, did not like me, why I didn't belong to one of their cliques. I grew tired of the monotony from just being friends with Jody, as I watched from afar the black kids clowning around, always laughing, telling stories, and appearing to be having the time of their lives. They seemed untouched by the brutality of the junior high experience, and I finally wanted to be a part of it all.

I made friends with Drew, one of the more subdued black girls at the bus stop. She had hazel eyes, caramel-colored skin, and smooth hair. She was daintily pretty. She was a part of the in-crowd of black seventh grade girls, and I tried to charm my way right into her clique by complementing her eyes.

I waited for the day Jody finally got sick and didn't come to school and asked Drew if I could sit with her group for lunch. She happily obliged. There were five different girls, including Drew, who belonged to the group, and wanting to be their friend was not something that would turn out to be to my advantage.

I walked earnestly over to their designated table during lunch, a step or two behind Drew. We passed the table where the evil ninth grade boys liked to sit without a peep from any of them. My Smurf-jacket-free body had escaped their ridicule. They hardly noticed me.

Drew and I stood in front of the lunch table full of girls, facing east, with the mild October sun at our backs, casting an angel-like glow upon our brown faces. I felt like a specimen underneath a microscope. There was Eva, who was a shining example of the overly developed seventh grade girl, made apparent by the huge breasts she had overtaking her body, sticking out from her chest past her feet. She was very popular with the boys. I was convinced the acorns I had for breasts were the product of some sick joke God decided to play on me.

There was Felicia, an inconspicuous-looking, dark-skinned girl with thick, coarse hair brushing her shoulders. She seemed nonthreatening and decent enough, not the type to stir up trouble. My eyes tightly closed and opened again when, to my dismay, Cleo, my arch enemy, was sitting quietly next to the girl whose demeanor told me she was the leader of the pack. Porsha had gotten pregnant and was sent down South to have the baby and escape the shame. Cleo had been left to fend for herself and hadn't done a bad job at it. She was second in command.

Yolanda, the obvious leader, sat like a panther at the head of the lunch table. Her skin was the color of coal, but her features were very fine. She had thin lips and a thin nose. She seemed to rule over the girls with a smoothness like butter. It was as if she'd never asked them to follow; they just did. No one laughed unless she did. No one admitted to liking the school lunch unless she did. She appeared to be wise and mature. I wanted to be on her good side, because I believed at that time she actually had one.

"Hey, guys, this is Sydney," Drew announced. They all said a marginal hello, except for Cleo. She leaned over and whispered something into Yolanda's ear. Yolanda looked at me, giving me a curious smile. I sat down to devour my food and noticed that all of them were watching me. Eva's thick lips whispered something to Felicia. I became uneasy and suspicious of what had just been said about me.

So this was it? This is what I couldn't wait to be a part of, this bullshit of a clique that I knew deep down would only betray me. But it felt good to be a part of something bigger than just Jody and me, so I would try to make the best of it. I told myself I would eventually fit in. I just had to kiss butt and be as nice as possible.

For months I hung with them in the morning by the girls' gym and ate lunch with them every day. Seventh grade and my misery seemed to pass by like water dripping from a faucet, never ending until someone decides to put a stop to it. I oftentimes had nothing to add to the conversations going on around me. I had nothing in common with the other girls. It was as if I stayed within myself, inside a self-made prison I could not find the keys to. I placed myself next to five charismatic, popular girls, but

I was in a verbal solitary confinement. I could never think up anything interesting to say. Was it because I was so different from them? Was my life at home so foreign that I could not carry on the normal conversations of a thirteen-year-old girl? What was wrong with me? Interesting words and phrases, stories and jokes, eluded me. I was a bore.

By betraying Jody, I'd inadvertently betrayed myself since she was the only one who truly liked, understood, and accepted me, and I had given her and our friendship up at a chance to for once be popular and well-liked. Jody was blossoming and becoming acutely aware of who she was in the world of junior high, and she carried on, bouncing right back, only to thrive from my leaving her. She joined the science club and made new friends, smart friends, worth-something friends, friends that would last her well into her fifties.

Our friendship ended as easily as it began, without words. One day at lunch Jody had called to me from the table we had always shared. I was at the new table I was now sharing with my supposed new friends. I kept my back to Jody and never turned around. She got the hint and left me alone. Maybe she thought it was a black thing. Maybe she thought she'd done something wrong. Maybe she knew I'd get what was coming to me.

Eva was having a birthday party at a roller skating rink. Word about it filled the school hallways like smoke. Everyone wanted to go. I thought, like everyone else in the group, I naturally would get an invitation, and I waited with anticipation for it to come. It never came. That Thursday, two days before Eva's party, I became frantic from not having yet received an invitation. I remained silent while the girls and boys around me discussed the impending event.

"So, are you going to Eva's party, Sydney?" Felicia, asked?

"Um, yeah," I lied, with my nervousness intensifying.

I knew I had to do something or I would suffer the embarrassment of the year. I'd look like an outcast for sure if I didn't get an invite to that party, so I hunted down the only person I knew who could save me. I waited after school near Eva's locker. I watched her come down the hall, breasts bouncing recklessly from side to side. I tried to wipe the worried look I wore off my face.

"Hey, Eva," I said.

"Hey," she said not looking at me, beginning to work the combination to her lock.

"Well, I didn't get an invitation," I said.

"Well, yeah, I didn't send you one," she said as a matter-of-factly.

"But I really want to go, Eva," I began to pathetically plead, and if she'd had a throne, I would have flung myself across it I was so desperate.

"Well, my mother said I could only invite so many people," she said.

"You can't invite just one more?" I asked.

"Nope. I can't. Sorry," she said dismissing me. In the last few months I'd been sitting with the group of girls, in that moment it was evident that I hadn't formed a bond with Eva any more than I had with anyone else. Not being invited to Eva's party was their way of telling me that I hadn't been accepted, I was being tolerated. My being a part of their group was all an illusion. They'd let me sit with them at lunch because I was fun to watch. To them I ate funny, fast, and had become the object of their amusement. When I started to eat, they would poke each other, watch and giggle. I had been oblivious to it all.

"Are you going to Eva's party, Sydney?" Craig, a boy in my economics class, who I was sure was destined to be gay, asked me later on that day.

"Yeah," I said.

"But I heard you didn't get an invitation," he countered in his dead-give-away lisp.

My world was caving in on me, and I couldn't see the sun for the rest of the day my mind was so foggy, my prospects so bleak. I stayed home that Friday as a way of passing the day without having to deal with not being invited. Felicia, the one I had underestimated as quiet and inconsequential, was behind it all. She secretly hated my guts. I never suspected there had actually been a Mafia-style conspiracy not to invite me. Felicia made the request, and the order was sent out by Yolanda.

I decided to have my own roller skating party on Saturday afternoon in my driveway, and I was the only one invited. At that time shoe skates were all the rage, and luckily I owned a pair. I was keeping myself company, doing figure eights in the driveway, wishing I had a friend. But I'd felt alone my whole life, and that cold, desolate place called loneliness was all too familiar. Returning to it wouldn't be too difficult. I'd been there before.

Monday morning while riding on the bus, doing my usual, looking the whole time out of the window at nothing really, I was able to forget about the party I hadn't been invited to. A wild pack of girls surrounding one of the concrete poles that stands just outside the girls' gym was about to remind me, though. I walked over hesitantly, pushing my way through them to see written on the pole in bold black: "Did you have fun at Eva Pringle's birthday party, Sydney?"

The fuck I did, I thought. I wasn't even invited. Horror and embarrassment began to boil inside my body, and the music from the shower scene in "Psycho" was playing in my ear, and I had never in all my life been as humiliated. Why did they need to add insult to injury? I had already not been invited. My eyes were fixated on the pole, reading it over and over again, with stress wrinkles protruding on my face.

"Well, did you?" a voice, so familiar it felt like a warm blanket, came from behind me, almost bringing me to my knees. I hadn't heard that voice in months. I turned to see Jody standing there before me, like she'd just won a bet.

"Did I what?" I said softly, my words cracking, barely able to form in and leave my mouth.

"Did you have fun at Eva Pringle's birthday party?" she asked with her finger pointing out each word.

"No, I didn't," I whispered, unable to look at her as I turned to walk away. I know Jody watched me for a long time as I walked aimlessly down a winding sidewalk behind the school gym, like a vagabond, passing every school building there was on campus. I didn't stop until I reached the end of it and there was nowhere else to go but back.

I reluctantly went towards my next class, while feeling angry with myself that I couldn't go back to being friends with Jody. The trust we once had was lost forever. I couldn't go back to being friends with Wendy. She was at a different school. I couldn't go back to that school because I probably wasn't even smart enough anymore after almost two-and-a-half years of an inferior public school education, which meant

I couldn't undo what I'd done to Carrie, which probably was the cause of all this madness anyway.

My head hung low, with my eyes halfway open, and my senses became numb when the next day, "Cydney loves Gene" turned up on another pole just outside the girls' gym. Gene was a boy in the eighth grade with disgusting, ashy skin, matted hair and dirty clothes. It was a disgrace to have to even breathe the same air as he did. They just aren't going to stop, I thought, standing in front of it. Someone came up to me and asked if it was true, did I really love Gene?

"I don't know if it's true or not. That's not me. My name doesn't start with a C," I said, as matter of fact. The very next day the exact same thing was written on the same pole using my name, only this time it had been spelled correctly, using an S.

I went to the P.E. teacher, Ms. Delusha, and asked her to remove everything. Ms. Delusha's wrinkles were so deep they were like ditches winding their way through her face. She was tall, agile, with spiky gray hair, and I figured she had to be like a hundred. The understanding look shown on her withering face told me she knew just how fucked up it all had been. Later on that day, as she was rubbing away my humiliation with her pitching arm, I overheard her accusing Cleo of being the graffiti artist.

"I swear, I didn't do it. Dang," Cleo pleaded.

"Yes, you did. I know you did it, and you're lucky I don't tell the principal," Ms. Delusha threatened.

It was fun to watch Cleo squirm, and I started to feel the need to watch the others squirm as well. I waited until lunchtime as Cleo, Drew, Yolanda, Eva, and Felicia were assembled at the lunch table. There is nothing more dangerous than a girl with nothing to lose, and at that moment that was definitely who I was. I stepped up to them with my head held high.

"I know what you all did, and I know none of you really like me. The whole thing was really mean," I began. They stared at me as if I had thirty seconds before I would lose their attention. The words about me on the pole flashed before my eyes, and I grew enraged.

"You bitches. What did I ever do to any of you? All I wanted was to be friends," I said angrily.

"Now, wait just a minute," Yolanda started.

"No, you wait. You don't have a dad, do you? You either, right, Felicia? Or you, Cleo, Eva, Drew? But I do." I paused to allow them to regain their composure, but I wasn't finished yet. The fear in their eyes was feeding my anger and I grew stronger.

"Felicia, I hear you live in a dusty, old, drug-ridden apartment, and your mother's never home." Yolanda, you're poor too, aren't you? Shall I go on, ladies?"

"No, you don't have to go on," Drew said, her eyes tearing up. "I've heard enough. And you're right, I don't have a dad. He split when I was a baby," she said with her tears falling. All I could see when I looked into Drew's tear-streaked face was Carrie's. And for the first time I felt sorry for what I'd done to Carrie, and I wondered what had become of her. Was she still traumatized by what I'd done? Were thoughts of me disrupting her sleep at night? Were there any scars left over on her bruised shins from my unforgiving kicks? Had she become withdrawn, untrusting, catatonic?

I closed my eyes, raising my head slightly up to the sky, with the sun radiating down on the back of my eyelids, asking God for forgiveness. I wanted his glory to reach out and touch me, wash over me, saving me from the self-made fiery hell I was engulfed in. My faith had indeed survived public school, and I knew God was watching.

"I'll never talk to any of you evil bitches again," I said. Yolanda stood up as if I had destroyed nothing. She used her popularity as a shield. She knew I was meaningless, an insignificant part of life at Crawford Junior High, a cockroach. I had only wounded her and the others with my words, and I was about to be shot dead with hers.

"Maybe all that's true, but just who do you have now, Sydney? Why don't you ask yourself that." She moved from the table, passing me by as if I ceased to exist. Everyone else filed in behind her, without so much as even looking my way. The next day Yolanda's question would be answered, as I could be seen sitting at a table eating alone, going virtually unnoticed, reclaiming my title as the invisible girl.

6

Staring out the school bus window on my way home, turning over the week's events in my head, I couldn't see my way past tomorrow. And, quite frankly, I didn't care if tomorrow never came. At that moment, I could understand why, at that time in the early '80s, so many teens were killing themselves. I had watched a TV movie the night before about two teens, a distraught girl and boy, who were so miserable and disillusioned by their dismal lives and clueless parents that over a period of a few weeks they plotted their own suicides. They died in the boy's car from carbon monoxide poisoning in the family garage. Their parents kept asking themselves, while crying over their dead bodies, "Why, why, why?"

"Because life for teenagers is fucking hard," I said, talking to the TV, exhausted, flailing my hands back and forth, before I became annoyed and abruptly switched it off. They were dead because misery is like a disease, and if left untreated, one day it just kills you. What would eventually kill me, I wondered? A deranged rapist, some sick child molester, a speeding car, or my fucking misery?

I woke up the next morning before school to see what had already been slowly killing me, Jade Greene, my mother, standing over me, pissed off that her calls hadn't awakened me, and she had to make a personal appearance in my bedroom.

"Get up, Sydney," she said sternly. "It's time for school."

I rolled over to face her.

"I want to ask you something," she began, softening her tone as her eyes met mine.

"You were pretty engrossed in that movie last night. You wouldn't ever try to kill yourself, would you?"

"No, Mom. I'll let you take care of that," I responded, disappointed and annoyed at the same time. I let my back return to the warm spot just below my pillow where it had previously been and rolled over, taking the covers with me. My mother waited for a second or two before she said,

"You know, Syd, you can be a real little bitch sometimes."

"So I've been told," I said beneath the covers.

I figured she just didn't want the stigma associated with having your own child commit suicide to fall upon her. Parents back then were always getting the blame. If she only knew that even with all I was enduring as a junior high student, with being unpopular and everything that went along with it, I would only have wanted to kill myself in order to get the hell away from her.

The natural scent from her body remained in my room for a long time after she'd left, a combination of orange rinds and vanilla. How is it that she was able to be everywhere? Every childhood photo I'm in, even if she wasn't photographed, she was still there. She's the clothes I wore, because she picked them out. She's my hairstyle, because she fixed it. She's my smile, because it is identical to her own. I can't escape her legacy.

I remembered a time when I did truly love her without fear or worry, when I'd give her the weekly flower that I picked for her, lifted out of some neighbor's yard on my way home from school.

"Here, Mommy, this is for you," I'd say, never knowing what her response would be. Maybe the sun didn't shine brightly enough for her that day or it was the wrong day of the week, and she'd just say, "Thanks," flatly, without so much as even looking at it or me. Maybe my dad had made love to her just right the night before, and they had plans for the weekend she was excited about, and she'd say, "Thanks, honey. That's very sweet of you." After being dismissed with a pat on the head, I'd turn on my heel and go wait on the porch for my father to come home, waiting, waiting, always waiting for something, anything.

She mostly spared me her affection, leaving me with more and more unanswered questions. My love for her at times was still unwavering, and I tried to remain optimistic through my doubt until I had turned about fourteen, when my mind became all messed up from the hormones raging inside me and the overwhelming trauma I had suffered from being in junior high. I was unsure of everything and sure of everything all at the same time. I began to reassess my childhood and take inventory. Daddy, good. Mommy, bad. Daddy, happy. Mommy, pissed. I probably should have been in therapy.

The first time I can vividly remember that sometime occasion when I did not love my mother, Lachlan had come cheerfully into the house, giving her a huge hug. "Hi, Mom," he said, "I had a great day today." He left and she turned to me, where I was sitting quietly next to her on the couch, telling me that with all the trouble he causes her, she wished sometimes he wouldn't hug her at all.

I was alarmed by what she said. Lachlan had no clue. I do not recall the last day I'd actually hugged her myself, but that particular day marked the day when I would stop. The flowers stopped, too. I never wanted her to be able to betray me the way she'd betrayed my brother. I began to believe she could not be trusted, that her love was not real, that she disliked us all, resented us because we'd kept her from her dream of becoming whatever it was she really had wanted to become; like maybe we were the reason she never did become that ballerina or jazz singer.

My love for her left me like an out-of-body experience, and I felt it float out of me and rest itself against the ceiling, waiting for me to retrieve it. But I left it there. She stopped being a special fascination to me and became my secret enemy. I'd lurk around corners to see just what the enemy was up to. Oh, I see you're washing dishes. I'll dart by you, without your having seen me. Um, talking on the phone? I'll sneak up behind your chair and pretend to strangle you with my jump rope and watch as you struggle to break free. I spoke to her less and less, thinking that anything I'd say she would use against me. She and I were in a war only one side knew about. I would not be her casualty. I would kindly say, "Yes, Mother," "No, Mother," while my dark-brown eyes hid a darker force raging behind them.

My mind still flourished in my father's love, but at the same time a part of it lay injured, near death on the floor of my soul. His love was sweet sustenance for my wounds, and I began to not need or want her. She had nothing to sustain me. Over the years, being around her had choked me like gas. She was always unhappy, and I believed I was the cause of it. After years and years of feeling unloved by my mother, I'd become a cold, calculatingly unsympathetic young girl when it came to her.

And years later, the stress from both Lachlan's sudden death and the separation from the man I would marry left me beaten and worn. I had weathered more storms than I'd been provided shelter for. The guilt I felt clung to me like I'd stepped in tar. Had I been a good wife? Had I been a good sister? Could I have saved my marriage? Could I have loved my brother more?

Lachlan's death and my mother's reaction to it was the last reason I needed to justify my not loving her. I watched her ever so closely. I searched her face to see if her tears were real, if her pain was crippling her body to the point of breakdown from the sheer exhaustion of mourning. I monitored her sleep patterns to be sure they were anything but blissful, a sure sign of indifference. My father's sisters rallied around my mother, taking pity on her, offering their concern and support. There was so much irony in the display since my mother had never liked any of my father's family members. She never stopped hating Uncle Bennie, my father's older brother, for divorcing Aunt Lucky, her own sister. She never forgave my dad's now deceased mother for warning him against her. And she always claimed my dad's sisters were racists and disliked white people. All of it false.

My father's younger sister, Olivia, the more striking of his two sisters, stroked my mother's head continuously until Aunt Lucky, my mother's favorite of all her sisters, could arrive. But I stayed away, keeping my distance, becoming the virtual fly on the wall. I couldn't help her through her pain. There was no one to help me through mine. I was alone. She had my father, and Chance, of course, who was still living at home. Casey was at best a basket case after having had to identify my brother's body. She and her girlfriend, as in lover, were huddled on a couch in the corner, with new matching haircuts, sobbing quietly.

"Jade, are you hungry?" my dad's other sister, Rita, asked carefully. My mother's head only left the pillow she had it resting upon, while the rest of her lay on the bed she bottle fed us in at one time or another.

"Yes," my mother answered, "I could eat something." I knew it. There was the final betrayal. I'd been waiting for it like it was a train I had to catch. She couldn't even refrain from eating to mourn my brother. Fasting at least long enough to raise suspicion and have to be put under a doctor's care would have been a testament to her despair at having lost a son. My aunt was actually on her way to get my mother some catfish from her favorite seafood restaurant.

My mother sat up to eat and asked for hot sauce. What else was she going to do, wear red and dance at my brother's funeral? Was this the way mothers mourned their children's passing, that unintentional slippage into the proverbial light, or in my brother's case there could have quite possibly been some darkness since he was a real piece of work.

My brother as an adult became full of absolutes. He absolutely loved being outdoors, fishing, and riding dirt bikes. He was opinionated, and you always knew exactly where you stood with him, which made the elusiveness of his death seem unfair.

"Your brother went over a hundred-and-fifty-foot cliff somewhere in the mountains in Boulder, Colorado. He was not drunk, and so they think he must have swerved for a small animal or something, causing him to go over the side of the mountain. He was ejected from his vehicle, breaking every bone in his body," is how my Aunt Olivia explained it to me while we were on our way to pick out his casket.

At the funeral home, where Lachlan lay waiting for his wake to take place the next day and the following day after his funeral, I entered the room where he lay. Two layers of a thick white sheet had been placed over him, with only his head exposed. A single light shone directly on him like sunlight through a forest, leaving the rest of the room in a glow of gray darkness. I moved closer to touch his face. It felt cool, clammy, almost damp, but firm. My tears were immediate, profuse, and I paid them little attention, letting them fall wherever they may, and they did, all over the white sheet covering him. I wondered if they would leave a stain.

As I gazed at him for the last time, the first memory I had of him - the time when I was five, he was ten, and he was in a good mood and hugging me, telling me he loved me - encircled my pounding heart like a bow, wrapping itself around it, tying in a knot. I stayed there, unable to look away, trying to find a way to tell him good-bye, with my grief intensifying. There was so much more left to say to him, that I was sorry this had happened to him, that I didn't understand what it all meant, that the enigma of why he was dead was harder to face than his actually being dead. But all my unspoken words were lost on his lifeless body. He would never know how much I loved him. I was sorry he had to die before I really knew how much I loved him.

Aunt Olivia came into the room and pulled me away, as if she feared I would disappear inside him if I stayed one minute longer. She had her arms around me, walking beside me with her hands on my shoulders, marching me out of the room. Damn her for that. I wasn't ready to leave. I was twenty-four, at the time, and the pain from his death would hang over me like a canopy, and every time I looked up, it was there, he was there. But surviving this meant I could live through anything. My father had warned me against going into the room, telling me it was something I would never forget.

"But I don't want to ever forget," I had said.

Two days later we gathered at the veteran cemetery, about seventy of us, sitting in white chairs, listening to a eulogy I no longer remember. An hour later Lachlan was lowered into parched earth, surrounded by randomly singed patches of grass riddled with miniature American flags left by previous mourners. It was a violently windy, blazingly hot day in the middle of July that smeared away my makeup and my composure. I clutched myself, closing my eyes to visualize and long for the return of frigid winds indicative of winter, along with Lachlan to come back.

7

Before Lachlan died, we had seen him maybe once every few months for, like, thirty minutes. So it was at times hard to remember that he was really gone and never coming back. It's not like I'd expect him to come walking through the door or anything like that. It's just that I never really got to know him as an adult. And the funny thing is I never felt robbed by his death. It just felt unfortunate and deplorably sad. And there wasn't the typical angry-at-God thing that people go through.

He'd made himself scarce, moving to Colorado with his wife and daughter. After his death, when I thought about this, it finally dawned on me that we were more alike than I'd realized. Our thoughts must have run in the same direction, away from our mother. The way he never came around, proceeding through our lives in the way a cyclone would, fast-moving. He would stay just long enough to cause my parents to stir with angst and guilt, then abruptly disappear for another long interval of time.

Lachlan left home at eighteen, joining the army, disdainfully telling my mother he would never be back to live in her house again. True to form, she'd said to him, "Yeah, right, Lachlan, you'll be back," causing him to want nothing more than to prove her wrong. The two of us were the middle children, with no real identity, holding no significance from being the first born or special sentiment from being the last. Our place in the birth order was nothing special; lost like the second and third layers of meat in between a sandwich, the taste we left went mostly unrecognizable. But I could recognize his actions in my own; sometimes I didn't love my mother and, at the time, neither had Lachlan, comfort at least for my sadness at having lost him before he could keep me from being alone in my lack of feelings for her.

When I entered my sophomore year in high school, Lachlan had entered the army. He wrote to me once, and sent me a hundred dollars, which I quickly used for albums and makeup. I ignored his message about studying hard. The girl I hung with, Drew, wasn't much into studying. Yes, Drew. We had had no choice but to gravitate towards each other after junior high was over. Yolanda, Felicia, Cleo, and Eva all ended up going to the high school on the rough side of town, Poly High. Our mothers continued to have us bussed across town, to the white side of town, to McMillan High School.

My first day at McMillan High School, after elementary school, I had really never hung with anybody else except for Drew, so finding a group to have lunch with was a daunting task against the backdrop of a campus three times the size of Crawford. I was caught in between crowds of kids, wandered around, searching for a familiar face, any familiar face to latch onto to have lunch with, saving us from the embarrassment of eating alone. I latched onto Brandy Rudolph, one of six or seven girls named Brandy, all Caucasian, I knew of back in junior high. I guess the name had been popular back in the '70s. This was a blonde, curly-haired Brandy.

"Oh, hi, Sydney," she said, apprehensively. "So I see you made it here to McMillan."

"Yeah, I did," I responded. "So what's up? I mean, what's going on?" I said, fumbling over my words, trying to get in good with her. She was looking around over my head, trying to avoid my eyes. I could tell she didn't want to get stuck with me. She was looking for her crew, and I wasn't the type of person she would normally hang with. I was just good enough for polite conversation during class, as we'd done in ninth grade.

"Hey, look, there's Drew," she said, passing me off as if she had just been saved from something. I bid Brandy farewell and made my way over to Drew, who was standing next to another Brandy, a Black Brandy. Until then, I didn't know they actually existed. To my surprise Drew looked happy to see me. The two of us went off campus to eat lunch, walking to Roundtable Pizza. We were both surprised and relieved to see one another. We left what happened in junior high mostly unspoken.

Without the others, Drew had a strong personality and was a lot of fun. She always had interesting things to say. The boys were intensely drawn in by her, struck by her large cat-like, golden-brown eyes and gregarious nature. I would stand next to her, looking off to the side somewhere, without commenting as she spoke to them with a finesse I would always envy. We shared secrets, talked on the phone constantly, and I trusted her completely.

While I was wading through the trash dump of junior high, I never imagined Drew and I would find each other.

"Phone, Syd," Casey, yelled. Since Drew and I had been calling each other, I had been competing for phone time with Casey, who, at the elderly age of twenty-four, shouldn't have been living at home anyway.

"Hello," I said.

"This is Drew, and I've decided something," she began.

"What?"

"I don't have a best friend, and I think you should be my best friend."

"Okay," I said, quickly and overjoyed. I smiled into the phone and nestled myself deeper into the couch, exhaling, ready for whatever Drew was going to say next. Then Casey appeared from out of nowhere like a pit bull.

"You're gonna have to get off the phone," she said, "I'm expecting a call from Odette."

"What?" I said, raising my back from where it had been resting. "I don't care if you're expecting a call from Michael Jackson, I'm not getting off until I'm done," I retorted, hopping off the couch, standing up with the phone cord stretching behind me, anchored by the base of the phone that was weighing it down on the carpet.

"Oh, and don't bother telling me because I already know I'm a bitch," I spat out smartly, shifting my head from side to side. Being Drew's best friend meant to me that I was back on the map, and I would be damned if my slacker sister was going to end my happy moment prematurely.

Casey lunged for the phone, attempting to take if from me, causing the bottom receiver to hit me in the jaw when I resisted. Reflexively, I took my other hand and slapped her across the face with it. The smacking sound it made was surreal. I had never really expected to hit her. I dropped the phone and took off running through the house with her following close behind. I could feel her hands scratching at my back and arms as I fled from her.

I had never been in a physical altercation with my sister, and my unknown fate caused my feet to carry me faster than I knew they could. That day she would not catch me. Before I could retrace my steps through the house a second time, she stopped chasing me, giving up on exacting her revenge. It would have required more determination than she could muster. She'd spent her whole life undetermined, and chasing me around the house was easy to give up on. There had been many worthwhile things that she'd already stopped chasing. By the next morning my sister acted as if nothing had ever happened. I figured her heavy drug use had erased parts of her short-term memory and considered myself lucky.

The last time I had been kicked off the phone for her to converse with this Odette person, I crept into my parents' room, softly raised the phone to my ear and listened in on their conversation.

"I swear, she keeps looking at me all day long," said a gruff woman's voice on the other end.

"Well, then maybe she wants your panties," my sister said, followed by coy giggling.

I was horrified at the connotations of what I was hearing. My eyes bulged from my head, and I hung up the phone like it was on fire. I wouldn't allow myself to believe my sister could be gay. I had seen Odette once in the past, and she had a raspy, Peppermint Patty, truck-driver voice, a short haircut, wore parachute pants, and a lot of military camouflage. I chased the thoughts out of my head shortly thereafter, giving up on them as quickly as Casey chasing me through the house.

And I was still chasing popularity, even after previous failed attempts in elementary and junior high. Drew got the bright idea that we should try out for the school's most popular cheerleading squad, JV Cheer. Neither of us had ever cheered before, so we did not exactly have the moves. Our grades were already sucking by October, not good enough for us to be picked because we'd bring any intellectual creativity to the squad. And we were, after all, dare I say it, unpopular.

The JV cheerleading spots at McMillan High go and had always gone to the most popular girls, and they are looking for girls with a certain charisma and attitude. Everyone knew this. I knew it and Drew knew it. She just didn't care, hence the reason why we would try out anyway and end up humiliated by the whole thing. Jade refused to buy me a new outfit to try out in, so after pulling something old out of my summer clothes box, I looked wrinkled, worn, and like I was too poor to even scrape up the money to buy the cheerleading uniform I would need.

During tryouts, as we stumbled through the required routine, we both fell out of our cartwheels. Drew forgot some of the steps, and I knew I looked out of place, which was true. I felt like I looked; bad. I was not peppy and deliriously full of school spirit. I grew tired of spelling the school's name each alphabet at a time as loud as I could. The whole thing wasn't me. Where school was concerned, I didn't rise to the occasion. I had no school spirit. School was a chore, something I had to do, not something I willingly involved myself in. The cheerleaders who sat in the bleachers looking for that special twinkle in the eye, perfected moves, and winning smile, saw right through me. I couldn't fake it. We left the gym with snickers coming from the other girls.

I'd been talked into trying out by Drew, who, at that time, I would have followed into a burning house I was so grateful to have her. But I knew we wouldn't make the squad, and I knew it was a total waste of time, that we looked like fools. Suffice it to say, we didn't make the squad, and Drew screamed racism right away. Her mother called the school, speaking to the principal, wanting an explanation for why only one black girl made it on a cheerleading squad with eight open spots.

The one black girl, Alison Beasley, had earned straight A's since elementary school and had cheered just as long. The call went nowhere. The principal didn't give an explanation, because there was none to give.

He told Drew's mother that the school was not racist, because the other cheerleaders made the decision, that she could file whatever she wanted to, and left it at that. But before he hung up, he recommended that we try out for the Cadettes.

"Fucking Cadettes!" Drew squealed into the phone when she called me. "How dare he."

The Cadettes was where girls who couldn't cut it as anything else went to cheer. They were all rejects from tryouts and also the ones who didn't make JV Cheer. The Cadettes took anybody and everybody who wanted to be on their squad, which made trying out for them just a sick charade, because anyone who ventured to try out got to be a Cadette. Their numbers were great, made up of the big and tall, short and fat, the bizarre, the unexplainable, the freaky. They were mostly laughed at during our Friday pep rallies, where they performed.

"Sydney, go tell your parents to call the school," Drew sobbed over the phone. "This is really unfair that we didn't make it. We didn't make it because we're black, and they don't want a lot of blacks on JV Cheer. I hate that school."

I was surprised at how much being on the JV Cheer meant to Drew and curious to know why she felt she'd even had a chance in the first place. She must have really thought highly of herself. She seemed to have that personality that would always have you setting yourself up for failure, like trying to and actually thinking you can win the New York Marathon when you've never run a day in your life.

"Please, just have your parents call. If enough people complain, they'll have to put us on the squad."

But I knew that our skin color had nothing to do with it. Drew was obviously suffering from all kinds of delusions, and I knew my parents would never make such a call. Blaming bad things that happened to me on being black did not fly in my household.

Seneca Greene and Jade McLearie had grown up in 1960's Oklahoma, and despite this hadn't felt held back because of their race. In fact, one of my dad's favorite stories he liked to tell on Thanksgiving, with plenty of family around to enjoy, is the time when he was a little boy at school, and a blonde, blue-eyed girl, who thought she was superior, ordered him to move out of her way as she was coming up steps he was going down.

"I just ran her little ass over. You should have seen it. Her books flew everywhere," he'd say, with clapping and boisterous laughter coming from my aunts and uncles. And my mother always said because her skin was so fair, she was never at the back of the bus and was able to use the black or the white drinking fountain.

"Yeah, right. Sure, Syd. Don't you think it's because you just weren't good enough?" my mother would say.

"Yeah, and it was going to cost $150. We can do something else with that money. And didn't you say they already have a black girl on the squad?" my father would testify.

I'd be wasting my time again complaining to my parents. To them there were worse things that could happen besides my not making some cheerleading squad, like my mother having to call me more than once for something, or my dad having to go in his pocket to give me five bucks.

I listened to Drew crying into the phone. I ended the call by telling her I'd ask them to call. Of course that didn't happen, but Drew's influence over me was still undeniable as she had been able to talk me into humiliating myself. She was the captain of our friendship, and I was the passenger who was seasick, desperately holding the side railing, trying not to fall in, using her as my lifejacket to help me get through tenth grade.

Of all my years, ironically enough, even after our disastrous first weeks of trying to become cheerleaders, tenth grade would become my favorite year of all my years in school. Going off campus to eat lunch was an adventure in itself. We'd leave through a huge wrought-iron gate, in a sea of other high schoolers hungry for food. We usually found ourselves enjoying burgers and fries at McDonald's, pizza at Roundtable, and burritos at Taco Bell. And there was the occasional fight that would break out when some kid had a beef or misunderstanding. As soon as we were safely off the school grounds, we acted like inmates on a field trip with no supervision.

I discovered that being anonymous in high school was just what the doctor ordered, and I began to embrace being unknown in a way I couldn't when I was in junior high. By Christmas of my sophomore year, I was still passing kids in the hallways and in the quad I'd never seen before. There were twice as many kids at McMillan as there were at Crawford. I didn't have to worry about ridicule or complete exclusion. For every popular person at that school, there was another pathetic soul nearby, more pathetic than I'd ever been.

There were the kids with bad skin covered in pimples, puss-filled, inflamed, and disgusting. At least I wasn't afflicted with that. Or the kids who were exceptionally overweight, looked down upon, and subjected to ridicule for wanting the fundamental enjoyment of a Twinkie. That wasn't me either. I wasn't one of the known or assumed sluts, or one of the creepy devil worshippers who wore only black clothes and makeup. And I wasn't walking around school pregnant. Being unpopular was not at all bad since I had plenty of company.

On some days, while on my way off campus to eat lunch with Drew, I would pass another face searching for a warm body to eat lunch with, searching to no avail and ending up sitting Indian style beneath a tree, with only the grass and the occasional bug flying by for company. At these moments I was happy that that face was no longer mine, but then I discovered kids were eating alone everywhere. Unpopularity was an epidemic here. It was almost popular to be unpopular.

One day when Drew skipped school, claiming she had nothing to wear, I found myself sitting on a concrete bench, after purchasing the dreaded school lunch, eating alone. As the sun-kissed breeze kicked up, passing over my skin as if I were riding on a swing, I tried not to feel embarrassed. There was something quite liberating about being able to eat alone, and I began to not think so much of becoming popular and was able to focus on just enjoying being a tenth grader as well as being a good friend to Drew.

By doing this I thought I would finally be able to atone for what I'd done to Carrie and Jody. Somewhere along the way, I realized how easy it would be. I let Drew share my locker. I passed with diligence the notes cute boys gave to me to give to her. Whenever Drew forgot to bring her lunch money to school or just wasn't given any, I would share the three dollars I had with her. Jade had been pretty good at keeping me supplied with cash, so I never had to let her go hungry. When she wanted to borrow my clothes, I made sure to remember to bring them to school so she'd have them for the next day. I was always there when she needed me. We had numerous sleep-overs and exchanged gifts. She was my true best friend, my first one ever.

On a typical Saturday night, as we were sprawled out on the bed in Drew's room, looking at teen magazines, playing albums and records, Drew would tell me how she wanted to have a large wedding, with two hundred people in attendance, in a beautiful cathedral, with her in a dress to rival Princess Diana's. Her sheer vail, adorned with diamonds, would hide her dainty tears. Her father, the one who'd never been around, would rush to wipe them with his musk-scented handkerchief. She wanted to marry a gorgeous black man that all woman would envy her for having. He would treat her like gold. They would be rich and admired. Yeah, Drew had grand dreams, and I listened on the edge of my seat as she revealed them to me, taking in all the things that fell out of her mouth like it could happen to me.

But that was Drew. She had all these thoughts and dreams, ideas and plans with no way to truly attain them. I knew she was full of it, that none of it would ever really happen to her. But as she spoke, I let myself believe, you know, the way you let yourself continue to believe there's a Santa even though you're eleven. But I also knew that as sure as she believed the sun would rise tomorrow, she believed in what she was saying, and I could appreciate that.

I didn't dream of having a big wedding with my dad walking me down the aisle, and there would probably be no church service. The idea of all those people watching me made my stomach turn, and if I did get married, I didn't know, at that time, if he'd even be black. Maybe I'd get married in direct sunlight at the top of a mountain, or on a white-sand beach, maybe on horseback. My life would not resemble a fairy tale in the way Drew wanted hers to.

Despite my terrible grades, I wanted to become a lawyer and fight to put criminals away forever. I enjoyed playing contemporary pieces on my piano, something I'd done since I was ten. I liked easy-listening music, the kind you hear in elevators, like Barry Manilow, and I was captivated and inspired by old books made into movies like "Gone With the Wind" and "To Kill A Mockingbird." I could not share these things with Drew. I was afraid of what she'd think of me. And I never let on that I was attracted to all boys, not just the black ones. I preferred to let her think I was someone I was not. I kept my real self a secret, further plunging into the unrealistic world of being Drew's best friend.

8

We were in the middle of our tenth-grade year. It was the cold and rainy season, and the sky was only filled with different shades of grey without the sun. I'd resigned myself to the fact that I could exist comfortably at school in Drew's shadow, and I was happy with that, happy with a grey area of existence. I found an identity in being Drew's best friend. My days of staring blankly out of the school bus window were long since over, having been replaced with deep introspective thoughts. I had also finally found something real and tangible to stare at. His name was Danny. He was also in my first period English class. I sat in the chair right behind him, sniffing the sweet aroma coming from the back of his neck. We had, ironically enough, been in the same kindergarten class together, and all these years later we ended up at the same high school, riding on the same school bus.

The memory of him had never left my mind, from when I first saw him sitting on a red carpet square when we were five in kindergarten. I remembered the last time I'd seen him, watching him walk hand in hand with his mother across the street, leaving kindergarten behind, on his way to a new grade and a new school. When I saw him on that first day of tenth grade, as he boarded the school bus, I recognized him right away. He was that little boy I never forgot. It was fate that sat him next to me, and I felt like I already knew him.

Danny was kind of geeky looking and went largely unnoticed by the other girls. He was tall, skinny, fair-skinned. He had dark hair inherited from his Filipino mother. His dad was a lanky white guy who ended up splitting on them. Danny was sensitive and caring, and my heart opened to him like a flower. He didn't need a lot of words with me; the way he chose me to sit next to every morning said enough. I knew he was meant for me, sent by the planets on that rare occasion when they had perfectly aligned.

But we were both very shy, and so even after we got to know each other, we hardly moved past innocuous conversation like, "So what did you have for dinner?" Danny had been my chance at true happiness in high school. He was my soulmate, the person I was supposed to one day marry, and the lack of confidence I had then didn't allow me to capitalize on what I'd been given. Oftentimes I would say something ridiculous and out of the blue that would make him pause and wonder where I was keeping my spaceship. Drew didn't approve of him because he wasn't black, so I kept my love for him a secret from her and ultimately from him. Funny how the things we do to ourselves are sometimes far worse than the things done to us by others.

"Sydney, Daryl Farrell asked me out on a date." Drew said at lunch, just as I was about to take my first savory bite of pepperoni pizza. I pulled the pizza back out of my mouth, immediately becoming annoyed and losing my appetite. Daryl was a tight-end on the football team, short, dark, with huge, deep-brown almond eyes. He was ruggedly handsome and had a nice, muscular physique. We both knew him from junior high. He wasn't someone Drew looked twice at then, because he was skinny, and wore cords and Wallabees and wasn't popular.

A few weeks previous, Daryl had come to my locker one perfect autumn Friday, asking me out on a double date. I quickly did what I knew Drew would want me to do and turned him down, disappointing him to the point where he left me with his almond eyes lowered and brooding, his head hanging down. He didn't understand how I could resist him. Now, since being a starter on the football team, he'd become extremely popular.

I watched him turn the corner, passing the last set of lockers, saying to myself, "There just went my popularity," and forgot about it.

"Of course you told him no, didn't you," is what Drew had said when she found out that Daryl had asked me on a date.

"Yeah. I mean, I don't like him or anything," I lied. I did what I felt she would have wanted me to do, turn him down. Her reaction was as I'd expected it to be, so naturally I was a bit perturbed at her memory lapse when I found out that he had moved on from me to her, and she had actually decided to go out with him.

"And guess what," Drew said with half-chewed pizza visibly rolling around in her mouth.

"Wait. Don't tell me. He's proposed and the two of you are running away together tonight? Oh, the suspense is killing me." I said.

"Are you done being a jerk? Because I want to tell you something."

"Okay. What?"

"He has a friend, Charles, who likes you."

The whole thing seemed suspect to me, and I tried to conjure up Charles' image in my mind. I had seen him before eating with Daryl and some friends at McDonald's. I didn't think he was a head-turner, and I vaguely remembered hearing something about him being interested in a very well-known, stunning black girl named Tonia. Charles was also on the football team. I knew I didn't have a snowball's chance in hell of winning him over Tonia. I summed up Drew's news about Charles as a cleverly disguised diversion from how wrong she was for going out with Daryl.

Once more, I was still plagued with a loss for words, and the thought of actually having a boyfriend was not easy for me to deal with. A boy would ask me for my number, I'd give it to him, he'd call, I'd say nothing. He'd hang up convinced I was dumb, and that was that. Being cute was just as worthless as being unattractive since I couldn't back it up with an intriguing personality. I was like a sundae with no chocolate syrup, whipped cream, or cherry. I looked good, but I didn't taste great, and there were bowls of ice cream everywhere on campus from which to choose. I wasn't sure I even wanted to be on the menu.

At times I found myself feeling indifferent towards the boys, skeptically picking them apart one by one, evaluating their clothes, hair, height and intellect. None was good enough for me. All I really wanted was Danny, but I had ruined that, and he had moved on, and Daryl Farrell had not been a worthy consolation.

Danny would call, and I was such a bonehead that I'd pretend I didn't know who he was I would get so frazzled, which caused our conversations to start off wrong. I was immature and still insecure about my looks. My love for him was overwhelming. His calls would make my heart feel like it would burst. After he gave up on me, I was left to painfully watch him from afar with his friends at school. At night I marinated in my regret, refusing to eat dinner until he called again. He had drifted away from me like a message in a bottle placed out to sea drifts from its author; deliberate, slowly, continuous.

My message to Danny in a bottle would read:

> You will never know how much I loved you.
> And although life's plan for me is that I go on to love others, you will always be my first.
> If a million years go by, I will never forget you.

Drew lost her virginity to Daryl Farrell, and then she decided I needed to lose mine.

"I think it's time for you to have sex," she announced one day after school from the top of her bed. I stared up at her from the floor, wondering were she found the nerve. At that time, I was really caught up in her, but my virginity was something that I wouldn't let her mess with. My father had warned me to refrain from having sex, telling me all boys really wanted was a warm place to stick their penis in. After such a blunt warning, I would decide when to have sex, not her. Two weeks later when Daryl dumped her and she wouldn't come to school, I was glad I hadn't been that stupid.

And then Drew got sick, so ill she was too weak to get out of bed and go to school. I ate my lunch alone for five days and deeply regretted how dependent I had allowed myself to become on Drew. I regretted how I hadn't bothered to make many other friends, especially friends that I could use as backup lunch buddies. School became my prison. I dreaded each day I went to school, knowing Drew wouldn't be there. Without Drew, I was alone. Drew had missed almost ten days of school when her mother finally took her to the hospital, where she went undiagnosed for another three.

"Sydney, this is Drew," she weakly began. I was afraid of the horror of what Drew might say next and I braced myself for it.

"The doctors think I probably have leukemia and I might die." At that point, Drew was crying, and then I began to cry. The thought of Drew dying was too much for me to bear. I began to try to figure out if there was a way that, if it were true, I could go and die with her.

"But, Drew, you can't die," I said.

"The doctors say I'm real sick, and I will be in the hospital for a long time. Sydney, I don't want to die."

"Drew, you're not going to die. You have to think positive. Okay. You'll get better. I know you will. I'll pray to God for you," I said. Drew hung up, and I pictured her in her hospital bed with tubes hooked up inside her, going every which way. I didn't tell anyone at school or at home. I carried it alone inside.

One day as Danny and I were the only two people walking towards each other down a school hallway, he sarcastically asked me where my best friend was. At that moment, I wished I could throw myself into his arms and beg him to give me another chance. But my pride being stronger than my heart's desire kept me from it, and I was left with only his comment burning my ears as he passed me by. I wondered if this was how my life would always be, great things, chances just passing me by. Danny was my greatest living regret, and I would have greatly benefited from having him as a boyfriend at that time, to see me through my pain.

At home I turned to my piano and to my love of music. I enjoyed the times when I was there alone and my piano playing was the only sound filling the house. I had outgrown taking lessons and was mainly learning on my own, but there was one last recital that I had been practicing for the past three months. My first two recitals, I had taken second place then first, and I wanted to go out with a bang, playing the song "Out Here On My Own" from the movie "Fame." I blocked out my best friend being ill and dug into my music. It would be my final performance and a whole host of my relatives were going to be there, the ones mainly from my dad's side of the family. But the night before I was to play my masterpiece, Jade was complaining about everything, arguing with anyone who crossed her path, on some kind of a premenopausal-induced rampage.

"All of you, ungrateful dummies. I'm so tired of you all. One day I'm just going to walk out of here. I swear I am."

I sat on the couch in the den not far from where she was, saying to myself that I wished she finally would make good on that same old promise I had been listening to since I was like ten. My father breezed through, and she told him how he was never around to help her. Chance passed by, and she told him he was always in the way. I tried to remove myself from her view, but I wasn't fast enough.

"And you, I'm not going to your recital," she callously stated.

I could hear my father in the distance asking my mother why she would go and say a thing like that, but it didn't matter. He was too late. The damage had been done. But I played gloriously the next day, bulldozing over everyone else, seizing first place. The prize I got from winning didn't matter. The self-esteem and sense of accomplishment I gained would last me forever. That day I was the shit. And my mother, with her negative attitude, and her destructive words and her ultimate presence there at my recital hadn't worked to ruin my moment.

I got home that night, and Drew called saying she was out of the hospital and home and going back to school.

"So why is it that you're back home and returning to school just like that? What happened to you having leukemia?" I asked, concerned.

"Well, Sydney, I just wanted to get out of going to school for a while. I was never really sick. I'm sorry if I scared you, but you know... Well, that's it. I'll see you tomorrow."

I hung up the phone and felt betrayed and foolish for worrying about Drew. I wondered what was exactly true, then, about our friendship. A part of my attachment to her broke off like a tree branch snapping, and just like that, I didn't need her anymore.

As our tenth-grade year came to a close, I turned sixteen and could see our friendship for what it really was. The one and only time during that whole year that I had no money for lunch, Drew did not share hers with me. With my empty stomach grumbling in protest, I watched her eat her lunch without offering any to me. I was quietly furious, mentally beating myself up for being so generous to her in the past. Here was my so-called best friend allowing me to go hungry. By seeing Daryl, she had also ignored the unwritten rule about not dating a boy who once admired your best friend. Maybe the only reason she'd slept with him in the first place was because he could have otherwise been mine.

When I asked her to bring clothes to school for me to wear the next day, she would mysteriously forget. And what really took the cake is when Drew got the chance to dance on "Soul Train," to actually be on TV, she decided to take someone else to the show instead of me. I was furious, and Brandy, who ended up being the one to go with her, was elated. I had too much pride to allow Drew to know how disappointed I was. I had wasted a year being her minion, devoted to a friendship that never really existed. My experiences with friendship left me disillusioned, feeling the consequence would always be the same whether I was a good friend or not.

In late spring, my parents announced we were moving from Sunny Beach to sunny Montara Valley, where I would finish out my days as a high school student, and they were by then very numbered. I was angry that all that needed to happen was for my mother to want to move and, there you have it, we would. What my father truly desired and wanted had always been an afterthought, like what would be the best thing for the family pet. I waited until the day we actually moved to tell Drew. The quiver in her voice let me know I would be thoroughly missed. I told her good luck finding another fool and hung up without giving her my new address and phone number. The phone call had left me feeling empowered and independent, until my first day at Montara Valley High, the most excruciating day I would ever endure at a new school.

9

Montara Valley, which was sixty miles east of Sunny Beach, was like moving from the city to the country. I had hit a brick wall, and after two days of hiding out in the library or bathroom during lunch, because it was impossible for me to make friends the kids were so different - I refused to go back there. My mother put her foot down and started kicking me out of the house every morning. I defied her by going around the house to the side door leading to the garage and spending the day inside our second car, my father's pick-up truck, passing the time by reading paperback novels and sleeping. I listened at the back door for Oprah to come on to let me know when I could come home, as if I'd been at school all day.

I intercepted letters from the school, and after two months, the lack of exercise I was getting caused me to gain fifteen pounds. I didn't carry the weight well, and I was beginning to look rather unattractive. My mother was offended that she needed to replace my old clothes with new ones that fit.

"Syd, come down here. Your sister and I are taking you shopping," my mother said with resentment in her voice from the foyer of our roughly seven-month-old house. Never mind that it was my seventeenth birthday, she was refusing to acknowledge my special day after the school finally stopped sending letters and decided to call, letting her know they hadn't seen me in months. But my father said we could celebrate my birthday anyway and go to my favorite steakhouse for dinner. I sat in the cab area of my father's pick-up truck, listening to my mother tell me that I was ungrateful, would never amount to much, and, news flash, wouldn't be allowed to buy anything that came in black.

"All you do is wear black," my mother said, "And I'm not buying any more of it."

"Why not? Ever since you moved me here, my soul has been in mourning," I said dramatically. "Besides, you're not the one who has to wear it."

"Hey, you'd better watch what you're saying, Sydney."

"Whatever," I countered.

"You're pretty big now anyway," she said, smirking towards my sister.

"Well, you're not so small yourself," I fired back.

Before I could say anything else or even blink, my mother turned around and rose up over her seat like a viper and began to pummel me repeatedly with her shoe. Caught off guard by the swift manner in which she delivered the blows, she was able to land at least three before my arms came to my defense. I tried hysterically to fend her off as she was aiming directly for my head, which she struck several times, forcing it to bang against the window. The worst blow she gave immediately raised the skin on my forehead, producing a welt the size of a golf ball. My sister screamed for my mother to stop, telling her we were going to crash as our truck swerved from side to side, narrowly missing a van full of girl scouts in the next lane.

Casey brought the car to a screeching halt in front of our house. I jumped out, fleeing to the safety of my room. I ran up the steps, flung the door open, fell to the floor sobbing, unleashing with each heave of my chest the despair I was feeling from having been assaulted by my own mother. I let the snot from my nose trickle down my top lip, mixing with my tears without wiping them away. I lay there waking and sleeping as the sun went down over the house, until I felt the weight of my father's shoes push into the carpet beside me.

"I heard what happened earlier today," he said calmly. "I can't believe what you did. And you won't be going to dinner." He left, closing my door. After a few moments I heard from outside an engine rev, car doors opening and slamming shut, and then the sound of a car engine trailing off down the street. The house was still and silent from its emptiness, and I realized I had been left there alone.

I reviewed my appearance, staring into the bathroom mirror seething, looking like a mental patient and panting, betting on the welt leaving a scar. I couldn't believe my eyes. I looked like a Frankenstein, created by a mad, out of control scientist who had really taken the time to mess me up good. I took a long look at myself, vowing never to forget. I didn't for even one moment blame myself, and I didn't blame my father for leaving me on the floor of my bedroom. She had obviously lied to him about what happened. I hadn't deserved what she'd done, and I knew she would not be forgiven.

After that day, like Medusa, my mother's gaze upon me turned my insides to stone, and I was never the same. She had crossed a line I had no idea existed, and once over, she couldn't come back. Between us there grew a divide as vast as the Grand Canyon. She couldn't come back to me, and I couldn't go back to her. She stopped me near the stairs one day and tried to apologize for hitting me. But her words slipped through me like a letter being mailed, falling to the bottom. She even had tears welling in her eyes that said she could quite possibly be sorry for once in her life. I looked at her, let her hug me, and continued to tell myself I didn't have a mother, that this thing holding me was an imposter, a fraud.

In her mind, she'd made up for what she'd done, and soon after she went back to her old ways. When she was angry, she told me and Chance we were going to be nothing, were worthless, and didn't care about her. I wanted to ask her what exactly that would make Casey then, since she was twenty-six, an absent, neglectful mother, and homeless, as well as jobless. She'd been a terrible parent to her son. We'd all been forced to take a part in raising him. And if that didn't make Casey worthless, I didn't know what did. But even then I knew I would be something. Worthless was not going to be used to describe me.

The following year I said, fuck it, left school for good, got my GED, and enrolled in a night school course that would be a stepping stone to my becoming a lawyer, to being able to prove my mother completely wrong and to get me out of her house forever. I got a job at Mervyns and met Jack, the man who would become Aden's father.

10

"Hello, Clarice," I said in a deep, throaty, breathy tone, standing at the foot of Aden's bed, as I tried to awake her from her quiet slumber.

She did not respond, so I got closer, and into her ear I said in my best Anthony Hopkins impersonation, "Hello, Clarice."

Aden, turned and twisted. "Mom, you know that scares me. Stop," she said, scraping sleepy eye out of the small crevices of her face.

"Time to get up, sleepy butt. Out of your coffin."

"Mom, you know I don't like it when you say that," she squealed.

Aden was born to me in the middle of a humid summer night, just a year and nine months after I'd married her father, Jack. I have the fact that we were in Vegas, it was our one-year anniversary, and a drink called a Bahama Mamma to thank. I was strung out on the floor of our '70s-in-sprired suit at the Maxim Hotel, and thoughts of birth control were on vacation as well. I can still hear Jack's laughter filling the room as I crawled on all fours beneath a spinning disco ball in a feeble attempt to get to the bathroom to take a much-needed pee.

Jack and I made Aden while having sex on a harvest gold comforter in an oversized bed with a mirror on the ceiling above it. I was in awe when I first saw it. As Jack gave me one of his rare good thrusts, my head flung back on the pillow in ecstasy and surprise at how good it felt. I opened my eyes to see our reflection in a mirror bolted to the ceiling. Jack's back was jerking, and my body was lost beneath him as we swayed in the bed. I focused clearer and my initial elation turned to disappointment as it became painfully obvious that I was not married to a male model. I was married to a plus-size man, five-ten, weighing in at 230 pounds.

We'd met at the Mervyns department store in the summer of 1989, the summer after I left high school, the summer I was never the same. I was a less-than-inspired associate working at Mervyns, totally into doing nothing more than collecting my check. All the rest was just a formality. My friend from the Montara Valley neighborhood, Kenya, had talked me into putting in an application since I was fresh from just being fired from a 50's-type diner for not showing up to work enough. I was a soda jerk there and a pretty bad one. The whole '50's diner thing didn't have as much appeal to me as my new boyfriend at the time, and he was the reason why I didn't make it to work. Although our relationship didn't last as long as it took for me to put on my bowtie and whip up an egg cream, it lasted just long enough for me to lose my virginity and get me fired from the restaurant.

Kenya was ambitious in a bizarre sort of way. She loved being a Mervyns associate. To her this was the best gig she'd ever had, after working fast food throughout her teens. She aspired to have a gold star on her badge, then ruby, then diamond. I just didn't give a shit; they were lucky if I even remembered to put the damn thing on before I left the house.

As Kenya and I stood in the Young Men's department folding Polo shirts, I balked at my badge, having just poked myself with it.

"I'm this close to getting the ruby star on my badge," Kenya said, showing me with her two fingers how close this close was.

"Yeah, that's great, Kenya," I said unimpressed.

"Don't you care?" she asked.

"Hell no, I don't care. When I graduate from this business school I'm going to now, I can get a cool office job and leave all this customer-service crap behind. You think I care if somebody gets away with stealing six pairs of jeans from here? I'm not chasing them down. I don't own any stock in this company, and neither do you. And what's with this secret shopper coming in to spy on us, giving us unfriendlies if we don't tell her to have a nice day? Forget that."

"And just to remind you, you already have one unfriendly, by the way," Kenya chimed in.

"So I forgot to tell the secret shopper to have a nice day. I gave her the right amount of change back. I don't care if this badge never gets a star on it. It tells people what to call me, and that's enough. And I don't care that everybody else has a gold star and I don't. Well, everybody except for the people who started like a week ago."

Kenya paused, looking at me through her hazel-colored contacts, with a less-than-thrilled look on her face, and then proceeded to dust the cash register, trying to ignore the truth in my dissertation.

"Well, I gotta finish paying for my braces, since Afenie said she's not paying for them anymore," she said. "I'm not rich like you. My parents don't just give me everything. As a matter of fact, hey, what do you know, I only have one parent. You come from a two-parent dream home. We ordinary folks needs da jobs dat da white man lit us have."

Kenya was on a roll now. I wasn't surprised, though. After she finished Malcolm X's autobiography, she had become a slightly militant, anti-establishment type. She'd recently joined the Bayside chapter of the "Free Geronimo Pratt" campaign and liked to boast that her mother, Afenie, had been a Black Panther. She also thought all black men who dated white women were sell-outs, we lived in a white man's world, and slavery was a cross we still had to bear, yes, even in the early '90s.

I admired Kenya's vast knowledge of civic issues, but I did not share her radical views. I thought being friends with her was very chic, because she was so different from me. I considered her to be my angry black friend. Everyone should have at least one.

She was right about my home, though. Money had never really been an issue for me. It was always somehow there when I really needed it. Kenya really needed and wanted her job. I didn't blame her. Her mother's presence was virtually nonexistent since she spent her workweek in L.A., reclaiming her lost youth and independence, leaving Kenya stranded from at least two of life's basic necessities; a dependable parent and a ride home. Being the good friend that I was by nature, I normally obliged.

The first time I drove Kenya home, I was taken aback by her home's appearance. It was a small two-bedroom off an isolated, dirt road. The house stood alone with no street lights or grass. My tires rolled precariously over gravel rocks that covered the area. It was something straight out of "The Grapes of Wrath," but Kenya was trying to make the best of it. I questioned whether I'd find my way back to the city, I had strayed so far from the main highway.

I found my way back to the neighborhood I lived comfortably in, with the lovely Jade and Seneca Greene, made even more unbearable by the recent and most unwanted return of the drugged-out slacker Casey, who, to show me just how much she really loved me, without my knowledge, put a phone in my name, and after running up the bill to an exorbitant, outrageous amount, decided it would be really fun not to pay it. She also wore my clothes. But I digressed.

Needless to say, I was lonely and unhappy living there. I was nineteen at the time, and I couldn't wait to get out of the house and away from Jade Greene. Her constant complaining was suffocating. There was no way to escape her there. Her voice permeated the walls of my bedroom, penetrating my skull, seeping into my brain like liquid into a sponge. I lay awake night after night in my bed plotting about how I could get away from her. Hiring a hit man was out of the question; I was broke. But little did I know my ticket out was about to walk around the corner, out of electronics, through housewares, and into my miserable little life.

11

One day at work, needing just one more unfriendly in order to be fired from my second job ever, yet increasingly complacent about the whole thing, I stood in the middle of housewares slacking off. At 10:30 in the morning, on a Monday, the place was empty. I walked to the toaster area and bent down to see myself in the reflection. I laughed at the way my nose and lips appeared distorted. I glided through the china department and did a few twirls. I went to the bridal registry, leafed through some magazines, and knocked a married-couple statue off its wedding cake perch.

As I was on my way back to the register, I heard footsteps behind me. I turned to see a fellow Mervyns associate coming towards me. He was dressed in an off-the-rack suit and slightly overweight. Any other time I would have turned right away, but something about his mustache and goatee told me he deserved a closer look.

I decided he was kind of cute, but I was annoyed by the delight in his smile and the bounce of his walk. Oh, great, here comes another fool who actually likes this job, I thought.

"Hey, why don't you do something," he said walking up to me, invading my personal space. "I know this place isn't busy, but you could, like, still do something."

How dare he address me in such a manner. Who the hell was this guy telling me how to do my job? Had he been watching me the whole time? I was thoroughly appalled. After I was done being stunned, I managed to reply with a haughty, "I am doing something. I showed up today."

He shook his head as he walked just past me, looking me up and down.

"Well, what are you doing yourself?" I contended.

"I work in electronics. I'm on my break now."

"Well, isn't that special. You work in electronics, and you're on your break now," I said mockingly.

"You're perverted," he replied.

I'd never been called that before, and I was instantly intrigued. I searched my brain to find the meaning in his accusation. Was I perverted? Is it really so bad to be? Was this a cleverly disguised compliment? I couldn't help but giggle a little inside, so I looked at his badge to find out his name. It was Jack Cassavan. But I frowned and wanted to vomit when I noticed the gold star stuck on it.

In the days that followed my initial meeting of Jack, I became his stalker, strategically placing myself in the break room whenever I thought he was going to be in there. Every day when I got to work, I checked the employee log to see when he was scheduled for breaks, and I made sure I would be in there at whatever hour he was scheduled to be. He was like clockwork and always right on time. Sooner or later I knew I would have my chance to talk to him again. I would be patient. I would wait there just like a spider. I had a plan, and he was it. I would weave a web of intrigue and lure him in with my wit.

After waiting a whole week for him to notice me in the break room, it still hadn't dawned on him what a coincidence it was that I was always in there at the exact same time that he was. It had all been a waste of time, because my chance to talk to him actually came when he was put in the Young Men's department for the day, where he ended up working with none other than Kenya and me.

We stood around the register, folding display clothing like three chirping Mervyns minions, gossiping about the assistant manager who'd just been busted for stealing.

"Yeah, late at night after closing she was taking jewelry home with her," Kenya said. I marveled at how fast she'd gotten the 411 since I didn't know about any of it.

"So, Jack," Kenya started.

"That's my name, don't wear it out," he said. How corny, I thought. What a nerd.

"So, what's your story? I mean, are you in college? Live at home? What? How old are you?"

"You want to slow down a minute?" Jack began. "Well, actually, I'm going to Chapman University. I'm twenty-four. And I'm seeing a shrink right now."

"A shrink?" Kenya and I said in unison. I was a little shocked by his candor. I would have taken something like that to my grave.

"Yeah. I just got out of a bad relationship, and she ruined my life, fucked me up so bad that I have to get help for it. I moved out of our apartment, and now I'm living back at home with my parents." Damn, I thought. He's obviously a little disturbed. Well, he has some issues, but he still seems nice, though, I reasoned.

"My parents are going away for a month in December, and I need a place to stay because they don't want me at their home while they're gone. Do you know a place where I can stay?"

I wondered what kind of a loser he was that his parents couldn't trust him to be left alone for a month.

"Well, I can't help you with that, but are you Hispanic, because you look kind of Hispanic," Kenya inquired. That was so typical of her. With her, race so mattered.

"I'm Italian. And my mother's a nurse. We live on a big hill in Bayside." The way he just gave up information should have sent bells and whistles going off in my head, but my nineteen-year-old mind was not equipped to register those kind of red flags yet.

"So how much do you make over there in electronics?" Kenya asked.

"More than you two bums. I get wages plus commission." I only vaguely sensed danger, but I also saw potential. It had been a while since I'd had a boyfriend, and I wanted to see how good this fish would fry up.

Something about him told me he would be successful one day. He was five years older than I was, and I knew I would learn a lot from him. He was in college, and he'd already lived out on his own. Perfect. I saw my days living at home with Jade as numbered. The countdown to freedom had begun.

"I don't know about him. Something about him is weird," Kenya said, her eyes narrowing as we stood in the Young Men's department, waving to Jack as he rode up the escalator back to electronics doing a dance with his fists.

"Yep, definitely weird," she said again.

That day after work, I passed by Jack on the way to my car. He was standing like a drug pusher in the corner of the Mervyns entrance. The way he was waiting there led me to believe he didn't own a car and was relying on someone to pick him up. I immediately became disappointed, since my high standards would not allow me to date someone who did not have his own transportation, so I ignored him. I hadn't even realized that he had been there waiting for me. I guess I wasn't the only one who knew how to stalk.

"What's up, skinny?" he called to me, as I breezed by and as his back left the wall he'd been leaning on. He started to follow me.

"Nothing. Just going home," I said over my shoulder, without changing my stride, anxious to get out of the hot sun.

"So why do you slack off at work so much?" he said, catching up to me, adopting my gait.

"Because I don't care about this job," I said.

"What do you care about?" he asked.

"My business school I'm going to. I'll be done in ten months."

"And then what do you want to do?"

"I want to be a lawyer," I said. He looked as if a light had come on inside his head, while he tilted it slightly to take me in from a different angle.

"You know, we should go out," he said.

"Yeah, we should."

After we exchanged numbers, I watched him turn out of the parking lot in his Mustang 5.0 through the windshield of my Toyota Supra. Impressive. Very impressive.

At nineteen, impulsive was my middle name, and I did not wait for him to call me. I called him the very next day.

"Halo," a woman, who I would later find out was Jack's mother, Gloria, said into the phone with broken English.

"Jack, please," I said perfectly.

"Who is calling?" she gurgled.

"This is Sydney."

"I tell to him you call," she said, before abruptly hanging up.

Something told me that the women who answered the phone wasn't the maid, and it must have been his mother. He's not Italian, because I was sure that was an Hispanic accent I heard, not Italian. What else did he lie about? Kenya was right. He may just be a little weird, I thought. Every chance I was given to change the course I was on, I ignored or overlooked. I was about to jump into the water with both feet, eyes closed, and no flotation device.

After Jack called me back, we bonded instantly. He was like no one I had ever met. He'd been places I'd never seen. I found out his father was the one who was Italian and his mother was from Argentina. We spoke on the phone every day, and we spent as much time together as we could. We became inseparable. When December came, Jack's parents went on the month-long trip they had planned to go on, leaving him alone with the use of the whole house. Since he could not find a place to stay, they had no choice but to leave him there.

12

The first time I drove over to Jack's house after his parents left, I was struck by how it did not sit on a hill. It was more like a slant and surrounded by a bunch of other houses like any other middle-class neighborhood. From the driveway I could hear music. I peered into the garage and saw Jack staring into space, playing the guitar shirtless, wearing shorts. Am I really going to go through with this, I asked myself? He's so strange. Yes. I hung a right, walked up a narrow pathway, and knocked on the door.

"I'm glad you came," he said.

"I'm glad you asked me to," I replied.

When I walked into Jack's room, I was struck by how clean and pleasant-smelling it was. He sauntered over to the stereo and put on an Anita Baker cassette. Then he came over to me and grabbing me by the waist, kissed me and began taking off my clothes.

I kept saying over and over in my head how I could not go through with it. I had only had sex a few times before and with the guy who'd help to end my soda jerk career. This guy was not my type. He wouldn't be any good in bed. I was naked on top of the bed as he pulled my legs open before he got on top of me. I stared up at him in disbelief but mostly at myself. The look on his face was of absolute assuredness of what he was about to do as he looked deep into my eyes. I tried to borrow from it to no avail.

His back had a thick slab of fat on it that didn't allow me to obtain a firm grasp. His shoulder blades were unapparent, lost in the wave of fat that washed over his entire posterior. I felt awkward, and I was inexperienced, so I lay there still, waiting, hoping to be pleased. I barely moved as he thrust inside me. He made faces like he was enjoying the feeling, and I looked at him with surprise. I could barely feel anything his penis was so trivial. But I continued to have sex with him, and he continued to want to have sex with me.

As I ignored my night school, we engaged in sex almost every day, everywhere in his parents' house. And I got better and better. As a result, I started to notice how good he wasn't, and I couldn't go on letting him be in control of our love-making. I took matters into my own hands and ventured on top of him. I discovered it didn't matter as much that he was so fat when I was on top. There I controlled our movements, our rhythm, and ultimately our pleasure.

"Don't get a big head or anything, but you got some nice curves, and you're great in bed," he murmured into my ear one night.

"Thanks," I said, with my head beginning to swell. Jack, despite his weirdness, began to consume me. Something began to come over me that I could not control. I stopped caring about anything else except for my new relationship with him. I forgot about my plans for the future. He became my future. I stopped going to my night classes at business school and started spending my evenings after work with him.

Eventually I was dropped from the school. I went crawling back to the administrator, begging to be allowed to start again at the beginning of the next semester. The next semester started in April, plenty enough time for me to get my shit together, or so I thought.

I was upstairs in the bathroom getting ready, and I had let my dad and my sister know that Jack, the guy I'd been seeing, was coming over. My mother was at some meeting for people who suspect they may be suppressing memories of having been molested. She wasn't sure she'd been molested, she only suspected. As if that would explain everything. I was glad she was gone, occupying her time, even if it was a waste of it.

I was pleasantly startled by the doorbell ringing, because I knew it was Jack. My sister went streaking by me in a revealing, silky, tiger-print bathrobe down the stairs. "What a bitch," I said loud enough for only me to hear. Did she really think she'd make any type of an impact on anyone who dated me? She liked guys who resembled those pesky windshield washers planted at the end of almost every off-ramp in L.A. that I wouldn't trust to walk my dog. Still, that didn't keep her from trying to get Jack's attention.

Jack stood in the doorway perplexed by what my sister was wearing. I introduced him to my father, who was lounging in the living room with a slushy Margarita in his hand. My father said hello, looked unimpressed, and said he was going to bed. I guess he was expecting Denzel. So Jack and I disappeared into the den to watch a video, leaving my sister standing in the foyer like a hooker waiting for her next trick.

Jack and I were getting cozy on the couch watching a video when one of my sister's low-life friends, who appeared to be clearly on speed or some other type of mind-altering drug, arrived at the door wearing a T-shirt, shorts, and boots.

He sat on the couch next to us twitching and perspiring, complaining of being hot even though we were now in the first weeks of December and he was dressed for August. He smelled of illegal narcotics, cigarette smoke, and that tangy, musty smell that you get after your deodorant has worn off. I glared at my sister, who was now properly dressed and lighting up a Virginia Slim in the chair next to me, as I sat pissed off that she'd bring him there when she knew I was entertaining a guest.

"You guys, this is Daren," she said with her elbow resting seductively on the arm of the easy chair, her lit cigarette balancing on her fingertips, her head cocked backwards in a suggestive manner, while she crossed her legs, reminding me of Cruella de Vil.

"So fuck'n what," I whispered to her with my teeth grinding together. "I don't care if his name is Louis Farrakhan, I want him out of here before I go tell Dad." I looked suspiciously at him, thinking he needed to be in a rehab clinic somewhere, and I almost offered to drive him to one when he and my sister abruptly got up to leave. Jack and I raced each other to the living room window just in time to catch a glimpse of them speeding off down the road on his motorbike.

"I don't know where she finds these people," I said to Jack, embarrassed.

"Yeah, and why did she answer the door in her bathrobe?" he asked perplexed.

"I don't know. Hey, what do you want to do?" I asked.

"I don't know. What do you want to do?" he said, smiling a smile I was all too familiar with. He began kissing my neck and fiddling with the button on my jeans. As he freed my waist from the bondage of the jeans, he slipped his hand into the moist spot forming between my legs. I slid my pants down, ready to take him inside me when Cesar, our Pomeranian, began to gyrate and growl as if to say, "I don't think so, buddy." We looked at him and laughed, and tried to go back to what we were doing. Cesar went into a frenzy, making some of the orange-red hairs growing out from his body fly loose from his jerking. He barked and jumped on Jack's now bare butt, nipping at it as if it were covered in fleas, clearly traumatized by what he was witnessing. We had no choice but to find another location.

The laundry room was close by. We had sex on the dryer that was still warm from towels previously drying. My dad was obliviously asleep upstairs, and my sister and her friend were probably miles away by now, either sprawled out on the highway or working as hostesses at a crack house somewhere. If I got my wish they were being slowly tortured in a Tijuana jail. I thanked Jack at the door for coming over, offered him a twenty for his services, which he summarily declined, and floated upstairs to my room, falling softly asleep, forgetting for the next eight hours who I was.

When Jack finally met my mother, far from perfect ended up being as close to it as I would get. This meeting would make the one with my sister and father seem like a trip to Disneyland. I decided to stop delaying the inevitable and told Jack to come over and meet my mother. I was proud of how young she looked and how pretty she was. I was used to getting compliments for her. At that time she hadn't let herself go and given up on making herself look presentable.

I looked intently at her as I introduced her to Jack. Their voices faded to the far reaches of my mind as they spoke of things people who just meet speak of. I wondered, tracing the fine lines of her face with my eyes, why her beauty did not allow her to escape the demons that undoubtedly lived inside her.

What haunted her? What did she fear? Why couldn't her beauty Band-Aid her wounds and help them go away? She only had to look in the mirror to find strength. There it was before her, the face of an exquisite beauty, who most women envied. She was lucky. She had a doting husband, a nice house. Why was she always unhappy?

I gazed at her, remembering the time when I was little, before I stopped loving her, when I was on one of my many missions to make her happy, and I followed her out from the house to a waiting car driven by one of her friends to take her to work.

"Have a good day, Mama," I said.

"How can I, when I have all of you?" she said, before closing the passenger-side door, leaving me standing in a swirl of dusty wind in the middle of the street. I could not appease her. I was jealous of her beauty then as I had not come into my own, and I wished I looked more like her. At that time, I only possessed her perfect, straight-toothed smile, which I saw little of.

She was smiling now, as Jack charmed her, her mouth opening into an easy laugh. My eyes followed its pattern. I was thinking how easily smiles fade away, and hers definitely was going to. I stopped to let my old memory fade, going back from whence it came, dissolving like sugar stirred into coffee, snapping my mind back into the present.

Jack and I sat in the den chatting about the Christmas that had just passed us by, as my mother retreated to the kitchen, where she went undetected by either of us. I mentioned that I'd bought a bottle of perfume for Kenya that I thought she'd really liked. My mother had been eavesdropping in the kitchen just steps away from where we were.

"You didn't buy that bottle of perfume for Kenya," she said annoyed.

"Yes, I did," I said, confused.

"Oh, no, you didn't. You borrowed the money from me and never paid me back," she said, becoming increasingly irritated.

I sat there for a moment, embarrassed, trying to replay in my head the course of events. And I was sure that, yes, she had given me money for gifts, but I was sure I had paid for Kenya's perfume out of my own pocket. I didn't know what Jack was thinking, and I definitely didn't want him to know what she was really like so soon.

"No, Mom, I paid for it myself," I said standing my ground.

"Hell, I'm always giving you money you never pay back," she said, blasting me. I couldn't believe she was actually doing this to me in front of the guy she knew I was seeing. I didn't want to seem like a wimp and a freeloader in front of Jack. I worried about what he was going to think of me, so I continued to defend myself. I stood up to better counter what she was accusing me of, and that's when she lost it.

"I'm tired of helping all of you. You never do anything for me. You're all ungrateful. I have the most ungrateful kids in the world." And I had never felt more regretful for being one of them.

I looked at Jack and told him we were leaving. We left her in the house shouting behind us. I stopped processing what she was saying and let her voice Ping-Pong in my head untranslated. Jack walked behind me, and when we got to the sidewalk, I let go of the tears that were always just under the surface, waiting to be released. I had never been so embarrassed. He hugged me and told me it was okay and not to cry, but I couldn't stop.

"I hate her," I said, choking through my tears, my nose beginning to stop up. "None of what she just said is true."

"Come on, you don't hate your mother."

"Okay. Where were you just now? You didn't just watch her do that to me in front of you?"

"I did, and I heard it all. But it's over now. Just forget it and move on."

"Forget it? Just move on? Oh, why didn't I think of that? Is that all I have to do? No, you forget your grocery store coupons, or the names of people you've met only once before, and to take video rentals back. You don't forget stuff like this. Tell me how do I forget being treated like crap in front of my friends by her ever since I can remember? I can't forget all the mean things she's said to me and the things she's done. If you're talking about forgive and forget, well, I don't have any of that, and I sure as hell don't know where to go to get some."

Jack was speechless. I could tell he didn't know what to say, so he simply guided me to his car, and we left to go to his parents' house. I rode in the car wondering if he'd dump me I had so much drama in my life. Maybe this was more than he could handle. I had a dysfunctional family way before it was fashionable, before Oprah aired her dirty laundry and let us all know we were all fucked up in one way or another. Until then, I thought my family was the only one.

Later on that night, Jack and I were in the midst of having sex. I reached in his nightstand for a condom and discovered there weren't any more.

"Jack, we can't do it. We're out of condoms," I said flatly.

"Just get on top of me," he grumbled.

"No, I can't. You'll get me pregnant," I said, beginning to get worried.

Jack reached over, pulling my waist towards him and maneuvered my torso onto his. He put his half-limp penis inside me, placed his hands on my hips, and began to pump.

"No, Jack," I protested, "You're gonna get me pregnant. Stop," I shrieked.

Jack held me tighter to keep me from getting off of him. I looked at his face and watched him grow agitated. I fought harder to pull myself away from him by trying to fall to the side.

"I'm not gonna get you pregnant, dummy," he blurted out.

A smack went off in my head, and my heart sank like an anchor. And at the same time, I did begin to feel dumb. I thought since he was older he knew something I didn't. I started to feel unlike a woman, more like a scared little girl. I did what he wanted, and I let him pump me without a condom on until he was suddenly pushing me off him before he came all over himself. He could have violated me in five other different ways if he'd wanted I felt so numb. I bounced a few times on the bed from his overweight body leaving it as he went into the bathroom to clean up.

I lay there wondering just what the hell was I doing, but I knew I could not leave him. There was no one else. It was him or no one, so I stayed, even though it was clear now for me to see that he was a jerk. I drove home that night believing I didn't have very many choices left in life. I couldn't know then that at such a young age, all I really had were the choices I would make. I chose him, and by choosing him, I chose my fate.

13

By the time New Year's Eve rolled around, Jack and I were bringing in the new year on the couch with drinks and Dick Clark. During one of the many commercials, Jack and I sat down to enjoy a pizza we'd just ordered.

"Hey, let's get married," Jack announced from across his mother's dining room table. I began to laugh from the other end of it, I'd never heard anything so ridiculous.

"You don't want to marry me," I said through my giggles.

"Yes, I do," he replied.

"Okay. Give me ten reasons why I should marry you," I said, getting serious.

"I only have five."

"Then I won't marry you. Besides, I'm only nineteen."

"So what. Come on, let's go to Vegas now, right this minute."

"We can't do that."

"Please. I want to marry you. I want to take care of you." Those were the magic words; he wanted to take care of me. And I wanted to be taken care of. So we drove the three-and-a-half hours in his Mustang to Las Vegas, through the desert, through the night. My motives for going with him were totally misguided, because all I really wanted was to be able to get out of my mother's house. I'd always pictured Jack and I living together in sin, not wedded in holy matrimony.

What would my parents say when they found out? I didn't care. I was hurting from an unhappy life I could not come to terms with. I wanted something new, something different, something more. I was being stifled in that house, and my sister's return only exacerbated the problem. I fought with my mother constantly. I could not talk to my father about it. He couldn't listen or understand through his perpetual defense of her.

So I would marry this man I barely knew anything about, this man I thought would be my savior, this man that my better judgment kept telling me he had something gravely wrong with him that I chose to ignore. But he could get me out of there, and at the time, that was all I cared about. As for whether I loved him or not, I thought I did, a little, but not nearly enough. He was my lottery ticket, and maybe the catastrophic events that came to pass were of my own doing for marrying a man I did not truly love, marrying for solely selfish, self-serving reasons.

We drove through the desert on our way to get married. We hardly spoke as the first two hours passed, and I became bored with the silence and the darkness, so I began to look for things to occupy my time. I opened the glove box to be nosy. The light inside lit up a picture of a girl I did not recognize. She had long, blonde hair rolling over her shoulders and a long nose. She had an odd face. There was nothing special or striking about her. Her looks were slightly below average. She looked about twenty-four. The size of the picture let me know she was proud of the way she'd been captured in it. I told myself this must be the ex I'd heard about, and I slowly grew annoyed and angry. An ex-girlfriend still alive in Jack's heart was something I had not contemplated, and I felt betrayed.

"Who's this?" I asked.

"That's Denise, my ex-girlfriend," he answered, his eyes darting quickly from the road to the picture and back again.

"How long were you together?" I asked

"Five years. Why?"

"Is she the one that had you seeing the shrink?"

"Yep."

"Why do you still have the picture, then?"

"Well, I don't know. I just do," he said, dismissing me.

I turned away from him and rolled the window down. The freezing desert wind stunned every exposed part of my body, ferociously blowing my hair back, muffling the sound in my ear. I forced the picture out of the window, letting it take ahold of the wind, flying away like a kite. I hoped the picture would be the first of its kind on Mars. Jack turned and looked at me like I was crazy.

"What the hell did you do that for?" he said, out of breath.

"Well, we're on our way to get married. I didn't think you'd still want it."

"Well, I did. You shouldn't have done that."

"Why? Do you still want to be with her?"

"No."

"Then you won't mind that it's gone," I said.

We should have turned around. But the Vegas lights are at their most seductive after midnight. They're the perfect mistress, tempting you to defy the sensibilities of going to bed at a decent hour, leaving your better judgment behind. They dare you to come closer as they're seen in the desert for miles before they're actually reached. They beckon with a persuasive glow made up of hopes and dreams of a bright, happy, lucrative future, wrapped around them. Just as a near-death experience would urge us, we went into the light.

We made it there around 3:30 in the morning, and began to search for somewhere to get married among the myriad of wedding chapels offering up quickie, cheap, unplanned marriages. After we secured a marriage license, we made our way to a small, white chapel on the strip, near a restaurant serving steak and eggs for $2.99, where I supposed we'd have our wedding reception dinner for breakfast instead.

The couple in line ahead of us smelled of cheap liquor and cigarettes and probably had no business getting married in their drunken haze, but there was no one there to give last-minute counseling to get them to change their minds. Las Vegas was clearly not a place for redemption, and these all-night wedding chapels were definitely not confessionals. They were open all night for a reason, to be the place that catered to the whims of the impulsive and lonely-hearted.

We sat in front of the person who would perform our marriage, my eyes red, my thoughts dishevelled, with my brain in an apparent fog since it never occurred to me to turn back after seeing all the other rejects in line before us about to make the same capricious mistake. I began to see the stubble on Jack's face bloom and transform into the five o'clock shadow it would later become from the late hour. He appeared to be a lot older than his twenty-four years. The sprinkling of sweat beads across his broad forehead revealed his nervousness as we sat there waiting to be joined in marriage. I wondered if we were what a mistake looked like sitting there in our wrinkled clothes, yawning involuntarily, obviously having just driven there without previous thought or preparation. I'd decided when my hand had touched the car-door handle that if I got in I would go through with it, and that is what I did.

At 4:35 a.m. on what would otherwise have been any normal Sunday, Jack and I were married. We skipped the steak and egg breakfast, traded it for an immediate drive home. Somewhere in that grey area that separates night from day, I thought about how I hadn't told my father I was getting married beforehand, and I twisted my head towards the passenger window, pushing it deeper into the headrest. With the sun coming up, I knew I would not tell my family at all. When they would eventually find out was something I wouldn't let myself contemplate. I just knew I wouldn't tell them right away.

The sunrise made a thin stream of light over the mountains across my pretty, newlywed face as we raced through the desert morning. By the time we'd crossed over the state line, it all had become like the irrational nature of a dream. I couldn't reconcile the fact that I had just gotten married to the man driving beside me, in the middle of the night, at nineteen, without telling my parents, and I actually went all the way to Vegas and didn't gamble.

After Jack dropped me off, the early morning air awakened my senses, and the reality of what I'd done was in stark contrast to what I was about to do. I wasn't going on some exotic cruise or flying to some romantic location for my honeymoon. I kissed my husband good-bye and quietly went inside, tip-toed up to my room and allowed my willowy thin, five-foot-five frame to slink into my twin-size bed, perfectly suited now to accommodate my twin-size brain. I fell asleep hoping my face wouldn't reveal my secret to all who would gaze upon it.

"Did you see what time she got home?" Casey asked in a hushed tone to my mother.

"No," my mother replied.

"I hope she doesn't get pregnant," Casey said.

"Well, she can screw up her life if she wants to."

Sure. Whatever. Like I was just gonna get pregnant. Just like that. Casey was the one who'd gotten pregnant and at the same age I was then. I listened to them in the kitchen from the top of the stairs, as their whispered voices echoed up to me like unintentional confessions.

Yeah, back in 1982, Casey had picked herself a real winner. She had a shotgun wedding. Her husband abruptly joined the army, taking her with him to Washington, where he was stationed, and where he proceeded to beat the crap out of her every day until the baby was born. She left his ass faster than a speeding bullet and came back home to Sunny Beach, to live with us. In 1987, Jade and Seneca moved us to ritzy Montara Valley. With her irresponsible ways and dysfunctional lifestyle, of course Casey followed soon after, bringing with her enough trouble to keep a small courthouse running.

So I'd married Jack, Aden's father, setting off a chain of events that would last a lifetime. I'd also returned to the scene of the crime a year later to celebrate a one-year anniversary that wasn't really worth celebrating and conceived Aden, but I didn't get what I'd bargained for by marrying Jack. Whether I had gotten what I deserved was still open for debate.

My father and I pulled up to an anonymous Montara Valley burger stand, waiting to order, with the sun the color of Tang setting in front of our eyes like it was a movie showing at the drive-in. The view through the windshield was flawless.

"You're not thinking about getting married, are you?" popped out of my father's mouth. I kept quiet, but, caught off guard, I almost jumped.

"Because I'm feeling like you're about to do something impulsive like get married."

"No, I'm not," I said without emotion.

In my late teens, I discovered my father could predict things, like earthquakes and the weather. He'd catch me just as I was about to go out the door and tell me to get an umbrella. There wasn't a cloud in the sky, the weather had been forecast for sunny and warm temperatures. But sure enough, it would rain. My dad would tell me, like, at dinner, "Sydney, there's gonna be an earthquake soon."

"How do you know, Dad?" I said with intrigue.

"I just know. Trust me."

Sure enough, on the evening news, a day or two later, there would have been an earthquake somewhere in California. Sometimes they were even in far away places, like China or Japan. My dad being clairvoyant made me idolize him even more. He was special, different, fun, and real, someone easy to touch and believe in. His predictions were a secret he only told to me, and I believed wholeheartedly in what he was saying. The secret we kept between us, our closeness from my devotion to him must have helped him survive in the desert of a marriage he was inhabiting with my mother.

By the time I had turned eighteen, when I looked into my father's eyes looking back at mine, I'd only see pride, yet I felt I had given him nothing to deserve it. My marrying Jack was nothing to be proud of; he wasn't rich or famous. Lying to my father was making my eyes water, but I said nothing. The food came, and we drove home.

And now my father's clairvoyance was no longer fun and intriguing. It was becoming something I should fear, as he seemed to know me better than I knew myself. I didn't want him to find out about Vegas, not one minute before I was ready to tell him. Although he was off the mark by a month, and the deed was already done, he had accurately sensed marriage swirling around in my puny brain. I wondered how the hell he became psychic, and whose fault it was that it didn't get passed along to me.

Jack and I still lived separately at our parents' house and continued to keep our marriage a secret. Back at work at Mervyns, we had to keep our marriage a secret. Married couples could not work together there, and we were saving up for an apartment.

"Are you and Jack together or, like, dating?" Kenya asked slyly while I began to ring up a shabby-looking man, unshaven, dressed like a an ex-war vet, who had brought nine pairs of expensive designer jeans to my counter.

"Umm, what gave you that idea?" I said halting my sale.

"Well, it's going around the store that you two are seeing each other. And somebody even said you two were married this past weekend in Vegas, but I told that person they should quit hitting the crack pipe."

"Kenya, let me finish ringing up this sale and I'll get back to you, okay?" I said trying to buy myself some time to come up with a good lie. I ignored the oddness of someone buying nine pairs of the same type of jeans and put them in one of the store's handle bags, placing it on top of the counter in front of the man.

"Sir, will that be cash, check, or charge?" I asked. The man made a sudden move and abruptly snatched the bag and bolted from the counter on his way out of the store. Kenya and I looked at each other, our eyes widening. I began to laugh uncontrollably as the man who changed from paying customer into thief was now running through the store like an es-caped convict, his head bobbing and weaving, dodging in between racks of clothing until breaking free through the front doors. Kenya chased after him, yelling for him to wait, stop, waving her hands in the air, calling for security, while I was being held captive by my laughter. She came back out of breath, her hair displaced all over her head. I saluted her for being such a loyal employee.

"How can you just stand there and laugh?" Kenya asked angrily.

"Well, it was funny. Didn't you see the way he ran? He grabbed the bag from me and just took off running," I said, continuing to laugh. "I can't believe the things people do."

"You really don't take this job seriously, do you, Sydney?" Kenya ac-cused while she put her hair back into place.

"You wear mini skirts and a ton of other things, even though you know they're against the rules. You never show up for work on time. You couldn't care less if the store is robbed blind. So why are you even here?"

"Well, let's see. To get a gold star on my badge? Oh, I'm sorry, that would be your reason. Mine is much more simple. It's because I get paid to be."

The next day I was fired in the human resource office by some chick named Kim on the second floor. She said it was something about my customer service attitude and abilities not being reflective of what the store thinks is in their best interest regarding security. My job at Mervyns had run its course. Frankly, I was surprised I lasted as long as I did, with my slacker ways and nonchalant attitude. Driving home from my old job, I scolded myself for not staying in business school. I had no clue what I would do next. Jack, being the good husband, said our situation was not a problem, he would just go back to making money selling cars, even though he'd promised himself he would never sell cars again.

He dropped out of Chapman University and went back to kicking up dust on a car lot in Santa Ana. We searched on the weekends for an apartment and found one in a quiet college neighborhood called Claremont. I told my parents I would be moving in with Jack, neglecting to mention our marriage.

"Oh, really," my mother said flatly, as if I could go ahead and move to the moon for all she cared. But my father took me aside later and said he loved me, would miss me, that I was still his little girl.

"She'll be back," I could hear my mother predicting to my sister in the kitchen as I packed my things upstairs. I was only taking my clothes and miscellaneous items since Jack and I had purchased furniture and everything else we'd be needing with the money he was making at the car lot. When I came back the next day to pick up some last-minute items, I was thrown for a loop as I rounded the corner to my room and found my mother and sister sitting on a couch I'd never seen before watching Lifetime, television for women. They had their feet up on a coffee table that used to be downstairs. Overnight my room had been converted into a den. I wanted to say, "You bitches, you couldn't even wait for my fucking bed to get cold before you moved in here."

Like cement drying, my new reality was beginning to set in that I wasn't a kid anymore. For some reason I thought I would be able to come back to my old room now and then to ponder my existence and to be reminded of who I used to be. But two unsavory individuals I despised more and more every day quickly erased me like sand blown away by the wind. I didn't let my emotions show as I glanced up somberly at the last piece of evidence that proved I had once existed within the room's four walls, my beloved George Michael poster.

I left the poster in what was no longer my room, descending the stairs leaving pieces of my former self behind one step at a time. With the erasure of my room, I felt detached and cut off, like the house wasn't even my home anymore. The next steps I went up led to the new apartment I would be sharing with my husband.

14

Our apartment was a small one-bedroom on the second floor of a three-story building. It faced the west, and the sun didn't show inside the apartment until half the day was over. I woke up in subdued sunlight I was unfamiliar with, and I was unfamiliar with waking up next to the body that was breathing next to me all night. Jack's weight caused him to perspire easily, and the tangy, spoiled-milk smell coming from his side of the bed let me know he should shower before bed. I looked at his smashed hair, half-open mouth, and shirtless body and decided to nudge him awake out of excitement from spending our first night together.

"What? I'm sleeping," he grumbled.

"Come on. Get up. It's morning. Don't you want to get up?"

"No, I want to sleep."

"Well, I'm a morning person, and I'm getting up."

I opened the sliding doors leading to the balcony and walked out, taking in the view. It was February, and the air smelled and felt brand-new. There were apartment buildings on all sides of ours. If everyone were to come out of their apartments all at once, I could possibly be seen in my nightgown by at least a couple hundred people. I looked up at the snow-capped mountains peeking out from behind the roofs of the apartments, taking the fresh air into my lungs. I was home.

Jack and I sat in our dining room, enjoying a pasta dish he created, getting used to our new surroundings, when voices from outside came bursting through the quiet walls we sat encompassed in. Voices were coming from people shouting downstairs in the courtyard.

"I'm tired of your dog shitting in the courtyard! You and your black girlfriend need to pick his shit up," a shirtless white guy with a beer and cigarette in his hand, tattoos of skulls and crossbones on his arms, was shouting from his first-floor apartment patio.

Jack and I looked at each other, then ran to the front of the apartment to better hear what was going on. We cracked the front door open, afraid we'd be drawn into the argument, so we listened and took turns watching through the crack of the door. Since we were living in our first apartment building, we were fascinated by the spectacle taking place down below.

"You're a racist jerk," a husky black girl yelled back from the grassy area of the courtyard with her white boyfriend holding the leash that lead to a small, quivering, shaggy, cream-colored dog.

"Shut up, you fat bitch," the man said.

"Hey, don't you talk to my girlfriend that way," the white guy said, taking steps towards the man.

"Nigger lover," the tattooed white guy yelled back, spitting on the ground. At that point, the girl was grabbing at her boyfriend, trying to keep him from crossing the grassy hill area to physically confront the angry white male screaming about their dog. I told Jack I was calling the police, and I went into the bedroom and picked up the phone.

"Are you kidding me? Put that phone down," Jack said, grabbing at the phone from behind me.

"Why?" I said, twisting around in the cord.

"It's none of your business what's going on down there."

"Well, what if it were you and me? We're an interracial couple. That guy could have it in for us next."

"Look, they weren't picking up after their dog, and he was mad."

"Oh, really. Well, what about his racist comments?"

"I'm gonna go finish my dinner," Jack said, leaving me in the bedroom. I stared at the phone for a second, then hung it back up. The shouting had stopped, and the courtyard was empty, but the incident stayed with me. The next day, the interracial couple moved out, and I don't know what happened to the angry tattooed guy. But Jack's views on race, which I never took the time to find out about, were starting to come into the light.

I passed my days by occasionally looking for work. I tried to return to the business school I had been going to, but my dreams of becoming a lawyer were now lost, evaporated into my subconscious when I had married Jack. He was an excellent bread-winner, so I was not motivated by the need for money to get a job. The money Jack was making took great care of us, and I spent it as if there was no tomorrow.

On my 20th birthday, Jack surprised me by bringing home a black cat that I, without hesitation, named Boo.

"Happy birthday," Jack said, placing Boo, who was at the time a tiny kitten, in my arms. I had never had a cat before, and Jack couldn't have given me a better gift. Boo squirmed around in my arms, trying to escape my hold, and he fell, spilling onto the carpet. He ran away, scurrying under our bed. I followed behind him. I knelt down and lifted up the bedspread.

"Hey, there little fella," I cooed. "Come here little guy."

Boo's eyes became enlarged and glowed in the darkness as he hissed, showing me his underdeveloped claws as I peered at him. I reached for him, searching for a paw to grab onto with which to pull him out from under the bed. He hissed again before scratching my arm, slightly breaking the skin. I ran water from the kitchen sink over my scratch that was beginning to sting.

"What's wrong with him?" I asked Jack, rubbing my arm. He was busy scratching his head.

"Just what kind of a crazy cat did you bring home?" I complained.

"Well, I guess the fact that he was sitting in the corner, facing the wall, away from all the other kittens should have told me something."

"Gee, you think?" I said, annoyed.

Boo never bonded with either of us. He preferred to ignore us unless he was hungry and wanted to be fed. He grew to be a large cat, with an oversized head shaped almost like a lion's. He didn't know how to accept affection, bulking up his shoulders and turning uncomfortably when I tried stroking him. Sometimes he'd even scratch and hiss at me for simply reaching out, attempting to touch him. I resented his inhabiting our apartment with the attitude of not liking us, leaving his hair all over the furniture, darting out the front door, his litter box stinking up the place. But he was my birthday present from Jack, and my thoughts of getting rid of him weren't as strong as my love for Jack. After all, he did keep me company while Jack was at work.

One slow weekday, I wandered around the apartment bored and jobless. I stepped out onto the balcony to get some sun with a fresh cup of coffee in my hand and heard voices coming from across the courtyard. My days, being filled with the emptiness of air, turned me into a vicarious snoop, and anything I could see and hear coming from outside my cocoon of an apartment made me run towards it.

"I said get out, you stupid whore," a guy's voice said from inside the apartment directly across from where I was standing. There was a slender, blonde girl slumped in a lawn chair crying with her face in her hands, on their second floor balcony. I stepped to one side to continue watching.

"But how can you do this to me?" she called to him inside.

"I'm tired of you. Get the hell out," he responded. The goings on of the other couples in the building was arousing my curiosity and shocking me at the same time. I had been fooled by the clean streets, clean air, and picturesque mountains surrounding the apartments. I soon realized that the people inhabiting the other apartments were anything but clean. They were rowdy, classless, undesirable, and different from me.

"Hey, you, over there," the man shouted to me from across the courtyard, as he was now standing on the balcony with his hands on his hips next to the crying girl. He had caught me watching.

"Mind your own damn business," he yelled to me. Startled, I stumbled back into the apartment, spilling coffee, just in time to hear a message on the answering machine from Jack saying he was coming home late. I sat in front of the television, watching "Love American Style." It was 1:00 a.m. and Jack still wasn't home yet.

"So where were you?" I asked as soon as Jack opened the door.

"Well, I went out with the guys," he said.

After receiving five more I'll-be-home-late messages, I grew suspicious of exactly what Jack was doing after work.

"You're coming home late again? Where are you going? And what am I supposed to do?"

"That's simple. I've been telling you to get a job."

"That's not fair. You know I've been trying. Nobody will hire me. The president you voted for started this Gulf War, and our country is in a recession, and now I can't get a job," I said sarcastically.

"Look, I'll be home later."

I hung up the phone, headed for the kitchen, and pushed Boo with my leg on my way there. He took a swipe at my ankle, and I threatened to starve him for a week if he scratched me again. I grabbed a Mountain Dew from the refrigerator, popping the top like I was a mean trucker dude, looking around for my girlfriend so I could smack her.

As I stood in the kitchen, gulping down my favorite drink, a pile of bills was staring at me from the dining room table. I decided to pass the time by paying them. I sorted the bills out one by one: lights, water, trash, phone. Phone. The phone bill appeared to be getting thicker with each month, and the bill amount was getting larger. I knew I wasn't making more than my usual amount of calls, so I decided to take a closer look.

I searched the bill, distinguishing between my calls and Jack's. There were no bells and whistles going off in my head looking at it, but there was a large number of calls made to a Pasadena number. I didn't know anyone in Pasadena, and for all I knew neither did Jack. When Jack got home, I asked him who he had been calling from Pasadena.

"My cousin Mario," he said.

"Your cousin Mario? You don't have a cousin Mario," I said.

"Yes, I do. I've just never told you about him because he lives kind of far."

"Jack, Pasadena is thirty minutes away," I said.

"Well, yeah, but.... well, that's who I've been calling."

I was suspicious of Jack's explanation, and the next day after he left the house, I called the number.

"Crogus residence," an old lady's voice said. I quickly hung up. I couldn't confirm the connection to Jack, but I knew it wasn't the number for any cousin Mario.

That night I told Jack we were going to leave all the windows open and just bundle up in bed to keep warm. I told him the brisk night air would be exhilarating.

"Say again why you want to leave all the windows open?" Jack asked.

"It will feel like we're outside camping. It will be cool. You'll see," I said. "It's called a freeze-out."

Jack reluctantly allowed me to leave open all the windows, which basically consisted of the slider and a medium-sized window in our bedroom.

"I better not get sick," Jack warned. "My boss will fire me if I miss too many days."

"Oh, you won't. Stop being a baby. Trust me."

Jack placed his large, flabby body in our bed, nestling himself in.

"See, isn't this great?" I said underneath three heavy blankets.

Jack woke up the next morning with the sniffles. I gave him a cough drop and kissed his forehead good-bye. He told me to get a job. But I already had a job all right, finding out who the hell he'd been calling. Before the dust left over from Jack closing the door could settle, my finger was punching in numbers on the phone.

"Hello. This is Denise," a girl's voice answered.

"I'm sorry. I have the wrong number," I said blankly and hung up. I stared at the phone number from Pasadena with a million thoughts dispersed into my head. I told myself he'd been calling his ex-girlfriend Denise, the one whose picture I had let fly away in the desert night.

I bitterly left the dining room table so furious the chair I was sitting in tumbled over behind me. I went for the bill drawer and flung it open, spilling its contents to the kitchen floor. I wanted to know just how long Jack had been calling her. I went backwards through the phone bills: April, March, February. Jack had been calling Denise from almost the very first week of us moving into our apartment. I couldn't wait to confront him.

"Syd, I'm home," Jack said, coming through the door, late as usual. At first I envisioned myself slowly entrapping him into admitting he'd been calling his ex-girlfriend, like a good detective would, but as soon as I saw him, all that was forgotten.

"What the hell is this?" I angrily spat, flying out from our bedroom, waving the phone bills in his face. "I know this is Denise's number, not some cousin Mario's. You lied to me. What are you doing calling her?"

"No. Wait. She called me first."

"Oh, really. How'd she get our number?" I said.

"Maybe my mother gave it to her," he said.

"Why would your mother do that?"

"Hello, because she doesn't like you," he said. "Look, Syd, I'm tired. Let's go to bed and talk about it tomorrow."

I felt put off, my anger thrown away like a balled up piece of paper, and it wasn't hard for me to decide to have another freeze-out. I lay awake in bed staring up at the star-like specks on the ceiling my eyes were forming into daggers aimed down at Jack, frowning, feeling betrayed underneath my pile of blankets. The wind howling outside was reminding me of vampires, werewolves and monsters.

It was about 35 degrees outside, and we were having a cooler than usual spring in California. I turned my head on my pillow to look at Jack, who was lying on his side facing the wall, soundly sleeping. I slowly pulled at the blankets until they tumbled off him, knowing he would not realize he had been uncovered he slept so deeply. Thoughts of what was really going on with him and Denise were continuing to brew inside me as I watched the tiny hairs inhabiting Jack's back begin to stand up and poke out, petrified by the cold air.

Jack woke up the next morning extremely ill. He was weak and couldn't get out of bed. His nose was plugged, head was pounding, throat was sore, and his body was aching all over. The wetness on his forehead told me he was definitely running a temperature.

"I'm sick, Syd," Jack groaned in bed, holding his body. "I can't go to work today. Call my job."

I called Jack's job for the next five days, telling them he was sick, and they fired him. The pain behind Jack's suffering eyes let me know there were a lot of evil words he wanted to say to me and couldn't because his illness had caused him to lose his voice. We had no health insurance, and I was forced to use over-the-counter medicines and home remedies to nurse him back to health. Jack ended up being sick in bed for three weeks.

"No more goddamn freeze-outs," was the first thing he said when he could finally speak again.

"Okay," I said cowering from my guilt. His being ill had allowed me to forgive him of the phone calls to Denise.

"What's she like? Denise, I mean," I asked Jack over coffee his first morning out of bed and looking for work.

"You shouldn't worry about her. She's not that great. She's had, like, five abortions."

I shocked myself while picturing Denise going into an abortion clinic for a fifth time. I had actually seen her with my own eyes a few weeks after we'd gotten married but before we'd moved in together. Jack had taken me to a house she was staying at in San Marco to pick up some old things she wanted to give him. Through the rearview mirror I could see her come around the back side of the car, then duck her head down in to greet me through the driver's side window. She had a strange look on her face as she shook my left hand, tilting it slightly, telling me hello before retreating back around the car into the house.

"She doesn't believe I got married," Jack said laughing, returning after a few minutes, getting back into the car, tossing some books in the backseat, starting the car engine.

"Why not?" I asked. "She did kind of turn my hand to look for a wedding ring I don't have yet. By the way, when am I getting that ring?"

"You'll get it," he had said.

We had been married for months, and I still didn't have a ring to prove it. And after meeting Denise I had discarded the memory of my meeting her down to the far reaches of my mind like a flicked piece of lint. But now I'd accidentally found out my husband was still contacting her.

"I don't want you to call her anymore," I said one morning while Jack got dressed.

"Fine. I won't," Jack said. At the front door Jack turned and told me we were close to having no money if he couldn't find a job, and with the recession being so bad, he probably wouldn't, and that he didn't know what we were going to do.

"It's important that you get a job," he said before leaving. I'd put in five applications at places like Home Depot, Food 4 Less, and Lucky Supermarket, and nobody would hire me, but I couldn't make Jack believe this. I spent the day sitting on the couch, contemplating my next move.

Jack called later on that day to say he'd found another job at a smaller car lot not far from our apartment. He left the number for his new job and told me he would be home late. I cleaned the apartment and went back to watching TV when the phone rang.

"Hello," I said.

"Is Jack there?"

"No, he isn't."

"Will you tell him Denise called, and can I leave a number for him to call me back?" she said. I was fuming, but I calmly, graciously took the number from her and called Jack at his new job.

"Hugo's Auto."

"Jack, please," I said to the receptionist who answered.

"One moment, please," she said. Over the phone I could hear Jack being paged.

"This is Jack."

"What the hell is Denise doing calling here leaving numbers for you?"

"Look, she's house-sitting for some friends near our apartment."

"And?"

"And I guess she thought I could call her if I wanted."

"Are you kidding me? Look, Jack, I'm not gonna put up with this," I said.

"It's nothing. I'm not going to call her. Hey, there's a party at a friend's house tonight. Do you want to go?"

"No, you go," I said, coldly declining the offer and hung up. Through his phone contact with her, she'd managed to let him know where she was staying. I figured she was trying to get him back. I was too young to know I should be packing Jack's things about now, so later on that night I sat in front of the TV watching "20/20" and arguing on the phone with Kenya.

"Kenya, you're so crazy," I said, laughing.

"I'm telling you, racism is everywhere," Kenya said in a whispered, paranoid voice.

"Well, you know what, Kenya, these are the '90s, and black people can pretty much be whatever they want nowadays. Sure there's racism, but it's nothing that getting an education and refraining from having children that you can't afford and staying out of jail won't cure," I said.

"Sydney, are you sure you're not a Republican? Because you sound like a Republican," Kenya said. The call-waiting was clicking on my end of the phone, and I told Kenya, to hold on.

"Is Jack there?" said a woman's voice.

"No, he's not. Who is this?" I asked.

"This is Denise."

I wasn't about to let this call go by unopposed, especially with all the gall this person obviously had coursing through her veins.

"You know what, Denise, I don't appreciate your calling my husband or my home," I said.

"Well, I'm calling to speak to Jack."

"And I just told you he's not here. What, you want him to come hold your hand while you're house-sitting? Yeah, I know where you are. Well, he's not going to do that."

"Oh, really. Well, why aren't you with him right now? Don't you enjoy a good party, or are you boring, Sydney?" I was pissed she'd actually knew and was using my name.

"Do you just like to stay home all the time?" she said snidely.

With that, Denise had pushed the wrong button and had chosen the wrong night to fuck with me. I sensed she wanted to really have it out, but I wasn't going to go the full twelve rounds with her, I was preparing for the quick knockout.

"No, I'm not boring at all, Denise," I began. "And what about you? Why are you home tonight? I mean, don't you have another abortion to go get?"

The click in my ear followed by silence let me know Denise had hung up, and I switched back over to Kenya to finish telling her how black people would be just fine if they would follow my formula for success, feeling more powerful than ever.

I fell softly into a blissful sleep with the windows open, believing I had devastated Denise into never bothering Jack and me again. I wanted her spirit to be wounded like a bird with a broken wing, limping, falling over to the ground with no choice but to wish that death would come mercifully and swift.

It was 1:00 a.m., the phone was ringing, and I was awakened by it with the realization that Jack had not come home yet to close the windows, as I'd expected. I answered the phone, barely saying hello, with my eyes remaining shut.

"What did you say to Denise?" Jack asked on the other end of it.

"What do you mean, what did I say to Denise?" I said opening my eyes, sitting up in bed. "She had no business calling me. And how do you know I spoke to her?" I said wiping my eyes. I could hear music playing and the chatter of people conversing in the background.

"She called me here at the party and told me what you said," Jack confessed.

"I think the real question is how did that hooker know where you were going to be tonight?" I said, now fully awake.

"I've been friends with these people for a long time, since before I was with Denise, and they invited her to the party also," Jack explained.

"How cozy." I said. "She called here harassing me, and I said some things I guess she didn't like."

"Some things you guess she didn't like? She called here hysterical, Syd," Jack said. A smugness was coming over me as I pictured Denise hysterical.

"Are you defending her to me?" I said.

"No, I just can't believe you would say something so cruel."

"Like I said before, she shouldn't have called here. When are you coming home?" I said changing the subject.

"I'll be there in twenty minutes."

"Okay. Bye."

"Syd."

"What?"

"Close the windows."

15

Jack's mother was a flaming racist. She did not like anyone who was not white. Yes, she was an Hispanic woman, a minority herself, but she felt as if Caucasians were superior to all others. She had been nice and cordial during our first meeting, before she knew we were married, but behind the scenes she was conjuring up trouble.

Jack's mother, upon her return from Argentina, had found remnants of me in Jack's room. I'd left a spare pair of panties in one of Jack's drawers, earrings on his dresser, and tennis shoes in his closet. She'd quickly confronted him about me.

"Who is this girl? She's American?"

"Yes, she's African-American," Jack had said. The conversation, as told to me by Jack, had taken place in the kitchen, where Jack admitted to our marriage, and whatever was nearest to Jack's mother went flying onto the floor. She smashed six picture frames and a vase before screaming out, falling over in a self-inflicted pain, with Jack rushing to her side.

"How could you marry a black person?" she wailed. "My only son is married to a black person," she cried out. She felt disgraced. And when Jack had revealed that she was the one who'd given Denise our number, I was far from surprised. After all, Denise was white and blonde, and I was this dreaded black person. Well, doom on Gloria. I told Jack I wanted nothing to do with his mother if she was a racist, which was just another something, if I had taken the time to get to know Jack before marrying him, that I would have discovered beforehand.

Summer came and went, and I was still jobless. We'd been married for ten months, and I'd only seen Jack's mother once, but she had been leaving messages on our phone all summer long in Spanish. I came home from the grocery store just in time to hear Gloria in the process of leaving another one of her infamous messages. I dumped the groceries onto the dining room table, letting my oranges tumble to the ground, and picked up the phone with her in the middle of speaking.

"Look, Gloria, it is very rude to leave messages on my phone in Spanish. You know I don't speak Spanish."

"Well, you need learn," she said arrogantly, as if she were happy to be getting under my skin.

"Well, I'm sorry to be the one to tell you this, but we're in America. You should be learning how to speak better English, Gloria."

"Excuse me, but I leave messages for my son, no por you," she said in a rude, dismissive way. I was blown away by her nerve.

"I'll make this real easy for you, Gloria. Leave another message on this phone in Spanish, and the only person who will be hearing it is Boo, our cat, who just so happens to be black, too. Now, you have a bueno day."

That night at dinner I was still upset about my run-in with Gloria, my encounter with Denise, and being jobless. Jack and I ate in silence at our dining room table, my newlywed innocence disappearing as quickly as the food being crushed inside Jack's mouth.

"Guess who's pregnant?" Jack said, putting an end to the silence. I looked up from my plate without saying a word.

"Denise," he answered for me. "She's pregnant, and she doesn't want her mom to know. I can't believe she got herself pregnant again," Jack said chuckling, while shaking his head down at his plate, stuffing meat into his mouth as if he'd gotten his hands on some hot gossip.

I awakened from my resentful daze, putting two and two together. One, it was safe to assume he was still in contact with Denise. And, two, another chance at revenge had just been handed to me on a silver platter.

The next day, I was positioned in my favorite place, in front of the TV, on the couch, watching a talk show that did little more than showcase deceptive acts. With the phone sitting on my lap, my face hovering over it, staring down at it as if it were a ticking time bomb I would detonate as soon as I got up enough nerve. I took a deep breath and reached for the receiver, pressing numbers into the phone like they were the code to a final destruction. With my breathing steady, the words perfectly situated and formed on my tongue, I spoke into the phone when the answering machine for the Crogus residence said, "Please leave your message at the tone."

"Hi, Denise. It's Sandy," I said, making my voice mimic that of an upper-middle class white girl's. "I heard you're pregnant. Congrats," I said. I was thinking Denise had better get home before her mother did.

At three o'clock, as the music for "The Oprah Winfrey Show" played on the TV set, the phone rang, startling me. I picked it up.

"What did you do?" Jack said angrily.

"What are you talking about?" I said, trying to sound surprised.

"Don't lie to me. Denise's mother is in the hospital."

"What?"

"Yeah. You or somebody left a message on her machine, claiming to be someone named Sandy, about Denise being pregnant. I can't believe you would do that," Jack said.

"Well, it wasn't me. Why is Denise's mother in the hospital, though?"

"Because she doesn't know or didn't know Denise is pregnant, and when she heard the message, she got so upset she began hyperventilating and had to be taken to the hospital. Please tell me you weren't the one who did it," Jack pleaded.

"I'm not the one who did it," I said into the phone like a robot. And we never heard from Denise again.

Years later I would learn that Jack had been misleading Denise about their relationship all the way up until the night he drove to Vegas with me. She had no idea about me, although she did know her relationship with Jack was on the rocks. The day she came out to the car to meet me, she was coming out to see proof of the bombshell news Jack had just dropped on her, that he'd gotten married. At the time, there was a certain hesitation, a look from her I could not place. It was a look I could certainly place now.

She had been a woman scorned, having lost Jack in one of the most abrupt, messed up manners there was. But that was Jack, and that was what he chose for her. Her calls to me were out of bitterness from feeling betrayed by him, feelings I was growing more familiar with every day. I didn't know at the time that she was actually the lucky one, the one who'd won. She went on, a year later, to find and marry a nice guy and finally get pregnant with a baby she would keep.

The year of my discontent was ending fast, and I no longer spent my days idly in front of the TV. I spent them providing excellent customer service to lower- and middle-income customers at Target. This job was even more detestable than the one I had at Mervyns. At least there I had kept my dignity by selling name-brand clothing, but now I was lowering my standards to sell things like chewing gum, toilet paper, and dish soap. I could not saunter in ten minutes past the time I was scheduled to be at my register. I had to clock in. There was no getting around the dress code, because everyone was required to wear the same thing: dull tan pants and a red shirt with "Target" slapped across it in white.

Surveillance was everywhere. Employees were watched on video cameras, and slacking off was caught immediately. I was on lockdown working at Target. There were no cracks for my faulty behavior to fall into. Everything was seen and everything was caught. As a temp, I knew Target would be looking to make me a full-time employee after the Christmas season was over if I was reliable and on time, but I wanted no part of that. It required too much butt-kissing and following of the rules, and I didn't want to do either.

I took customer after customer, feeling resentful of them and their squirming, whiny children riding by in the red Target shopping carts, leaving their germs behind on my counter, spreading colds and flu, opening up candy before it was paid for, basically making my job harder than necessary. I wasn't there to make friends, and I didn't for the whole three months I was there. I kept quietly to myself. I was shrouded in obscurity and enjoyed my reputation for being standoffish. I was happy to be left alone. As I shoved items across the scanner and took money from hands, with each dollar I took, I counted the shopping days left until Christmas and my time working at Target.

I may have been someone who had an aversion to people and following the rules, but I was proficient at executing a sale. I had the shortest line because I was the fastest worker. The faster I got customers in and out, I figured the sooner I could get them away from me, especially the smelly ones. When I had no one in my line, I was told by the floor manager to find customers that weren't even there or to rearrange the candy shelf to keep busy. "Hey, didn't you just see me go through fifty people in five minutes? Can't I take a breather?" I said to myself. I bent down to take the Mars Bars out of the Hershey Bar shelf and squeezed them so they couldn't be sold. In my mind, I was the best worker they had and too good for this bullshit job, doing menial, brainless work. At home, Jack was overjoyed at my working at Target. You would have thought I had landed a job working for the NAACP. My finding a job meant our first Christmas would be happy. Jack was still coming home late, and I was still left alone to simmer in my anger. I went out occasionally with Kenya, but I was slowly coming out of my denial and into the realization that I had made a grave mistake with my life, and the magnitude of it was eating away at me.

After the episode with Denise, any trust I may have had for Jack was lost, and I would never find it again. I questioned everything he did, and our arguments were verbal assaults that left me feeling defeated and mentally exhausted. I sat in the closet of our empty bedroom and cried at night after arguing with Jack on the phone about his unwillingness to come home at a decent hour. The voice of my mother stuck in my head, of her saying, "She'll be back. She can screw up her life if she wants to," kept me from going back home where I belonged.

I hid my anguish from my father, deciding to live in my own private hell. I'd visit him, look into his knowing eyes, and be unable to tell him I was hating life, had made a mistake, and desperately needed him. I couldn't stand to see the look of him being worried and afraid for me. I preferred to pretend all was well.

I had been devastated by Denise, and instead of hoping to send her to a psychiatrist, I was the one who needed one. In the aftermath of it all, I began to feel self-conscious, and I hung on Jack's every word to let me know he still wanted me. But what I was getting from him was a daily dose of how I was gaining weight and that he'd never been with anyone as big as I was. The other women he'd been with never had a problem controlling their weight, he'd say. When I'd attempt to get him aroused by strutting around in my favorite sexy outfits, he'd remain uninterested, telling me to move from in front of the TV, I was blocking his show. I stood in the bathroom mirror, inspecting my tummy, my butt, my legs. With everything still firm and in place, I thought I looked good, lust-worthy.

His rejection caused me to want to have sex with him as much as I could to validate my attractiveness, and I pounced on him, ravishing him, his penis, sometimes with him continuing to watch TV, until it was left too raw and tender to be functional. When there was no sex to be had, not much else remained, and the boredom of our marriage left me uninspired. With my better judgment impaired, I went along mainly in a fog of dissatisfaction I could do nothing about. Looking at myself in the bathroom mirror one morning, I saw a loser.

Jack came home one average Thursday night, slipping in stealthily next to me, trying not to wake me up. He wanted nothing more than to be left alone and to go to sleep. As I tried to initiate a dialog of where our marriage was heading, Jack rolled over with his back to me. Lit up in neon light, my eyes caught a glimpse of the time on the clock radio. It was 2:00 in the morning. A nasty rage filled inside me, boiling over like an unattended pot of greens. I stomped out of bed, turning on every light in the apartment. I turned on both televisions, the stereo and the dishwasher, which together sounded like a train wreck. I ran around the apartment like a madwoman, with my transparent nightgown flowing behind me, telling myself this bastard was not going to come home, ignore me, and fall into a blissful sleep. Not this time.

Jack finally confronted me in the kitchen, looking worn-out, wearing his favorite faded Led Zeppelin T-shirt and underwear, his hair smashed to one side. I had turned on the faucet and was on my way to turning on the blender.

"What do you think you're doing?" Jack said.

"I'm tired of you coming home like this. I'm not putting up with it anymore," I said, shaking from the cold of the apartment, tears trailing down my face.

"You're going to turn everything off and go to bed!" Jack yelled over the noise.

"Fuck you. No, I'm not," I screamed back.

Jack's face, from top to bottom, turned three different shades of red, and he stormed around undoing everything I'd just done, determined to be allowed to go back to bed in peace. I defiantly went behind him, changing everything back. Jack got ahold of me, grabbing me by the neck, forcing me back into our room.

As I cried out in pain, he slammed me into the bed, telling me not to move. He got in bed next to me, and when he let go, I flew out of bed again, going into the kitchen, beginning to randomly pull drinking glasses from the cupboard, violently sending them smashing to the kitchen floor. Next I threw bowls and plates down. I freed my overwhelming sense of sadness with each crash of glass to the ground. It was a momentary release of pain. I was crying out to a man who was not listening.

I waited to be grabbed again by him, could almost feel it before it happened. I wanted to have the crush of his strength and anger bear into my skin, proof that at least he cared enough to want to hurt me. Unfazed by my anger or my tears and unwilling to tolerate my tantrum for one more second, Jack went for his pants and jacket and keys and left. I turned and stopped, surprised by the unexpected slam of the door. I stood in our cramped kitchen alone, staring at nothing, with everything in disarray around me, surrounded by shards of broken glass spread everywhere around my feet, sweat penetrating my nightgown, sticking it to my skin.

I suddenly felt the cold in the apartment my body had before ignored. Having no choice but to recognize the worthlessness of it all, and with the tenant below me thumping on the ceiling, I withdrew from my actions and retreated to the closet to cry in the darkness.

I was digressing back to the young girl I once was, having left being one behind too soon. I didn't just cry, I hollered. I sat slumped in the closet feeling sorry for myself, not wanting to admit my mistake, because I didn't really want to go back home. I wondered what would become of me, how I could get out of facing my mother's words, and I contemplated suicide, unable to face the truth that, yes, I had fucked up and pulled a Casey.

But if I wanted to be honest, I never intended to be married to Jack my whole life anyway. He was a stepping stone to a better one. In time, when I was able, I had, in my mind, planned to leave him. He was supposed to be a temporary situation that somewhere along the way I must have fallen in love with. Perhaps this had become all too clear to him in the course of our marriage, turning into a deep gnawing in his stomach that made him feel I did not truly love him and he was being used.

By 6:00 a.m. the thin light slipping through the cracks in the closet was reminding me of a world about to go on outside with or without me, in the rushed sound of people going to work. I emerged believing that if I could get through one moment, I could get through another and then another.

So I came out of the closet and used the thought of the life I would have after I was able to live without Jack get me through the day, and someday, I thought, I'll be able to take care of myself and I won't need him. I'll have everything I want. But how to go about getting it? And how long would it take? While I was at it, I may as well have been asking myself when Jesus was coming back.

One week later, on a dank, dark Christmas morning before the sun came up, I left Jack in bed and softly slipped away to see my dad. He had always been an early riser, and I knew he'd be up having his coffee. I drove the thirty miles there without seeing another car on the road. It was as if I was the sole survivor on a deserted island. Driving alone on the rain-dampened highway gave me a pure, uncontaminated sense of myself, and I transformed into a real person again, feeling able to control my life and my destiny like I was controlling my car and the highway it maneuvered over.

I reached my father's door with the intentions of ending a lie I had been living, a lie I'd let rise and fall like the sun. With my decision to visit my dad as impulsive as it was, I had left wearing my pajamas, having put only a sweatshirt on to cover my arms, slippers on my feet, my hair uncombed. I turned the lock that I let keep me out, allowing myself back in again.

I found my father with the vapors from his coffee cup polishing the front of his bald head, sitting in the living room, waiting as if he had been expecting me. With one look at him, there was no turning back. My legs buckled beneath me, and the gravity from the enormous amount of guilt I felt forced me to him.

I broke down into my father's lap and arms, gently clawing at them, drowning my face into his warmth. I used his love for me to calm my fear and ease my guilt, to send me to that place where nothing matters, like when I was five. I relished in the luxury of being alone with him, having stolen moments from everyone else by showing up at such an ungodly hour.

His scent brought me back to life and feeling as if I did not deserve our time alone without the truth sitting between us, so I spoke the only words that could set me free.

"I got married to Jack months ago, Dad. And I'm sorry I didn't tell you. I wanted to, but I knew you'd tell Mom, and I couldn't face her. I'm happy sometimes, but unhappy more. Please forgive me."

I confessed with my face hidden in the curve of his body. He stroked my back, softly breathing in and out, without saying anything. The irony of it all was that I never needed to ask for his forgiveness. His silence told me he'd already forgiven me. I just needed to forgive myself. I lay there against him for some time, smelling the mixture of ingredients making up the way he smelled; like faintly of firewood, men's cologne, the tools he used for his work as an electrician.

The sun broke into the room, illuminating the Christmas tree and decorations I would be seeing for the first time. My head left my father, and I sat up at the sight of the largest box under the tree. It was labeled from my mother to me. We had not been alone. The box from her to me had been occupying my father's mind the whole time. I was angered at her gesture and untrusting of what she attempted to have it mean.

"See," my father finally said, "she does love you." At that moment seeing wasn't believing, because I had been with the real thing all early morning long, and the fact that he was still campaigning for her was disconcerting. He told me one day I would need her, but he may as well have been speaking Portuguese, because I didn't understand.

She called to him from their bedroom upstairs, and I counted the seconds it would take for him to leave me and go to her. This was where duty and love collide. Which one would win? I didn't really have to wonder. My losses here were immense. I couldn't bear to watch him go. I took the box and let myself out.

I sat in the apartment staring at it in front of me for a long time. I looked over at Boo, who was laying out on the carpet next to the couch, to see if the red and green colors of the box or the fancy dangling bows on it could arouse him, make him come closer to me, but he remained unsurprisingly aloof. Jack was still asleep in the room, filling it up with his smell of spoiled milk and bad breath. I closed the door.

As I sat there alone, with the box before me, I thought about giving my mother the benefit of the doubt that maybe she was capable of changing, and I started to get excited about the possibility of what the box held. My mother was very good at giving the gifts nobody wanted, like underwear and dress socks. But I allowed myself to feel like a child again and let the anticipation grow within me. I ripped open the box like I was back in our house in Sunny Beach, and it was Christmas morning, the fireplace raging, and I could taste the thrill of opening up the gift I'd always wanted.

My mother, never one to disappoint, had given me bath towels. Five of them. They weren't even my favorite color. They were white, colorless, with no imagination, like the way she felt about me. What made her think I needed bath towels? She'd never even been to my apartment. I threw the towels down to the bottom of the closet, leaving them in a rumpled pile; like her, I wouldn't be needing them.

And, Jack, he gave me that wedding ring I'd been waiting a year for, so small I had to squint to see the diamond. I gave him underwear and dress socks.

16

Rhubarb sauce was my favorite thing the school cafeteria served for lunch when I was in the sixth grade. I hadn't eaten it or thought of Jody, the person who shared my love for it, in years. But it seemed too easy when I decided to name the kitten Jack gave me Rhubarb. He was the exact opposite of Boo. His dark eyes looked at me happily, his ears pointing out with the anticipation of meeting my arms.

He was white with black spots parading all over his tiny body. He had a pink nose and white whiskers, and I loved him from the moment Jack surprised me by making him appear from behind his back. I carefully took him from Jack, and he didn't try to get away, having decided to stay folded in my arms. Rhubarb was the glue that would hold Jack and I together until our first anniversary. I hadn't been as thrilled all year.

Boo was not as thrilled, having grown accustomed to walking around with his antisocial mood setting the tone for the apartment.

But Rhubarb was prancing around, discovering new objects of varying size, shape, color and texture, curious about everything and me. He'd sit perched on the stool top in the bathroom watching me brush my hair and apply my make-up. I was flattered by his interest.

Boo was not as taken with Rhubarb, and he took swipes at him, sending Rhubarb tumbling over, banging into the walls. Rhubarb eventually won Boo over by creeping up to lick his face and falling asleep under his belly. I had Jack, our apartment, and my two cats. And that, for now, was enough.

"Hello," I said, answering the phone totally unsuspecting.

"I would like to speak to my son." It was like a voice from the dead. I handed the phone to Jack. Gloria was back, after not calling since the answering machine episode. When Jack got off the phone, he informed me that we'd been invited over. Never mind that Christmas had come and gone three days ago without a peep from his family; they were ready and wanted to get to know me. I immediately thought, no fucking way am I going there, until Jack said they wanted us there at 3:00 o'clock, which meant I would have to miss work, which meant I was out of that Target hellhole.

The scent of Jack's parents' house was not the one I remembered from the year before, when they left for Argentina and Jack was the only one breathing inside. It was now filled with the smell of mothballs, his mother's cooking, and her cheap perfume, the kind old ladies wear.

She was in her middle 60s, her body was big and round, and she had long, thin, blonde hair, which she wore pinned up in a bun behind her head. Her gray-green eyes, deeply set with thick lashes, hovered above high cheekbones and full lips that told me her face had once been beautiful before it was overtaken by aging.

But none of this really mattered. The woman hated the sight of my deep-brown face. The way her lips puckered together every time she spoke let me know it was paining her to be in my presence she so disapproved of me. I felt I was being shoved down her throat like a gym sock. I wondered how many times the word "nigger" had passed over her lips, and how Jack, having been raised in a racist household, ended up with me. I chalked our marriage up to partly being a twisted swipe at revenge Jack took against his mother. I had found out enough about her to know she was someone who could make you want to jump out at her and bang the life from her skull or do something just to piss her off, like marry a black person.

I sat in front of the dinner she made directly across from the man Jack would later become, his father, Sal. This was a man of few words,

although he was fluent in Spanish and Italian. Not having had the pleasure of hearing the sound of his voice yet, I didn't know what to make of
him. He gazed at me, motionless, his arms flanking his dinner plate, peering at me through his thick-framed glasses, looking as if he hadn't decided
anything yet about our marriage or my blackness. Sal was keeping his
views on my being black cloaked in mystery, and he did seem largely unaffected by our marriage. Absent from his face was the pinched, tortured
look I saw in Gloria's. This gave me hope and a comfortableness with
him that brought back my appetite. He was giving me a chance. Silence
in most people made me uneasy, but in his, for the moment, at the dinner
table, I felt calm.

"So, Synnie, you work for, uh, Target, is it?" Gloria asked, as if she
didn't want to say it, like Target was some seedy strip joint. I was mortified
by the way she was attempting to say my name and how she had abbrevi-
ated it. And I could have sworn Jack had mentioned something about her
favorite store being Kmart, which would explain why her house smelled
of mothballs but didn't explain her arrogance.

"Um, yeah, but not for long. I'm just there through the holidays," I
said, squirming in my chair and feeling as useful as a dirty rag. Her strong,
overbearing personality dwarfed mine, and the words coming out of my
mouth were shy and awkward. I stiffened and felt more like the loser I
was.

"So you have no college," she said, shuffling food around on her plate
with her fork, "and you expect me son to take care of you. What you plan
do for money? Me son say to me he need second income. You no have
money, barely can you pay you bills."

I could have shot Jack in the head I was so angry. I looked over at him
to see if he was bracing to defend me, to defend us, and the hurried way he
was looking down, eating his food let me know I was on my own.

"We're doing fine," I said, wimping out, unable to say much else, so
I just took it. But inside I told her I did go to college, a business college,
but had fucked it up to marry her creep son, that I wasn't happy working
at Target, and I wasn't about to stay there even if it meant we were evicted,

which we eventually were. I ached my way through the rest of dinner, realizing I'd married a mamma's boy who would never defend me.

When dinner was over, Jack's father did nothing to assist Jack's mother in the kitchen. He remained at the table like a king, with his wife doing her supposed duties around him. So I kept my unhappy ass in my seat also, following the actions of the king, refusing to be anything other than the kind of wife I really was to the male chauvinist I had married. Jack's father looked at me as if I were a foreign object he was trying to figure out, and I smiled at him. He said something in Spanish I did not understand and left the table to go into his office.

"Why didn't you help my mother in the kitchen?" Jack said when we got to the car.

"She didn't ask me to help her," I said.

"But you already know women.... I mean, you're supposed to clean up after dinner."

"Oh, really? Well, what ancient scroll is that written on?" I asked, annoyed and preparing for a fight.

"And why didn't you defend me? And how could you let your mother make it seem as if I'm just some sponge using you as a meal ticket?" I asked, jerking my seatbelt across my chest.

"I didn't pay attention to what she was saying," Jack claimed.

"Well, I was paying attention. She insulted me, and she insulted us, making it seem like we're irresponsible. I don't appreciate the things that she said to me. Why didn't you say something?"

"Because she's going to pay for us to go to Vegas for our anniversary."

You see, everybody's got an agenda. Even me. My agenda was to somehow grow up and not need Jack anymore, to endure this, survive it, to achieve something other than this disastrous marriage. Jack's agenda was to get whatever he could out of his parents, to manipulate them into feeling sorry for him so they would give their money, even if this meant hurting me. His mother's agenda was to send whatever insult she wanted my way, to make me seem inept, to have Jack and me both look like a dubious pair.

Our Vegas-style marriage left Gloria feeling robbed, cheated out of giving her baby boy, and only child, a suitable wedding. She was horrified by the manner in which we were married. She would have wanted to be surrounded by her friends, able to show off her good taste in decorating and at putting parties together. She prided herself on having the proper etiquette but didn't mind insulting me on a regular basis. Her friends were pleasant towards me and found nothing about me to be unlikable, as she had warned. They said in Spanish that I was very, very bonita but too skinny.

I, of course, lost my job at Target for not showing up or calling the night I was supposedly accepted into Jack's family. I went back to pounding the pavement, woefully looking for a job. I hated the routine of asking for an application, filling it out, going on the interview, waiting to hear back. I found the whole process to be degrading, having to admit you were jobless by appearing in front of someone, who couldn't care less about you, silently begging. I envied, at that time, everyone and anyone who had a job.

With the appearance of an eviction notice on the front door, as well as Jack's crimson-colored face before me, out of sheer desperation, I took a job cleaning houses. I figured I was a good housekeeper, a neat freak, and felt cleaning houses should be a piece of cake.

Wrong. We worked in crews of four, with two taking the bathrooms and kitchen, and two vacuuming and dusting. I quickly found out that a lot of people have disgusting ways of living, but I did my best to clean away the grit and grime they paid us to get rid of.

I rode in the back of a car with three other women, all illegal aliens, being driven by an El Salvadoran woman named Reyna. She had two kids and was married to a white guy who occasionally beat her up. Maria, from Guatemala, lived in a cramped apartment with her alcoholic husband and six children. And Maria, who was Mexican, hated salsa music. She lived with her boyfriend, whom she supported. She told me she learned English by listening to Bruce Springsteen records.

I enjoyed the new experience of being around them. I was having a cultural immersion that I thoroughly enjoyed, and I was learning Spanish. The way they would duck down in the car whenever they saw an INS truck pass reminded me of when my license was suspended and how I would stiffen whenever a police car passed by. They were deathly afraid of getting picked up by immigration and deported. They all hated either their husband or boyfriend. I realized we weren't so different. They had the same problems I did, same goals and dreams. We were all just trying to live and get by.

The man who owned the cleaning business was an evil weasel. He was a short, lanky, greasy man with a compulsive blinking problem, mixed in with an uncontrollable twitch. His name was David, and he refused to give us a lunch break, so we ate every day in Reyna's car while we were on our way to the next house to be cleaned. They didn't complain and neither did I. But I knew by law it was illegal not to give us a lunch break. I figured I'd stay quiet about it until I maybe needed to use it against David, if he ever tried to fire me or something. He sometimes sent us to homes that hadn't been cleaned in years, that were going to take hours, and then not pay us for the overtime. We were just pieces of meat to him.

One day after a hard day cleaning houses, I came back to the apartment, tired, hungry, dirty, and realized I hadn't had my period all month. I checked the calendar, figuring out it was two weeks late. I stared at myself in the bathroom mirror wondering what I'd done, how this could happen.

My eyes rolled through flashbacks of our anniversary in Vegas, the night I had been heavily drinking and did not use birth control. You could be pregnant is what I told myself, looking into the mirror. No. Not pregnant. Shit. I ran to the market just behind the apartment and bought a pregnancy test. I did what the box instructed and peed over a white device about the size of a popsicle stick and waited on the stool for it to change color.

When Jack finally came home, he found me slumped on my side with half my body curled around the toilet, staring blankly into the air, with tears streaming down my face, and the test with a pink line across it resting in the palm of my hand. Rhubarb slept quietly on the top of my head, and Boo was licking himself in the doorway.

"Oh, my God, you're pregnant?" Jack screamed, running his hands through his hair, pacing back and forth over the linoleum. But I couldn't respond. The whole time I had been trying to convince myself I was trapped in a hellish nightmare from which I would awaken. Trapped inside me was the word "no" being said over and over again, pounding in my head, thumping and thumping and thumping. I was barely twenty-one. I didn't need nor want a child, especially not with the jerk I was married to. Jack picked me up and put me in bed. I went to sleep and got up for work the next day.

For days we didn't talk about my being pregnant, acting as if not speaking about it would make it go away. Until one night Jack finally told me he thought I should get an abortion. "Just like Denise," I thought. I knew that some of those pregnancies Denise aborted had to have been his, if not all, and I wasn't Denise. And no matter how scared and disappointed I was, I would not be turned into her.

I woke up the next morning with Jack standing over me like the Grim Reaper. He said I had to get dressed; he was taking me to an abortion clinic to be evaluated so I could terminate the pregnancy. Intimidated, I got dressed, putting on whatever, and I got in the car. When we got there, there were protestors swarming the area, almost blocking the entrance. Women, as well as men, were out front picketing, begging girls going inside the clinic to reconsider what they were about to do.

I sat on the passenger side of the car with my fingers straddling the door handle, unable to move them, looking into the many faces of the protestors who seemed to be wrought with concern I did not understand. Never having seen anything like this before, I thought it all to be rather bizarre. I searched their faces for answers for why they were there and began to see an eerie obsessive nature about them and their cause. I wondered what they stood to lose by a woman legally terminating a pregnancy inside her own body. How could the despair of the protestors be greater than that of a woman who is faced with an agonizing decision that will haunt the rest of her days? But they had succeeded in making me feel guilty for being there.

When I began to cry, Jack grabbed my arm, shaking me, and told me I'd better get out of the car, that he didn't want a baby. But I didn't budge.

The protestors were beginning to turn their attention to us, descending upon our car, with pictures of aborted fetuses on their picket signs. They began to plead, "Don't do it. Don't do it. Don't do it." Jack sped off from the clinic, and we went back to the apartment.

"You'd better get that abortion. I'll leave you if you don't."

"How can you say that?" I cried.

"Because I don't want to have a kid. I don't want to take care of and pay for a kid. You'd better do it," he said, walking out on me, slamming the door behind him.

I had cried enough tears, and I knew I was determined not to go through with any abortion. I decided in my mind, as devastating as it was, from the moment I saw that pink line telling me I was pregnant, that I would keep the baby. Pink to me signified that I was pregnant with a girl, and she needed to live, to breath, to grow. I prayed the life within me would be exactly that, a girl. I needed to give her the love my mother never gave me.

I would bond with her, look deep into her eyes and speak the words "I love you" straight into them and watch it reflect down to her unblemished soul, healing my own. I felt I would be giving new life to us both. I knew how to love her, because I had always known how I would have wanted to be loved by my own mother. This love for her would give me the courage to stand up to Jack and tell him I was keeping the baby, and he could leave if he wanted to.

"Damn," he said. "I thought if I told you I would leave that would break you and you'd get the abortion."

"Well, sorry, asshole, it didn't. You're going to be a father, so get used to it," I said wryly.

17

Like my marriage, in the beginning, I kept my pregnancy a secret from my parents, mainly from my mother. It was my way of staying in control and also a glaring sign of my immaturity. Jack, with deception being his middle name, didn't disagree. He wasn't happy with my being pregnant anyway, and he usually didn't get in the way of how I conducted my affairs with my parents. I'd kept my job cleaning houses and remained very slim from slaving away all day, until my sixth month, when I began to show from my pregnancy, with a large bump protruding out from my body underneath my T-shirts.

If the girls I worked with knew, they didn't let on that they did, so I continued cleaning away the filth of others, wiping away their dirt, denying my own. But I couldn't deny anything after we entered the worst-smelling house ever. The people who lived there were cat owners who rarely, if ever, changed the many litter boxes throughout the house. The smell was toxic, with the fumes of cat-box odors, and I could not stand to breathe the air. It was our last house of the day, and we needed to be done by the time the homeowners returned.

Reyna panicked and called David when I refused to stay in the house and clean. I had lasted a half hour before I became nauseated with the smell that had permeated my hair, my skin, and my clothes. I fled with my hand covering my mouth and told the girls they'd have to finish without me. When David arrived on the scene, he confronted me as I sat in the passenger seat of Reyna's car.

"So what's the problem, Sydney? You too good to clean this house?" he said slyly, twitching, blinking his eyes.

"No. I just can't take the smell," I said.

"Well, who's gonna finish what you started?" he asked, like a prison warden.

"I don't know. Maybe you should get somebody else out here," I said, coming out of the car, standing up to him. "We've already been working ten hours today, and you know you're only going to pay us for eight," I said sarcastically. My belly was protruding through what I thought was doing a good job at concealing it, my T-shirt.

For a month now, unknown to me, wearing baggy T-shirts hadn't been hiding my pregnancy at all, but I hadn't noticed until I caught a glimpse of myself in the windshield while I talked back to David. With that, I knew it was only a matter of time before my parents would find out.

David continued blinking at me for a moment and disappeared back into the stink-infested house. I waited patiently in the car for the girls to return, regretting mouthing off to David. We headed back to the company office to refill our cleaning supplies. David called me into his office over the PA system. Without mentioning my pregnancy or even looking at me, he gave some ridiculous reason for firing me, saying I'd missed cleaning a spot on some woman's kitchen floor. He was dismissing me like I had been nothing to him.

My vow to blackmail him for not paying us overtime and not giving lunch breaks went out the window. I was too pregnant to muster up the strength, and I was semi-relieved to be able to go home and kick my feet up. But as the off-ramp for my apartment came closer, something was steering me towards Montara Valley, and before I knew it, I was coasting down my parents' street, about to tell them finally, after six months, that I was pregnant. With one glimpse of my sister's car in the driveway, I floored it and sped past.

I spent my last pregnancy months sitting idle in front of the TV since I knew no one would hire me. Without our second income, we were evicted, asked to leave, had one of those humiliating notices for all to see put on our door that meant we were total scumbag losers that couldn't pay to live there, just like Jack had always warned. We moved out in the middle of the night, with the help of one of Jack's friends, my eighth month of pregnancy, into a two-bedroom apartment two miles away that had a first-two-months-free special.

I didn't allow myself to think about my injured self-respect from the embarrassment I felt from being evicted. Except for in the middle of the night when the baby was kicking and I couldn't sleep, and I lay awake staring at the empty walls of my unfamiliar surroundings, next to Jack, with only my thoughts. Had my life really come to this? Had I really sunk this low, with a baby on the way, in a bad marriage, and no money?

The new apartment we moved into was overflowing with young families that Jack enjoyed getting to know and I ignored. When Jack went to work, I became a hermit, embarrassed to let anyone see that I was pregnant, especially since I looked only sixteen. Time was being kind to me in a way I was unable to appreciate, having been mistaken twice for a high school student and teenaged mother-to-be.

I shunned my parents, my siblings and even Kenya, as my weight ballooned to 170 pounds. Boo and Rhubarb were my only ties to the outside world, when I was forced to go to the market to buy their food and cat litter.

On one of my trips back, to my horror, Jade and Seneca showed up at my apartment building. I closed my eyes and prayed as I took anxious steps towards them that when I reopened my eyes the two ghostly apparitions I had seen would be gone. I was still unable to leave the comfort of my own denial, while they were obviously ready to face theirs, having driven here unannounced. They knew me too well.

The look of disbelief on my father's face and the validation on my mother's, as they stood in my apartment doorway looking at me, let me know I had waited too long to tell them. My father seemed to be short of breath from the impact my appearance was having on him, and he lost the footing on his six-foot frame and slowly fell over into my mother. She broke his fall and seemed to be annoyed and accused him of theatrics.

"I don't know why you're acting this way," she said, "I told you the girl was probably pregnant. Psychic my ass." My dad looked as if he could use a glass of water.

"When were you going to tell us you were pregnant?" my dad asked, before taking a huge gulp.

"Never. I mean, I don't know. I'm not that happy about it," I said, pacing in the living room.

"And Jack?" my dad asked.

"We're dealing with it. Okay?" I said.

"Well, I think it's great," my mother said surprising me.

"You do?" I said.

"Well, yeah. We can help you, and we will. Don't worry," she said. Feeling as though I'd just made a deal with the devil, I excused myself to go to the bathroom so they wouldn't see me cry.

By the beginning of my ninth month, my pregnancy was mired with feelings of wanting it all to be over with. The last days of pregnancy are actually harder to get through than the months and months that go by of waiting. Sleep was next to impossible. I was plagued at night with leg cramps so severe the pain brought tears to my eyes. I came to being within two weeks of my due date, and I was overcome with wanting the baby out of me. My wretched existence was an affliction, a cross, if you will, that I could no longer endure, carry, or bear.

The sixth sense that most pregnant women have that tells you your baby is coming told me my baby was not coming, not ready, and I feared my due date would come and go and I would still be pregnant. My baby was holding on inside me, her unwillingness to be born speaking to me, as I had felt no early contractions or false labor pain, something a lot of woman feel sometimes even in their eighth month.

But, God help me, I could no longer suffer the pregnancy, the growth within me. I became desperate, almost irrationally fixated with giving birth. I stared at the calendar I had been crossing off days from, counting seven more remaining until the baby was due. I would not emotionally make it. I knew this to be true, could feel it in my gut.

A memory of reading or hearing somewhere that cod-liver oil was good for causing contractions resurfaced in my head, and without too much further thought, before Jack could come home to stop me, I was at the market and back home again, wrapping my mouth around the bottle of cod-liver oil, downing the gooey substance like I was an alcoholic. I waited in my favorite spot on the couch, left side in the corner, feet on the coffee table, watching "Entertainment Tonight," waiting for something to happen, anything. All at once, I felt a sharp pain, a menstrual cramp like Godzilla would have, that threw me forward towards my knees. Then pain from the need to have a strong bowel movement began to churn inside my stomach.

I called to Jack from the bathroom, on the stool where I was trapped, when I finally heard him come home an hour later.

"What did you do, now?" he said.

"Nothing," I gasped.

"Sydney, tell me what you did. I saw the cod liver oil in the living room," he insisted from just outside the bathroom door.

"So."

"Well, did you drink any?"

"No."

"Dammit, Syd!"

"Okay! I.... Ouch. Oh, it hurts. I took the cod-liver oil to bring on the contractions so I would go into labor and have the baby," I said, groaning, barely able to speak.

"Why did you do that?"

"Because I'm tired of being pregnant. I want this over with already," I said.

"If something happens to my baby, I'll...."

"Oh, just get the hell out of here and leave me alone!" I cried.

I was in the throes of having severe contractions, and as much as I wanted to have the baby, I was not prepared for the excruciating pain it brought with it. Jack drove me to the hospital, verbally chastising me the whole way there, telling me what an idiot I was. But his words sunk inside the overwhelming amount of pain I was in. I couldn't even speak to tell him to shut up. When I had been checked into the hospital and placed in my room, I was given an epidural that numbed me from the waist down. I felt nothing after that.

A short time later, Jade and Seneca arrived and waited the rest of the evening, the next morning, and into the night it took for my baby to be born. Turns out using the cod-liver oil to bring on my contractions prolonged my labor, making it last of a whole day. I went through two shifts of nurses, and I was exhausted.

They tried to prep me for a C-section, but I refused to sign the release paperwork. I knew I was young, healthy, and strong enough to birth my baby naturally. Her life was not in danger, and I sent the nurse who came in with the foul bright-orange paperwork away. My obstetrician gently explained that I had not dilated enough centimeters in order to give birth naturally after being in labor 24 hours. I asked her for more time, which she granted, and I asked God to make me dilate. One half hour later, I was dilated and pushing my baby out.

She was born beet-red with a cone head and scrunched face. She weighed six pounds and had eyes like an Eskimo, with a crop of black hair on her head that continued its growth down to her forehead, just above her eyes, that made her look like a baby werewolf. She was the perfect mixture of Jack and me, with only traces of us found in her distorted face that made her also unique unto herself. Her skin was almost white. I was a little surprised by it. But Kenya, when she came by to visit, said the slightly darker tips of her fingers told what her true color would be.

"Don't worry," she said, as if her words were about to solve everything, "she'll end up being light-skinned. She won't stay this milky white color."

"Kenya, she's healthy, and that's all I care about."

"Then why are you getting annoyed when the nurses keep checking and rechecking your hospital bracelets to make sure she's yours she's so pale?"

I continued to listen to Kenya as she predicted doom and gloom for my biracial baby, telling me to expect her to be identity confused, discriminated against by blacks as well as whites, and how she would not feel as if she belonged anywhere.

"Kenya, I don't want to hear anymore of that racist shit. She'll be fine. Besides, she has me for a mother."

I decided against breast-feeding. I was twenty-two, and I didn't want deflated balloons for breasts, plus I'd read that it was better to breast-feed but not mandatory. It wasn't like half her brain wouldn't develop.

The next afternoon after I gave birth, I was famished, having been unable to eat since I had first been admitted to the hospital. I sent Jack, who had been unnaturally hovering over me since I went into labor, to McDonald's to get me a fillet-o-fish and strawberry shake, my favorite meal. Shortly after, a happy little nurse came bouncing into my room.

"Time to name the baby," she said whimsically. I was caught off guard but pleasantly surprised. Sure, I'd fiddled with a few names. Rachel was a name I'd always loved. My dad had suggested Yolanda. Not. Jack was gone. We hadn't talked about name possibilities, and I didn't know what to do.

"I'll just leave this right here for you," she said, "And I'll come back for it in a few minutes."

She placed a form in front of me on my hospital tray and left it for me to stare at. I started to tell her to wait, that the father wasn't here, but then my horns began to show and something else within me took over, and I let her leave. I was a new mother, and the hardest part was over. I'd already given birth, and naming my own baby was like icing on the cake. I had fought to keep this baby, been brave enough to almost end up a single mom to do it, and I suddenly was without the need to wait for Jack to come back.

I gave to my baby girl what some would say is a boy's name, Aden, to represent strength, wanting her name to somehow keep her strong, as strong as I had to be to bring her into the world. She made my lousy marriage meaningful, validating it, making it impossible for me to regret ever again.

When Jack came back, although annoyed, he didn't get too upset, saying he would name our next baby. But I knew then another baby with Jack there would never be.

When the nurse brought Aden back in to me from the nursery, I searched her fragile body again, counting her ten fingers and toes, thanking God for them all, looking down upon what I believed to be the only chance I would ever have to be a good mother.   And not until after the nurse wheeled Aden out of my room to return to the nursery for the night, did I stop to catch my first real breath. I released it slow and easily.

I found myself turning my head to gaze out the hospital room window, wondering what God had planned for me next. The moon glowing in the sky, surrounded by dense darkness, alone, proud, and pure, reminded me of what my future could be. Because like the moon, while driving in my car, my future would appear to be following me instead of my following after it; it was, for now, left in my teenage upstairs bedroom the night I drove to Vegas and married Jack.

18

When I brought Aden home, I brought the sins of my mother home with me. The mistakes she made with me, I would avoid. I was conscious of everything I felt she left me without. And my wounds, still left unhealed by time, with the birth of Aden they only became more apparent, as I was determined to raise Aden differently. I would break a cycle that began three generations ago with my mother's grandmother, Dagmar Armstrong.

She had been a white woman, slight but strong-willed and strong-minded. She had been wild and rebellious for Muskogee, Oklahoma, in the early 1920s. She became romantically involved with a strapping, young black man named Thomas Calhoun, who did odd jobs around her family's home. Disgracing her parents, who were wealthy and highly respected in the community, Dagmar secretly had seven of her eight children with Thomas as the father.

She and her half-breed children were disowned by the entire Armstrong family, shunned by the community, and Thomas was almost lynched and therefore forced into hiding. But Dagmar persevered, raising her children virtually alone and without the added perks that came with the privilege of having been born white.

But her youngest child, Maggie, was the product of a torrid love affair Dagmar had with a rising black minister. They met in church and fell in love. The minister promised to take Dagmar with him to California, where he believed life would be easier for a black man and a white woman together, where they could be married, if she would give up on Thomas. And so it was that she did. Unfortunately, shortly after Maggie was born, the minister left for California, only to marry another woman.

My mother told me the story of her unconventional grandmother over and over again as I was growing up. My mother had greatly admired her grandmother Dagmar for having bucked a racist society that strongly disapproved of her interracial relationships. Dagmar loved the way she wanted, without concern for the racial tension boiling over around her. She lived with her eight children in poverty on a non-working farm after being completely disowned. But Maggie was the one who paid the worst price for her father's betrayal.

Dagmar avoided Maggie, giving her little attention, silently blaming her, as Maggie was a constant reminder of her mistake, of what she'd lost. Maggie's brothers and sisters resented her for having even been born. With that story, my mother also wove in the story of Maggie, her mother.

Maggie's story was quite the opposite, far less romantic, far less admirable. Maggie was a tall woman, with striking features, inheriting her white grandfather's prominent nose and thin lips. Her eyes were oddly narrow, and her skin was the color of buttermilk. The way her family treated her left her cold and mean. And maybe she had to be, growing up as a mulatto woman, an outcast in Muskogee, enduring the racism she surely had to live with back then. But my mother had made no excuses for her and told me stories that did not paint a pleasant picture in my young mind of my grandmother.

My mother was the fifth of eleven children born to Maggie and also into poverty in Muskogee, Oklahoma. Maggie made sure to avoid the same fight-for-love struggle of Dagmar. She married a man who was also mixed-raced, who resembled herself. She married Julian McLearie, a gorgeous, almost-white-looking man, whose father had been Irish and who's mother had been Creole. He was a traveling salesman, but his ambition was stymied by Maggie's callousness.

She had a mean disposition and was uninterested in having the finer things in life. She enjoyed drinking, and the nightlife of going to bars.

Sometimes she didn't come home for days, leaving my mother and her sisters and brothers to fend for themselves.

She was known to spend some nights in jail after getting into fights with other women over other men. She had a reputation for being a floozy, a loose and easy woman sexually, which caused Julian to flee, going back and forth between Muskogee and Oklahoma City. My mother said he was a good, loving father, just not around enough to save the children from their destructive mother.

She was a brutal disciplinarian. She'd tie the boys to trees before she beat them with leather straps. She beat the girls while they were still asleep in their beds for not cleaning the kitchen to her satisfaction.

The money Julian sent home, Maggie quickly spent on boyfriends and lovers, leaving the children without clothing and food. My mother and her brothers and sisters were close and took care of each other. My mother helped with the little ones after her father left for good and never returned. She spoke of sleeping three to a bed, walking a mile in the snow to school, and wringing the heads off chickens on their farm.

And across the way from my mother's farm, off a narrow, dusty road, lived the little boy who would become my father, Seneca. My father said when he was a little boy he remembers being fascinated by my mother and her brothers and sisters. He said her house was overrun with kids, roaming everywhere, that their house was filled with chaos, that Maggie had a bad reputation in the neighborhood.

My father came from a family that resembled my mother's in the slightest way since his father was also in and out of the home. But that is where the similarities ended. He was only one of five. He was not born into poverty. His Aunt Ruby owned a store that kept him from going hungry. He told me interesting stories of his childhood, of trying to catch snakes and firing his BB gun while growing up also on a small farm. He had a loving mother, loving brothers and sisters, and he was unaffected by the cruel nature of racism. He grew up happy.

Happiness was never something my mother alluded to when she told me of her hardship growing up as Maggie's daughter, something she seemed to despise. As the years of remembering these stories, since they were told to me often, wore on, I grew tired of and became indifferent to them. They began to go right through me. I wondered if they were being used as an excuse for why my mother was the way she was, the kind of mother she'd been. I thought if Maggie had been so bad, how could my mother have allowed me to be baby-sat by her when I was four?

Maggie took care of me for a short time while my mother went to work, until one day I fell down stairs made of rock in her apartment, splitting open my top lip. It took Maggie forever to even make a move to pick me up, and she didn't take me to the hospital. My cut required stitches, which I got only when my parents picked me up, hours later, with a bloody mouth and took me to the hospital.

That's why I can attest to the fact that Maggie really was cold, as cold as the dismal, dank apartment she lived in, as frosty as her hands felt on me. Her curtains were always drawn tightly shut, keeping out the sun, containing her frigid heart.

More proof of her ruthless nature came when she tried to dispose of Annie, my mother's oldest sister. Annie had always been a little off. I could tell, even as a young kid, that something was amiss with her. The way she spoke, looked and acted, it wasn't completely normal. She laughed a lot and sometimes for no reason. She was heavy-set and applied her make-up recklessly, overloading her eyelids with baby-blue eye shadow. Her hair was awkwardly short and uncombed, and the perfume she wore seemed to be used to mask a musty body odor that did not wash away with soap. Yet she managed to keep a clerk job at a Goodwill store and give birth to two children.

For pure financial gain, Maggie had Annie put away, institutionalized, committing her to a mental hospital. Maggie quickly took custody of Annie's two children, and applied for welfare to receive money for them. Maggie did all of this without telling anyone. My mother was devastated and fought hard to get Annie released. In those days it was easy to have people committed and difficult to get them out.

After my mother was able to successfully have Annie released, she rented a small white house across the street from ours for Annie to live. My mother kept watch over Annie like a devoted sister, but Maggie was granted permanent custody of Annie's children and turned them against their mother.

However, Maggie couldn't stay away from Annie, and frequently showed up at Annie's house to harass her. My mother had warned Maggie to stay away, but Maggie was not someone easily intimidated. One early autumn Saturday afternoon, as I stood in the front yard wondering what to do with myself, I watched from across the street as Maggie pulled up in her lime-green Cadillac that used to belong to my mother's father, that Maggie stole from everybody else by lying about being Julian's wife after he had died, when she knew they'd been divorced for years.

She parked in Annie's driveway and got out, wearing her trademark hooded red-and-black cape with matching gloves. I was unaccustomed to speaking to her, so I didn't want her to see me. I had decided she was forbidden, and I ducked behind a tree to keep her from noticing me. I crouched there, watching with a gnawing feeling in my gut like a storm was coming.

My Aunt Lucky was visiting, and I had been alone outside, annoyed because she hadn't brought Minnow along. As she and my mother came out into the yard, screams came from Annie's open front door. My mother and aunt sprang into action and raced across the street to Annie's. I was paralyzed. I didn't know what to think or expect. I entertained thoughts of calling for my father, but I did nothing instead. I kept my eyes fixated on Annie's front porch, waiting, waiting, as my mother and aunt went up Annie's steps, across the porch, disappearing into the house.

From where I was, I could hear rumbling, like furniture being tossed, and muffled arguing, then louder shouts echoing across the street. Next thing I knew, Aunt Lucky and Maggie broke through the screen door like two wrestlers. They struggled on the porch, twisting and turning. I wasn't quite sure what Aunt Lucky was trying to accomplish when she snatched Maggie's wig off during the scuffle. I worried about one of them or both tumbling down the stairs off the porch, and that's when I ran to get my father, who was inside our house, unaware of the fight taking place at Annie's.

He streaked across the street, and when he got to the porch, he pulled Aunt Lucky and Maggie apart. My mother finally tore outside and stood on the porch, commanding it like a junkyard dog.

"You stay the hell away from my goddamn sister," my mother barked.

Maggie drove off like a drag racer, in a puff of smoke, and that was the last I would see of her before I became a young adult; because from then on, she would be omitted from birthdays and holidays, recitals, births and even funerals. If Maggie was going to be somewhere, my mother made a point for us not to be. Maggie was erased from our lives like chalk on a chalkboard, only not forgotten. Her stories and my mother telling them would remain. Although my mother spent years not communicating with her own mother, she spoke of her often as if she still did, keeping her spirit alive.

Years after, when I was a young adult, long after the dust had settled, while visiting Minnow at Aunt Lucky's, Maggie sat in a wheelchair, looking feeble and barely lucid, in what used to be Minnow's room. Aunt Lucky had forgiven Maggie long ago and took care of her when she could no longer take care of herself.

"Hi, baby," Maggie struggled to say, in a small, quivering voice as she reached for her dentures.

"Give me a hug," she said, this time easier, after her teeth were in place.

I was taken aback by how fragile and innocent she looked, not as how I'd remembered. I thought to myself, this woman couldn't hurt a flea, as I bent down, granting her request. Her body was warm, thin, and inviting. I didn't know how to feel for her. Here she was, finally defeated by time, a threat to no one, and barely remembering my name. It appeared to be too late for her, for me. All those years of not knowing her could not be returned and transformed into sympathy. She was no longer the demon my mother always talked about, and I felt sorry for her physical condition as she looked genuinely happy to see me after so many years had passed by.

My eyes rested upon her for the last time when I left Minnow's. I didn't look back, and she never haunted my thoughts like she haunted my mother's. And when she died, I didn't go to her funeral, ending up one of two people who couldn't make it, couldn't be bothered, made it an afterthought like whether to have dessert or not, ultimately deciding against it. My mother was the other person who wasn't there. I guess I didn't go because I had never pictured myself there, standing amongst all those sometime mourners who looked past her abuse, pretending she was something she was not.

I had heard there was a large turnout, attended by people whom I'd written off the face of the earth. It all left me rather intrigued.

"You mean, Uncle Danny's ex-wife's daughter Jackie came?" I asked my sister.

"Yeah. And you remember Aunt Mallorie, whom we haven't heard from in ten years and weren't sure was even alive anymore, well, she resurfaced," Casey replied.

She held a copy of my grandmother's obituary in her hand. I took it and began to read. Who was this Maggie woman anyway? It was too late for me to ever truly know. But her obituary gave the brief outline of a woman who, from the sweet picture on the front, appeared to be some loving old lady, devoted to her children and grandchildren. I was shocked to know that I was one of Maggie's thirty grandchildren. I didn't know she belonged to a church, spent time working for a Jewish family, and had actually given birth to twelve children, not eleven. A boy, Elvis, died just hours after being born. He would have been her youngest child.

I came to realize the real reason I hadn't gone to her funeral was because I felt as if I didn't know her, and my mother's years of telling me what a bad person she was had tainted my opinion of her. But reading her obituary had made her come to life as a real person. I regretted not going to her funeral after reading it. She was and had been a part of my history, but like so many other things in life, I couldn't get it back, so I forgot about it all until I gave birth to Aden.

19

Leaving the hospital, with Aden being held in a car seat by her father, I walked out into sunlight so bright my eyes immediately submitted to the rays, squinting halfway closed. I had a sliver of vision to guide me to our car, where Jack was standing next to the car door he had opened for me. He was being unlike himself, having morphed into someone I hadn't seen since our early dating days, a sometime considerate and loving person. I was careful not to enjoy it too much. My distrust wouldn't allow his kindness to invade and melt my heart, as I knew, like all good things, it would come to an end. And it did, about three months later, when Aden's newness wore off like relatives overstaying their visit.

Jack would not help with Aden, refusing to bathe, diaper, or even feed her. He said it was the woman's job to take care of the children. This wonderful information had come to him filtered through the mouth of his mother. She was truly the thorn in my side, the monkey wrench in my plan, the fly in my ointment, and I blamed her for everything. But she had nothing to do with my aspiring to be and ultimately succeeding at being a good mother. Anything less, I would only have myself to blame, so I took on the duties of taking care of Aden alone, while Jack went to work.

For the first two years of Aden's life, I was a stay-at-home mom. We discovered Sesame Street together, Barney, Mr. Rogers, and plum-flavored baby food. I'd never had a baby before, and Aden had never been one before, so her first steps were also mine. Her first understandable words, at two years old, dog and mommy, were a new awakening for me. Her first unsolicited display of affection, when she came over and gave me a surprise kiss on the cheek, was overwhelming, and I began to need and depend on it like I depended on air to breathe. As mother and daughter, we had bonded.

And then there was Jack. Only he can tell you what was truly swimming in his mind, what festered inside him as our child grew, while he grew distracted by other things he felt were more important. He continued to come home late, and we continued to argue. But this I did know, Jack wanted more.

He hated the cheap blue compact car that his mother co-signed for that made him look like a squeezed sausage driving in it. He hated his job and our apartment. He wanted a house. He was ambitious, and he had dreams of owning his own business.

My comfort with just being Aden's mother was enough to sustain my existence, however small. The only dream I had, at that time, at twenty-three, was being a better mother than the one I'd been given. I likened it to a bad hand being dealt to a gambler.

Jack told these things to his mother, and she bought a small house in a god-forsaken town called Paradise City that we rented from her. With Aden's birth, Gloria had a newfound respect for me, since it was clear to her I was an attentive mother, and she loosened her dislike for me, telling me to think of the house as my home, which I did.

Jack drove sixty miles east from there to L.A. for work and continued his routine of inattentive husband and father. I put Aden in preschool when she was two and a half and worked doing data entry at Sears. I went to work, I came home, I took care of Aden. That was my routine. The only help Jack would offer was dropping Aden off at her preschool on the days I went to work early, and used the time at home to his advantage to talk on the phone with a girl he was trying to screw. Yes, Jack was cheating on me.

Being of a young age has its advantages and its disadvantages, and not being able to quickly spot a cheat is a definite disadvantage. And my young age is why I was naive for so long to the fact that my husband wasn't coming home because he was cheating. This thought never crossed my mind. Was it because I believed I was God's gift, because I trusted him, because I didn't think he was the type of person who could do that to me? I'm not quite sure.

But I never imagined Jack would actually cheat on me. The signs were there for me to see like huge billboards on the freeway, but I chose to ignore them. Excuse after excuse for why he couldn't come home on time began to pile up until it was a mountain blocking my way.

"I called your job last night around 9:00, and no one answered the phones. You didn't get home until around 12:00, so where did you go, because you certainly didn't come home?" I asked him.

You're probably wondering why I didn't just track him down with his cell, but bear in mind, this was 1993, before cell phones were widely used. He didn't have one.

"The phones are turned off at 9:00, which means I was there, the phones just didn't ring," he said. His excuse had bullshit smeared all over it, and I was becoming suspicious, and like the true Aries that I was, I let him believe that I believed his lie, while the detective inside me was about to go to work.

One miscellaneous Saturday evening, I decided to see what would happen if I called Jack while he was still at work, to tell him I wanted him to take me out, that his mother agreed to baby-sit for us. He sounded apprehensive, but told me to call him when I got to his mother's house. I got there and made the call, as I was instructed.

"Hey, um, well, look, I have to work late," Jack said.

"What do you mean you have to work late?" I asked.

"Just what I said, I have to work late."

"Well, what time are you getting off? The store closes at 9:00, so how about we still go? You can't be working past 9:30," I offered.

"Look, I'll call you," Jack said before he hung up. I sat at Jack's mother's house, trying to look happy, pretending all was well. I played with Aden until I looked up at the clock and saw that it was 10 o'clock. I called Jack's job, and there was no answer. I called again at 10:15, and again there was no answer. Then I called at 11:00, and there was no answer. I bundled Aden up and drove home to Paradise City. My tears fell onto the steering wheel, and I knew deep inside that my husband was probably cheating on me. But denial is a powerful thing, and I was still knee deep in it.

I put Aden to bed and instinctively went through the past phone bills I always kept for the duration of a year. Just like years before, when I had stumbled upon Denise's number, there were L.A. calls placed early in the morning after I left for work, while Jack was still home with Aden. I dialed the number and a middle-aged Hispanic woman picked up the phone. I hung up and waited for Jack to get home. My anguish was almost unbearable, as two more hours passed by before Jack finally drove up at 1:30 in the morning. I caught him coming through the door leading from the garage to kitchen.

"Why! Why! Why!" I said in a frenzied, screaming voice. I banged my fist on his chest to vent my frustration, my anger and my fear. My hair and make-up were a mess because I was a mess. I had been crying for two hours, and I was bordering on mental instability. All Jack could do was grab my wrists and hold them while he started to explain where he had been with another lie I wasn't listening to.

"Why are you doing this to me?" I whimpered. Then I got angry again. "I hate you! I hate you!" I spat, followed by another sobbing, pleading, depleted, lingering, "Why," I said to him, as if I didn't require an answer. There wasn't one. But who would want to be with the emotional wreck of a person that I was? I was almost on my knees, begging. I melted to the hard kitchen floor and continued to cry. Jack stood in front of me, giving me a good view of his wing tips. He was about to say something that would send my heart into cardiac arrest.

"All I'm doing here is hurting you," he began, looking down into my sad, sorry self.

"And I don't want to hurt you anymore. But I'm not cheating on you. I do think, though, that I should just leave."

I quit crying long enough to process his words. The possibility of staying in the house alone with Aden scared me. Believing in what he was saying, I told him I would leave instead. I would go to stay at his mother's house for a while, to give him time to think. I figured I would find a way to get him back later. If I didn't have him, I had nothing. My pride would keep me from going back home to my parents and keep me from telling them what was going on. But little did I know Jack's mother was having problems of her own.

I got to Jack's parents' house on a gloomy Sunday morning. I walked into the house with Aden and saw a noticeable difference in Gloria. She looked every bit of what I knew she wasn't; self-conscious, anxious, worried. I studied the harried way she was making coffee in the kitchen for Jack's father. I sat at the table, while Aden played with her toys nearby. I was sleepy from the night before and a bit in a haze.

Sal walked by Aden and me like he couldn't be bothered, on his way out of the sliding glass door to his car. Gloria asked him in Spanish if he wanted coffee. He simply waved his hand in her direction, without looking at her, as if to say fuck off, and kept going until he reached his car and drove away.

Gloria looked as if her world had been blown up. She turned and bent over the kitchen sink, crushing her stomach against it and began to cry. I rushed to her side and placed my hand on her back and asked if she was all right.

"No, I'm not all right," she snapped. I turned to walk away, then turned back when she said, "Do you know that bitch, Mercia?" she said a bit more calmly, raising her swollen eyes to meet mine.

I nodded my head for yes, only I didn't remember her as being a bitch. I remembered Mercia as the lady who lived on the corner who was Gloria's best friend.

"Well, she and my husband are having an affair," Gloria said, breaking down again.

I thought, oh shit. What the hell have I just stepped into? Jack's dad was cheating on his mother with a woman who lived, not in another city thirty miles away, not some random woman at his job. No, she lived on the corner. I was blown away. I quit thinking of my own problems and sunk into Gloria's.

"He say I can no compare to Mercia. He say she no fat like me. He say she no nag him like me," Gloria sobbed in her broken English.

We were both now seated at the kitchen table and were looking out the window into the backyard at nothing. The look in her eyes was distant and faraway. She was hurting. My heart went out to her, and I wished then that I was a smoker so I could give her one of my cigarettes. This was a strong woman, whose strength I was watching disintegrate before my eyes. Like an elephant being brought down by a lion, something about it was remarkable.

20

Gloria had been so proud, and now every morning she was being reduced to groveling for Sal's attention, pleading with him to take his morning coffee as he always had before the affair. If he would only drink the damn coffee, she could live on it the rest of the day. She was clinging to anything that would make her feel he hadn't totally left her.

She didn't know some people are gone before they actually leave. My husband had left me months ago, only I hadn't seen it. And yet there we sat, the two of us, looking out the window, waiting for our men to return like they'd marched off to war to fight for some noble cause.

In the next few weeks after I moved in with Gloria, she and her problems were a magnificent diversion. Separated from Jack, but watching Gloria marinate in all her pain and anguish, listening to her chastise herself for being the epitome of the perfect 1950's wife, taking care of Sal's home, ironing his shirts, matching his socks, cooking his meals, washing his dishes, for simply being a good, loyal wife, reminded me of what a fool believes.

She was angry with herself for being his maid for thirty years, for doing what she thought to be her duty, for believing they would die together, for still needing him, and for thinking her loyalty would make him dependent on her, so dependent that he would never even think of leaving. She never contemplated how easy she was to replace. Just like a broken glass, I thought.

But the days would pass, albeit slowly, and Gloria and her life began to evolve. Sal had moved out, taking enough clothes with him to last like he was on an extended vacation. He grew tired of Gloria's neediness, of her desperation. It was so apparent to me that he was detached and moving on. I would hear Gloria cry in her bed, followed by water running in the bathroom.

One morning at the kitchen table when she finally noticed that her only grandchild and I had moved in, she wanted to know what was wrong with Jack and me. I told her how Jack was not coming home at night, that we hadn't been getting along, and how this separation was going to bring us back together.

"He have other woman," she said with the simplicity of adding two and two.

"No. You don't understand. He says he's not cheating. We just need some time apart," I said, trying to convince her as well as myself.

"This, I tell to you, Synnie. Listen to me. He have to him other woman," she said, her words all switched around, as if I needed to get a grip and smell the coffee she was still pouring for Sal that he was still not drinking.

"You know, Synnie, every morning before I leave bed, I cry," Gloria began to explain to me as if she was getting used to her new situation.

"But then I make it to bathroom, splash water on face, I look in mirror and say to myself, 'Gloria, you must get up and get on with you life. You and you life must go on.'"

Her words made tears brim at the bottom of my eyes and began to chip away at my rock of denial. I looked at her and could see remnants of the old Gloria. This gave me hope for my marriage when it should have been giving me inspiration to leave it.

"How have you been?"

"I've been okay, Jack," I said.

"I'd like to talk to you about something. Do you think we could get something to eat?"

"Sure," I said. I thought Jack was coming to get us, take us to eat, and then take us home. I showered, put on something nice, got Aden dressed, and waited for Jack.

We sat in a booth at Sizzler, eating All-You-Can-Eat-Shrimp.

"So, um, well... you know, Syd, we could still be friends."

"I don't want to be your friend," I said dropping my fried shrimp back onto my plate. It toppled off the plate and bounced on the table.

"I want us to be married. I don't want to be a single mother," I said as I began to grow concerned and worried.

"I know, but I just need... well, we're always fighting," Jack said, as his palms began to get sweaty and perspiration began to form on his wrinkled forehead.

"Come on, it will get better," I said weakly.

"You don't understand. I want a divorce," Jack said with enough force in his voice that let me know he'd made up his mind. It was up to me to change it. So I began to cry. I wiped the tears on my cheeks and looked around to see if anyone was watching. Out of the corner of my eye, I could see our server looking over at us from a few feet away, a petite brunette, just cute enough to get noticed by my husband.

"Jack, please," I said. I grabbed his hand and squeezed it. He pulled it away.

Something told me he was enjoying watching me beg him like a fool in the restaurant. Why else would he bring me to a crowded place to tell me he wanted a divorce? That's news you tell someone in private or near a police station.

"No, Syd. No," he said. He sounded as if he had no control over his own decisions.

"But you can't do this," I said louder. I was squirming in my seat across from his. My foundation and mascara were beginning to race each other down my face.

"Would you guys like a refill on your drinks?" the server asked, interrupting us. My eyes shot at her. I wondered how it was she could come over and interrupt when it was obvious we were in a heated conversation.

"No, thank you," Jack said politely. I went back to pleading, begging, with my pleas intensifying.

"Just... Jack, please... Jack, don't do this," I said. Half my body was hunched over the restaurant table. My growing frustration at not being able to change his mind was consuming me and fueling my desperation.

"Would you please stop crying. I've already decided what I'm going to do," Jack said.

"Do you guys need anything else?" the server asked.

"No. Now, will you please just leave us alone," I snapped. "That's it," Jack said, searching for the money in his pocket. "We're leaving," he said dropping a five dollar bill on the table. I waited for him to turn his back, and I ruthlessly snatched up the money, smashing it into my purse.

"Is there someone else? Because if there is, fine, we're over," I said to him in the doorway of his mother's house.

"If there was, I would tell you," he said flatly, and he turned to leave, and I believed him.

Jack didn't concern himself with what was going on with his parents. He seemed preoccupied and far removed from us all. I told Gloria that Jack wanted a divorce.

"Is that right?" she said unfazed. She was bent over in her bedroom closet shoving clothes that belonged to Sal into heavy-duty plastic garbage bags.

"Well, if he no going to have family, he no need house."

I smiled broadly. Gloria had made the move to my side. My eyes lit up, and I began to see a light at the end of my tunnel.

"And he's cheating, too," she said.

"Oh, Gloria, no, he's not," I said. She stood up and looked at me as if she was wondering what fairytale I was living in.

I went about my business, with time on my side. None of the decisions that had been discussed between Jack and me were mine to make. I just had to wait, and so I did. And one week later, he called.

"Hey, how are you?"

"I'm fine, Jack. How are you?" I said with confidence.

"How's my mom?"

"She's doing fine. You know, your dad finally moved out, your mom thinks you're cheating, and she says that if you don't want your family, then you don't need the house," I said, like I was a TV reporter.

"I want you to come home," Jack said.

"I thought you'd never ask," I said smugly.

I went home the next day, and as I drove down the street, reaching the corner, there was Gloria, and Sal and Mercia out in Mercia's front yard. Gloria's large body was standing over dumped garbage bags of clothes, shoes, ties and belts in the grass. She was screaming obscenities. Sal was pointing at Gloria, and Mercia was quivering behind him, using him as a shield. I turned the corner and drove home to Paradise City.

I didn't know the only reason Jack wanted me back home was because he was lonely and felt isolated living all the way out in Paradise City alone. He was also afraid of what his mother was busy filling my head with. He knew that she was telling me the truth, that he was cheating, and that was the last thing he wanted me to know. He also hadn't bet on his mother taking my side regarding the house.

When I got home, we went back to the way we were as if I'd never left. Jack came home late night after night. I left him letters on the kitchen counters, pouring my heart out to him, telling him the importance of family. They went unread.

A couple weeks after my return, Jack reconnected with his mother and began to spend time with her, while his father remained with Mercia. He'd always had a strained relationship with his father, and Sal was not missed.

There is no other human being I have ever come across that has shocked and perplexed me more than Sal Cassavan. After thirty years of marriage, he abruptly dumps his wife, leaves his home, most of his belongings, and moves in with a woman living on the corner, who just happens to be his wife's best friend. He proceeded to run up every credit card he and Gloria had, buying expensive clothes and jewelry for Mercia. He ravaged their life savings, spending it on lavish trips to exotic locations for himself and Mercia.

He was sixty-eight years old and having the mother of a midlife-crisis. Gloria was beyond words. She only found out about his spending when bills and pay-up letters began to protrude through the mailbox. He had ruined their credit. Any sadness she had inside her solidified into hatred. She got an attorney and filed for divorce. She was a cafeteria worker from the time she first came to America from Argentina, never bothered to master the English language, and couldn't make enough money to support herself. What took a lifetime to build was gone in a matter of weeks. Her life, as she knew it, was over.

"Jack, what's wrong with your dad?" I asked over breakfast one sunny morning after I'd been home for about a month.

"How should I know? The man never paid me any attention my whole life," Jack replied.

"I can't believe what he's done to your mother."

"Yeah, well, she's not so innocent either. You women think you're all so innocent," he sneered.

I was happy to be back home, and Gloria would have to solve her own problems. But the unjustified bitterness I detected in Jack's voice that morning caused me to wonder, and I got the phone bill out of the mail and I searched it for an L.A. number, the same number that I'd dialed weeks before. Saturday morning, when Jack left for work, I dialed the number again. Waiting for the rings to go by before someone picked the phone up was like waiting for lottery numbers to drop. I was so anxious I could pee.

"Hola," a young girl had answered. Her accent was a thick, Mexican-American-from-East-L.A. accent, like Cheech Marin's, with a little bit of Charro mixed in.

I wanted to be straightforward with her, so I simply asked,

"Do you know a Jack Cassavan?"

"Yes, I do," she said.

"I'm his wife," I said.

"Well, you know, he's a fucking liar, you know," she exploded. I couldn't believe the way she spoke. It made me chuckle, and I began to wonder about her I.Q. It was hard to be angry at first; she obviously couldn't hold a candle to me. Jack had not upgraded, he'd simply gone slumming.

"Yeah, I knew he was married. And he's a fucking liar," she said.

"Wait a minute. Who are you?" I asked.

"I'm Luz Garcia."

"How old are you?"

"Turned twenty yesterday."

At that point, I began to get mad. This young, stupid little tramp had been fucking my husband. He'd ruined our marriage to be with someone who sounded as if she hadn't finished eighth grade.

"How long have you been dating my husband?"

"A few months. He told me he wasn't married."

"Well, he is, and you've been fucking a married man."

"Oh, no, I haven't. Wait a minute. I'm a virgin. He's been trying to sleep with me, but I had a feeling he was married."

With that, she turned everything into a different ball game. But it didn't make it any better. He was still cheating even if he hadn't been able to stick his dick in her yet.

I sat on the couch, with the calmness of warm bath water flowing through my veins. There would be no tears, no begging, pleading. I knew what I had to do. I was not a woman who would tolerate cheating. It was the ultimate deal breaker. Jack came home already aware that I'd found out about his relationship with Luz. She'd told him I had called her on the phone. Turns out she was the receptionist at his job. This he admitted to when he came home, and I told him I knew he was cheating, that I'd spoken to her, that I wanted him to pack his things and get the hell out, to leave, that he could have his divorce.

He began to put her down, which is so typical, complaining that she was from a strict Mexican family, and everywhere they went at night, they had to take her little brother with them. He said she lived with her mother, and they were from a lower-income suburb of L.A. called Hunts Park. All of this was of no consequence to me. I wanted him gone.

His head hung low, and he seemed sorry he'd been caught. I kept my cool. I even sat on the bed to watch him as he packed his things. He seemed tired, like he'd been on death row for eighteen years, had run out of appeals, and it was now time for him to die. He told me he was tired of moving. But his words went right through me. My anger was so deep, so strong, it couldn't produce tears. I couldn't have cried if somebody was paying me.

I thought it would be hard to watch him leave through the door, but once he got there, I only felt the need to tell him, "You'll pay one day for what you've done to me. Nothing good will come your way until you make things right by me, and I don't even know how you will begin to do that."

Without turning around he said, "Neither do I."

And then he was gone. The stillness of the house sent chills through me. Then passing Aden's room on the way down the hall, her baby-powder scent warmed me up again, and I was calm. I would start again. I knew Jack didn't have the recipe for giving me what I wanted, needed, and deserved. But parts of me must have continued to love him, because I couldn't get out of bed the next morning.

In the coming weeks, after I kicked Jack out, it was a depressing struggle just to get dressed and out the door. I was a bundled knot of emotion, and I fought a battle with myself not to cry in front of my computer screen at work in the morning. I lost every single day.

I'd be tapping along on my computer, entering data at Sears, filling orders, and then it would hit me, I was alone. I'd try to talk myself out of it, saying things like, "Sydney, you can get through this. It's not the end of the world. You're not the only woman whose husband cheated on her, left her for some trashy bitch."

And then my sadness would spill out like water from a busted balloon, and I was competing with tears to keep my composure, wiping them away, ruining my makeup, angered by my lasting weakness. I was mourning a marriage that I felt was over. I didn't know how I would go on without it. I began to mourn as if someone had died, because I was dying inside. My insides felt like they were rotting, and I lost my appetite.

Driving in my car, there were songs on the radio I could no longer listen to, they were too painful. Anything that was sung slowly, with feeling and about love, brought me to near nervous breakdown. I felt as if I needed, wanted, just had to crash. I was in a serious grieving stage, like nothing I'd ever experienced. TV shows that I used to love and enjoy about marriage and romance were abruptly switched off, exchanged for the pessimistic, cynical view of the evening news, where I welcomed the stories of rape, robbery and murder.

Without having friends at my job, I sat alone in the lunch room, embarrassed by having to wear clothes that were out of style. I wore the same thing week after week. I envied the girls in the stylish outfits, who were skinny and beautiful. I was so envious I found myself gazing at them, staring, feeling like a double outsider, someone who didn't belong inside or out. They seemed to do it all with ease, an ease that eluded me and caused me to miss work. I was put on probation and told I couldn't miss any more work unless there was a valid reason.

I sat at home feeling like I had years before, when I used to sit in the closet of my apartment, too afraid to face what a mistake it had been to marry Jack. Why couldn't I just go back home to my parents, where I would find support? Because my last words when I walked out the door were, "I'll never be back."

Only I'd told them to no one. I didn't need to prove to anyone that I meant what I said, because I believed it myself and truly meant every word of it. I would die first before I went back home. So I'd told those words to only myself, and my soul was listening, and I would sell one of my eyes before I'd go back home again.

21

Jack moved in with Luz and her family. He slept on their couch. His mother refused to allow him to stay with her. She said when Jack left for work in the morning, it was giving her flashbacks of his father.

As for me, with my father's help, I inched my way towards getting on with my life. I leaned on him heavily, without shame and embarrassment, when I'd call him to come over in the middle of the night, when I couldn't sleep, because I was afraid.

I didn't care what my mother thought of me or my suffocating need for him. I didn't care that he was leaving her to go to me and how it must have looked. For the first time, in all my years alive, I had real proof of the enormous amount of love my father had for me. It stared me back in the face every time I opened the front door, the door through which Jack left, and my father was standing there, waiting for me to fall into his arms, waiting to catch me. He held me while I cried.

He told me I would be okay. He looked into my eyes, clear back to the far reaches of my wounded soul and told me, "Sydney, you will be all right." And it was so hard to believe, but I tried. For him, I would try.

One rainy summer night, with the rain pounding against the house like stones, he said the most profound thing up until then I'd ever heard. "Sydney, he's not going to want her after he realizes you've moved on. So move on."

It was like someone flicking on the lights, and the dark cloud following me began to dissipate. But I found out the fastest way to get over someone is to replace their warm body with someone else's; replace their words, their likes and dislikes, their smile, with someone else's. I started going out again.

On a steamy Saturday night, while I was at a club with Kenya and she left me to go take some puffs off a joint in the bathroom, I met Tim. He was thirty-two. And he saw something in me no one else had in quite a while.

I was wearing a form-fitting, short-sleeved, long, cream-colored dress, with horizontal black-and-white stripes, that was in style at the time, that hugged every curve on my young body. I wore it with confidence, like I didn't give a damn. I made the rounds around the club, acting nonchalant, like I was too good for so many, basically trying to seem unapproachable. I glanced around and saw the guys checking me out and, at the same time, wearing intimidation on their faces like neon signs. I never intended to meet anyone. I just needed to get out. The juicy look in their eyes was enough for me that night.

I walked alone through the crowd, searching for Kenya, when I felt a strong hand grab my arm. I stopped and looked at the hand like I could melt it with my x-ray vision and then into the eyes of the only man savvy enough in the room to know how to get my attention.

"What's your name, gorgeous?" he said, still holding onto me.

"Why do you want to know?" I said back, trying to make my voice sound mysterious through the booming sound of the R&B music raging around us.

"Well, my name is Tim."

"How long are you going to hold on to me, Tim?"

"I just want to make sure you don't get away."

"What makes you think I'll get away?" I asked.

"I saw you when you first came in. All the guys were checking you out, but they were all too intimidated to say anything."

"And why aren't you intimidated?" I asked.

"Oh, I was, at first, along with everybody else, until I kept watching you and then figured out how to approach someone like you."

"What's someone like me?"

"Someone not easily figured out. But I did it. I've figured you out."

By this time, I was smiling broadly with all my teeth showing. I was amused, charmed, intrigued, all of those things at the same time. This was the first man beside my father who'd been able to figure me out, to see right through me and my charade. We danced all night and exchanged numbers in the parking lot.

Tim was shorter than Jack, and darker. He was a black guy. He was a smoothly rich, dark-chocolate color, a real black man, something I'd never had before. He lived in Van Nuys, an hour-and-a-half away from Paradise City. He fucked me harder than anyone I'd ever been with, which was only one other guy besides Jack. I was in heaven. I had waited until we'd known each other a month before I had sex with him. My heart still had a scab on it. After we both had come and he was still on top of me, he'd look down at me with lust in his eyes and say, "I don't know how Jack could have ever left you, you're so beautiful." And I'd be flattered as hell, saying to myself, I don't either.

Tim introduced new sexual things to me that I never knew were possible, like coming three times in one night. He had a thick tongue and luscious, full lips, and when he went down on me, I swear I saw and heard angels trumpeting. Jack? Jack, who?

My mind was recovering, and I was getting the pep back in my step. I couldn't have cared less where Jack was or what he was doing. He came by on occasional weekends to pick up Aden and tried to forge a friendship with me I was not interested in having. I couldn't be bothered. I had learned finally how to move on.

And then the rent came due. My low income was not enough to sustain mine and Aden's existence in the house. Gloria said if I couldn't pay the rent, I had to move. A spider, when chased, runs away only until it's cornered, then it decides to take a stand and prepares to fight. I was cornered, and I fought back by having Casey move in with me. She had a job working nights at a convenience store, so our schedules conflicted enough for us to seldom see each other. It took a month for me to realize some people never change.

It had been years since I'd lived under the same roof with Casey, about five. And since I'd had little contact with her while I was busy being married and living my own life, I had forgotten who she was. I remained optimistic because my options were limited. There was no one else I could trust to live with me. She was all I had.

Kenya and I walked into my empty house to find Jack sitting cross-legged on the floor watching my TV. The T-shirt he wore was a burnt-orange color, stretched out around the collar, and faded. He looked like a homeless person, unshaven and shabby and still very much over-weight. His presence stopped our laughter. I was surprised to see him there. I had never asked him for his key, because to me he was gone for good, living happily in L.A. with his barely-legal, barrio bitch. He looked as if he had something he wanted to say to me. But I didn't care to hear it, didn't want to know, couldn't bear to hear the words, "I want you back, Syd," pass over his evil lips. I could see the longing in the demeanor of his body. I heard my father's voice prophesying,

"Don't worry, Sydney, Jack's not going to want that girl after he real-izes you've moved on," and a smug half-curved grin of vindication began to form at each side of my mouth.

When Jack looked up into my narrow, almost Asian, dark-brown eyes, from the floor where he sat, his face said a thousand words that he could not: That he still loved me, that he wanted to come back home, that I looked beautiful, that he was being eaten alive by his decision to leave me for that girl. He seemed surprised as he looked me up and down that he hadn't found me sitting scrunched in a corner of the house like a crack head, chain-smoking Newports. No, I looked great, and happy, and over him.

"Hey, Jack. What are you doing here?" I asked him with sincere surprise.

"I was just leaving," he said.

Good. Get the fuck out then, and put my key on the kitchen table while you're at it, is what I wanted to say. I was making love every week-end to a man I was not ready to give up yet, not for Jack and his bullshit penis. My body was being savagely pleasured, ravaged, and devoured by a bucking bronco of a man, who knew how to satisfy me in fifty thousand different ways. I would have shot Jack dead before I gave Tim up. So I let Jack leave even though I knew what he wanted.

I would take Jack back when I got ready and not one minute before. I deserved Tim's strong stubble on my cheek, his mouth on my breasts, his hands dipping into my hips, his thick, throbbing penis stirring in my body, making me feel like a goddess. I knew he and I wouldn't last. He had two kids for Christ's sake. But I didn't have to think about that just yet. I was in my early twenties, having fun, living on the edge based in my own reality. I had successfully liberated my mind, my body, my soul, my heart, ultimately myself, and the feeling was priceless.

22

Casey was to me what black is to white, a complete and utter contrast, an opposite that couldn't be farther from the same. I, unfortunately, had to find out the hard way that my older sister still enjoyed associating with the lower segment of society that only paid attention to who's going to be duking it out on "Ricki Lake" over someone's baby's daddy and how to get the most mileage out of your food stamps.

She had a friend who spent a whole month in a mental institution, pretending to be crazy, being evaluated, poked and prodded, in an attempt to be proved mentally disabled so she could collect a state check for the rest of her life. It worked. Another friend had some kind of a weird emotional disorder that caused her to pick at her legs until small open sores developed, leaving them riddled with scars. Some of her friends had criminal records and had been in jail for crimes ranging from driving on a suspended license, petty theft to welfare fraud.

So I was baffled by how likeable she was, how gregarious and charming. I began to notice as people I'd seen coming and going on the street where I lived for months, who had not even bothered to wave to me, were now making my sister the toast of the neighborhood. She was being invited to drink beers in garages, to watch boxing matches in living rooms, to pool parties. I remained an uninvited bystander, an uninteresting nobody.

It was as if I was a slab of concrete on the street, people just rolled right over me. What did they see in her?

I resented her popularity. This was my neighborhood. She was just here because I needed her to help me pay my bills and keep me from going back home. She wasn't supposed to be making friends with my neighbors. I told myself they would see, would find out for themselves what a total disaster she was.

A few weeks later, at work, I got a call from my neighbor, telling me that my garage had been burglarized. This came as an extreme shock since I had drilled my sister many times on not leaving the garage door open. It was supposedly done in broad daylight, with her inside the house. I thought that that was a bold move. They had allegedly backed into my driveway and proceeded to load Jack's electric guitar, his amplifier, and his large tool chest into the back of their truck. It only started to smell fishy when I asked my sister if she'd heard anything or even made an attempt to call the cops, and she said no.

During my interrogation of her, she confessed that she'd quit her job three weeks prior and admitted to not having the money for half the rent. Jack called a week later to say he'd found his guitar sitting in a pawn shop window in downtown Bayside. Casey denied having any involvement in the garage theft. I told her to pack her shit and leave. My next-door neighbor said it was real funny how my sister didn't seem concerned when he went to the front door to tell her two men had just driven off with items from our garage falling off their truck. I figured she knew exactly who had robbed us.

It only took my sister a month to drive my life farther into the ground. Why did I think she'd ever change? I couldn't pay the rent by myself. I was sinking. My parents, pissed off that I was throwing my sister out, believing nothing that I told them about her, weren't interested in helping me. I felt nothing while she stood in my kitchen, juggling clothes, bags and shoes in her arms, telling me what an evil bitch I was, vowing to never speak to my cold, unfeeling ass again. As I watched her leave and get into a Cadillac emitting a plume of exhaust fumes into the night air, I wondered when it would all end.

So when Jack came over later that night, easing up behind me, catching me off guard, placing his hands around my waist, inching his fingers softly towards the front of my lower stomach where Aden once grew inside, whispering he loved me in my ear, saying he didn't want a divorce, I collapsed into the security of what he was offering like I was falling into a net that was going to save my life. I closed my eyes, and I let myself fall, and fall, and fall again. I would be taken care of by him, by his money, by his ability to make things happen for us. But I wasn't giving in, I was giving up.

He wasn't selling cars anymore. He had been promoted to the finance department of a car dealership in L.A., doing car loans, where the big bucks were, and I was impressed. I had had enough of being a single mom, had been left disillusioned by the men I met while I was out there dating again. None of them had been as smart or goal-orientated as Jack. And his ambition, it was intoxicating.

He talked about us maybe moving to Argentina for a couple years, about his dream of wanting to own his own finance company, and about knowing someday he'd be rich. I envied as well as admired his dreams. I looked up to him. He was, after all, five years older than I was. I'd been with him since I was nineteen. I didn't know anything else past him, and I couldn't see myself with anyone else. Blaming myself for his infidelity allowed me to overlook it for the time being and allowed me to take him back, but it never really went away.

Still, he couldn't be trusted, because he wasn't trustworthy. And I didn't want to be stupid, not one more time, so I tried to protect myself by never forgetting and remaining suspicious. The feelings of betrayal I had and my animosity towards him and what he'd done hadn't subsided. They were with me always. I wore them like a winter coat. I'd been scarred for life. I told myself it was my fault for being too difficult, that I had driven him away, that obviously he came back for me, which meant he really did love me. Crap. All of it crap.

With the money Jack was making, after he left the job where he was working with that tramp, Luz, we were able to stop renting his mother's house and buy one of our own. We took over the payments on a little house in Montara Valley for $7,000 and nestled into domesticity once again. However, we were still a revolving door of emotional instability. By the time we'd been married five years, we'd moved five times, and our problems moved with us, infiltrating every feeble attempt we'd made to stay together.

And then the Internet revolution began. We got a computer, subscribed to America Online, and a whole new world was opened up to me. I began to take classes at the local community college. Just two classes, English and Psychology. I thought maybe I wanted to be a marriage counselor. I knew I was intelligent enough to do something real with my life. I was jealous of Jack and his career, his money, the charisma and confidence he had developed from being a high earner. I wanted what he had so much it made me almost hate him more for being successful than for being a liar.

Jack didn't say much about my going back to school. He didn't seem to mind that I wasn't working, since I was at least in college. Yet not being able to trust him became a residual effect from his affair, and it permeated every aspect of who I was. One minute I'd be studying Freud and the next I'd be wondering who Jack was flirting with at work, who he was maybe trying to screw. I questioned everything he did, checked his pants pockets, his wallet, searched his car for long strands of hair or a tube of lipstick, accidentally left by whoever wasn't supposed to be there, any evidence that he was cheating again. I hated calling him at work and having to speak first to the receptionist. Her soft, sexy tone put me on edge and on the defensive. I listened intently to her voice, trying to detect any ill will towards me that would allow me to link it to a possible affair with Jack.

Like I would have left him anyway. I didn't need to die to go to hell, I was already there, put there by my own weaknesses, setting my own self on fire, torching my own soul. I would even ask him, when an argument got out of hand and out of my control, "Are you cheating again, Jack? Just admit it!" Like he was dumb enough to. Why would he admit anything, so he could be in for more of my petty bullshit? Of course, he wouldn't admit to cheating on me, and I wouldn't have either. It was a joke to him. He knew I wasn't going anywhere.

With an anonymous phone number on a small, jagged, somewhat ripped yellow piece of paper, almost overlooked and tossed into the trash, because of a grease stain seeping through it from front to back is how our next break-up began. It had a phone number on it and had slid out, I assumed, from Jack's pocket and fallen, weaving back and forth in the air like a feather would, before it eventually landed unnoticed by him on the kitchen floor. I leaned down to pick it up, thinking I would throw it away, careful not to put my fingers on the grease stain, when the numbers written in pencil, with three of the numbers severely faded by the grease, caught my eye and captured my curiosity. My eyes grew large, my heart started pounding, my anxiety level elevated, as I thought to myself, oh, God, please, not again.

I stood behind Jack, who was eating a meatball sandwich, his favorite, at the kitchen table, with the paper in my hand. I knew if I dialed the number, I would get hurt. I knew if I dialed the number, there would have to be a confrontation. I knew if I dialed the number, I would have to leave or he would. I knew all of these things, and I was afraid of them all, but I was more afraid of what I wouldn't know if I didn't dial the number at all.

I angrily stared at the back of Jack's head, imagining myself bashing it in with a shovel and afterwards burying him in the backyard, then devising a plan for getting away with it. I told myself I'd been watching too much "Law and Order" and shoved the paper into my bra for later.

"Hello, Supreme Auto."

I hung up, not being able to place the voice of the woman who answered the phone from the number written on the greasy piece of paper. Jack didn't work at Supreme Auto, he worked at Raceway Honda, and he was at Raceway Honda now. I didn't know what to think. I thought this was a long shot, but I called back and asked for Luz Garcia.

"Luz doesn't work today. She'll be in tomorrow," a woman said.

My legs became weak underneath me. I felt dizzy, and everything around me went blank for a few seconds while my mind braced itself for the truth, could absorb it, could process the fact that Jack had a piece of paper with Luz' work number on it. I asked myself how it was that Jack

was involved with that girl, still, after everything. She was no longer innocent. She was fully aware that he was a married man. I wondered why
he ever came back. "Simply because you let him," I answered myself.

23

I had finals to take in my classes, but I skipped them, and sat on the couch all day. With that one action, I ruined my eventual way out of my disastrous marriage, and a semester of my time and hard work went down the drain, because my husband was cheating on me again, and I thought why even bother with anything. I would still be nothing without him. My dream of becoming a marriage counselor disappeared inside the two Fs I got for both my classes, since I didn't take my finals.

The next day I went to a temp agency and applied for work. They sent me to the Department of Child Protective Services, where I was put to work as a clerk. Jack seemed mildly annoyed, two weeks later, when he found out I'd dropped out of school. He seemed as if he never believed I would finish in the first place, like he had come to expect that I would not make much of myself, so why would he be mad? But I was mad. I was furious, by the way, and I was about to transfer my anger from Jack to Luz.

I picked Aden up from daycare, and after she was fed, and playing contently in her room, I went into the bathroom, closed the door and made a phone call. I waited for the tramp to answer.

"Supreme Auto," she answered.

And I let out a blaring scream, a screech, a hideous noise that I was hoping would shatter her eardrum. I don't know how long it took her to hang up, but the sound coming from my mouth lasted about five seconds, about as long as my lungs would allow. Afterwards, I felt good, like I was getting somewhere. I knew Luz had answered the phone. Her lowlife way of speaking, that uneducated way she formed her words was unmistakable and had left a lasting imprint in my head.

This became my routine, and I did it once a day, every day, the same way I took a shower. Got ready for work, check; got Aden ready for school, check; made obscene phone call to wretched whore, check.

I had sank down to her level and humiliated myself into becoming a crank-caller, and I hated her for it. But like everyone else, I did have an ego, and Luz, with her still speaking to Jack, was beating the hell out of it, so I was unable to let it go. I should have been, since I wasn't about to leave. And because I was in pain, nothing was ever going to make me feel better until I could say some things to her that were burning a hole in my chest.

I called one morning before I left work, waited for Luz to answer, but before I could scream anything at all, she said, "I know it's you. You're Jack's wife, and you don't even know who you are fucking with." I was categorically unfazed by that. She could eat shit and die for all I cared and take her dumb threat with her.

"I can't believe you're still involved with my husband, you moralless jump off," I said in the lowest tone I could muster.

"Well, you know, I can't help it if he keeps calling me."

"Oh, yes, you can. You're not so innocent in this," I said.

"I'm not the one who has the wife, he does," she countered.

"Well, now you know for sure he has one. But you know what I hope, you low-life nothing, pathetic excuse for a woman," I began, figuring it would be half a second more before I heard a dial tone, expecting it to be in her personality to hang up, but she didn't, so I kept going.

"I hope when you're married to the man of your small, insignificant dreams, that he cheats on you with some disgusting tramp and hurts you the same way I've been hurt."

And with that last sentence leaving my mouth, so did something else. I didn't have the need to scream into the phone at her anymore. I was able to let it go, to let her go, finally, and I was the one who made the first move to hang up, not her.

"We're not involved or anything. When I changed jobs, she did too, and she wanted me to keep in touch with her." Lies. All of it lies. "I won't talk to her again, if you want," is what Jack said when I finally confronted him about the phone number.

"I shouldn't have to have this conversation with you," I said with a tight ball of frustration mixed into every one of my words. "Why do you think it would be okay for you to talk to the woman you were once cheating on me with at all? I mean, do you have rocks for brains or something? This is so beyond stupid. I'm so tired of you and of this," I said.

"Oh, really. So you're tired?" Jack said. "You know, Luz told me how you were harassing her, calling her job and screaming into the phone, blasting out her ear. I can't believe you would do that. That's so third grade, Syd," Jack said, half laughing.

"You bastard. How dare you speak her name to me, in this house, in that way. Who the fuck cares about what Luz says. She can't even spell harassing. She's a liar. I never called her. She needs to get a life. You know what, this is bullshit. Fuck you and fuck her."

"Oh, it's fuck me now? It's fuck Jack?" he said, his voice growing angry and louder.

"Yeah, you heard me. And you know what? Why don't you just pack your shit and go live with your mommy. You know that's what you want to do anyway." And as fast as I said those words, I wished they had been connected to a fishing line and I could reel them back into my mouth from where they came. But it was too late. Jack was in our room packing, and my pride was keeping me from stopping him.

A few hours later his mother confirmed for me when I called her that Jack was, in fact, not there, and she hadn't heard from him. I wondered where the hell else it was that he could go and why didn't he go to his mother's. Sal had been gone out of the house for at least a year and had moved to Florida with Mercia six months ago. His mother was all alone.

"I just want you to know I'm at a friend's house in Huntington Beach," Jack said over the phone. The calmness of his voice frightened me.

"Why didn't you go to your mother's house?" I said unable to mask my surprise.

"Because I knew that's where you expected me to go."

"When are you coming back?" I asked.

"I'm not coming back, Syd. It's over, and for good this time. I'm filing for divorce tomorrow." After he hung up, the word "tomorrow" echoed in my head over and over again for about an hour.

I called in sick for work the next day and the next and the next. I spent the days on the Internet, reading news stories and getting updates on movies, and entertainment, and concerts I wouldn't be going to. Then I went into a chat room. The Internet was in its infant stages back then, before child molesters and evil-doers had discovered it, back when it was safe to give your real name and even your phone number online.

I usually started out writing something irritating and controversial, that I maybe only partly believed, just to get the people in the chat rooms stirred up and annoyed so they'd respond to me. I enjoyed their angry words pointed towards me. That day, I think I said something about being appalled by Jessie Jackson. A guy who was calling himself Draper responded by asking me what race I was, and that's how we started up our conversation.

Draper was a white guy and about to graduate from Berkley with a degree in engineering. I was intrigued by him and his intelligence. He seemed easy to talk to despite how smart he was. Something in the words he used, the way they danced on my computer screen, told me he was probably attractive.

I lied and told him I was single, but I didn't lie about being a mother. And I was, after all, soon to be single after my divorce from Jack. We had a lot in common. We were both Democrats, both knew all the names of movie stars, knew the words to most of the songs being played on the radio, and we both wanted more than just typing words back and forth on a computer screen, so we exchanged numbers over the Internet.

One minute later, Draper called me. I raced to the phone. Technology rules, I said to myself. We talked for three hours. He told me in a couple months he would be driving from San Jose, where he lived, about an eight-hour drive, down to L.A. to visit friends and wondered if he could see me.

"I think I need a photograph of you first," I said.

"Oh, sure. Right. But to be fair, you have to mail one of yourself also," he said.

"Not a problem," I said.

I tore into the envelope that enclosed his picture. There was something sincere and honest about his face. He had gentle brown-colored, wavy hair, a goatee and a mustache that grew nicely around his olive-colored skin and lips, below his dark-blue eyes. This Internet guy was gorgeous. He was tall, and slender, and looking at his picture made me feel like I could replace Jack with him faster than I could replace my air fresheners.

"Draper, you're gorgeous. When did you say you'll be here?" I asked as soon as he picked up the phone.

"Sometime in July."

"Okay. That sounds perfect."

"And, Sydney," Draper began.

"Yeah," I said, hesitantly, hoping there wasn't some kind of a problem.

"I think you're beautiful."

I knew the drill, had done it before, was by now very used to it; Jack would be picking Aden up every other weekend. I prayed he would have her the weekend Draper was coming.

"If you can't pay the mortgage, you will have to move out," Jack said.

"I'm not leaving my home because you want to be an asshole," I said.

"Syd, we are getting divorced, I am going to file, and you'll be getting your papers real soon," Jack explained and slowly, as if he were explaining something to a small child.

"Sure, Jack," I said.

"Look, the house is already a month behind. You either find a way to pay it or get the hell out of there," Jack said.

"Why? So you can have it? No way. Go to hell, Jack."

I wasn't thinking clearly. All the bills were past due. I was running around in some serious denial state of la-la land. All I wanted to do was to meet Draper. I wanted to be allowed to open myself up to knew possibilities and not have to think about Jack and the kind of life I was actually leading, a false one, because I had a mortgage I wasn't even thinking about paying, and I was risking a foreclosure that would be a black mark on my credit for the next seven years.

Every morning I dropped Aden off at her daycare and drove to San Bernardino to work, where I argued with my co-workers, did my job poorly, and hated every minute that went by that I was there. The girls had it in for me. For some reason I was not liked, but I couldn't have cared less. I guess my fuck-you, and fuck-you and fuck-you attitude towards some of the girls was to blame, but what was I really anyway? A shell. An empty paper bag holding nothing but a lot of hot air, a waste, a nothing, a nobody going nowhere but to bed with Draper.

Draper stood in my doorway on the hot July afternoon that he arrived, handsome, towering over me, taking my breath away. God, I don't deserve him, I thought. This guy is so out of my league. I hugged him, letting my arms fall around his neck like two heavy ropes. It hadn't seemed appropriate to do more than just that. He had a smooth, like Kiefer Sutherland voice that reminded me of Miles Davis and jazz and was turning me on. The first thing Draper wanted to do was to cook for me.

"Would you like that, Sydney, for me to cook for you?" Heck, yeah!

"Sure, that would be nice," I said trying to keep my composure steady. I was trying to play it cool, but this guy was blowing my mind. No man had ever cooked for me. I couldn't wait to fuck him. At the dinner table Draper traced my full lips with his index finger and told me how beautiful they were. He seemed to be intrigued with my black features as if they were artifacts recently dug up out of one of the great pyramids of Egypt. He felt my hair while I munched on the chicken Caesar salad he made for me.

"Hmmm, your hair, it's so soft," Draper said, "and fluffy." I began to feel self-conscious by the way he was noticing our differences. And I had been uncomfortable with him while we were shopping for groceries at the market. I was careful not to look around too much. I didn't want to see anyone staring at us who could be thinking something like, there goes a white guy with a black girl. Well, what the hell is that? Draper went about the store choosing the freshest chicken and the crispest, greenest lettuce, and didn't seem as if he were embarrassed to be seen with me, although

I knew by the way he gazed in wonderment at me that he'd never walked through the supermarket with a black girl before.

But Draper and I never did have sex that weekend, the timing just didn't seem right. We hadn't had enough time to get to know each other, I wasn't enough of a slut, and he was too much of a gentleman, and the whole weekend was too pleasant for a steamy seduction to take place.

What we did end up doing is what I like to call a slow type of seduction, an extra-long-lasting session of foreplay. We never even kissed until the second day when it was time for Draper to get in his car and go.

I walked him to his car and gave him an overly dramatic I-don't-want-you-to-go-yet hug. But this time when I pulled away from him to look into his eyes, the timing was right, it was dead on. Our eyes locked, and without giving it any further thought, and because it felt natural to, our lips met and we softly kissed, moving our mouths together in a slow, sensual rhythm. He pressed me closer into him with one hand and cupped my face with the other, and I went with it, with him, went with the intensity of the kiss as it increased while he sank his lips deeper into mine with unrestrained emotion I'd never felt before.

I sensed an awakening, a change taking place within me. I, for the first time ever, was feeling passion, the passion from a romantic kiss that warms your heart and makes everything in your eyes hazy with stars. I could feel the desire raging inside him, it was burning through the way he was holding and kissing me. I never wanted him to stop.

"Wow, where did that come from?" I said coming up for air. He looked down, still holding me and smiled.

"I don't know," he said. "When can you visit me in San Jose?" he asked, taking a deep breath to replace what had been taken away.

"I'll have to call and let you know," I said, placing my fingertips to my lips. I watched his car as it drove away out of sight and remained in the place where we had just stood together for a long time after he left, but I wasn't into the long-distance relationship thing. To me, it was a road that would lead to a dead end, but I decided I was willing to travel on it at least for awhile.

When Jack came into the house that night, he had a look on his face as if he was about to win something. I took Aden, who had been sleeping steadily, from Jack's arms and put her down in bed. I figured Jack would show himself out and be gone when I walked back into the living room. Instead, he stood there with a manila envelope in his hand, smiling.

"I warned you this was coming," he said.

"What are you talking about, Jack?"

"The divorce papers. Here they are. Take them." I was stunned. My heart began to pound like an African drum. I was afraid of divorce papers, never having seen them before. I didn't know what to think. I felt as if the wind had been knocked out of me. I took the envelope from Jack and began to read the legal documents inside, while Jack crept out the door. The papers said his reason for wanting a divorce was because of irreconcilable differences. He did not seek custody of Aden, he only wanted visitation. He also wanted sole possession of the house, which meant essentially that he wanted for me and Aden to be removed from our home.

"Oh, this is some bullshit," I said. But when I looked up, Jack was gone.

"You will not get my house. Do you hear me?" I said running out of the house to where Jack was next to his car door with his hand braced on the door handle. He looked startled, as if he were surprised by my reaction. I bent down and grabbed two fistfuls of the gravel rocks and dirt that filled the planters in the front yard and hurled them at his windshield. The dirt and rocks splattered on his car, making a dust cloud.

"Hey, don't you do that!" Jack squealed back, with his voice quivering. He hurried to get into his car and swung recklessly out of the driveway. I went back into the house furious, breathing heavy, crying hysterically, and slammed the door. I lay awake all night, not knowing what to do. I was truly afraid of what was to come.

The next morning I paid fifty dollars for a consultation with a family law attorney. "See, it's like this, he can ask for the house, and that's exactly what he's doing, but that doesn't mean he'll get it," the attorney explained. After hearing that, I felt like an enormous fool for having spent the night afraid.

"And he wasn't even supposed to serve you with those papers. He was supposed to have someone else do it, which legally makes them void. He clearly was only trying to upset you. Don't get upset, ma'am. The wife and the children normally are awarded the house, and you can ask for spousal support in your response. I'll bet your husband didn't think of that one while he was trying to hurt you with this," he said.

"No, I'll bet he didn't," I said blankly. I wanted revenge for what he'd done to me, how he had scared me into thinking I was a soon-to-be homeless person. I had no idea how the legal system worked. He had the power to hurt me because of what he knew that I didn't. But what he didn't know is that I was tired of being stepped on and taken advantage of. I had started out with him as just a nice, normal girl, with hopes and dreams for the future. None of that was apparent anymore. I had been living in a cocoon from which I was about to emerge, but when I did, I wasn't going to be leaving it a butterfly.

I was in the shower a day later when the phone rang. Each ring sounded more urgent than the last. So I hopped out of the shower to answer it. Standing there wet with a towel wrapped around my body, my baby brother Chance said,

"Sydney, Lachlan is dead."

"What do you mean, Lachlan is dead?"

"Just what I said. He's dead."

"Was he shot?"

"No, he had a car accident. You'd better get over here."

I hung up and called Jack where he'd been staying, an hour away.

"Well, that's too bad about your brother, but I'm not coming back out there," Jack responded. I'd never been let down as suddenly and as severe in all my life.

"I'll come get Aden this weekend if you need some time."

There are no words to describe the days that followed. But I was alone, totally, completely alone, and I had never existed in a lower place. But a lot lower, there was that I would get. I just couldn't see it yet.

After I buried my brother, I returned Draper's many calls to tell him I couldn't set a time for when I would visit, that my brother was dead, and my life was on hold. I wore my grief all over my body, losing ten pounds from my already undernourished state.

The house was going into foreclosure, but our court date was still two weeks away, and I wasn't mentally functioning. Jack began to bring Aden home late on Sundays, creating an excuse to stay over. We started out watching TV together, then playing cards, then just talking. I never told him what a disgusting person I thought he was for not being there for me when my brother died. I simply added this slight to the pile already full with so many others. When he asked me if he could come back home, I told him sure, but I wanted to visit a girlfriend of mine in San Jose first.

Getting off the plane in San Jose, I ran so fast into Draper's arms I nearly knocked him over. He had been standing there, waiting for me to get off the plane like I was a sailor returning home after being out to sea for six months. He wanted me, and I wanted to be wanted. We had been waiting for this for months, and once we were back at his apartment, we didn't waste any more time. He picked me up inside his apartment living room, my legs came up and straddled his waist, and he gently carried me into his bedroom.

I lay on my stomach in his bed with my head turned sideways on a pillow. Slowly he pulled off my clothes. I felt blissfully relaxed, leaving my worries behind. I would let him violate me in a hundred different ways I so didn't care. He raised the lower half of my body off the bed by placing his hand underneath my belly, and easily guided his penis inside me from behind, and slowly kissed my back. I was already wet with anticipation that he slipped right in me. This new sexual position and the way it felt sent a tidal wave of joy through my whole body, and my mouth opened and my eyes closed tightly shut at the feeling.

I could feel Draper's chest resting on my back, his hot breath blowing in my ear and the weight of his strength as he groaned with pleasure. After that, I never wanted to go home. But I did go home, two sex-filled days later. And when I looked back at Draper, on my way to board the plane, I was leaving behind what could have been and going back to what never should have been, Jack.

We struggled to get the house out of foreclosure, but we were forced to sell it, and we were also forced to move in with, of all people, Gloria. There was a bright side to all of this, though. Gloria lived on a little less than half an acre of land, in a six-bedroom house. There was a small kung fu studio not far away where I could study and live out my dead brother's Asian dreams while finding a new one of my own.

24

The one thing that I hold most dear, that has been the most long-lasting, most precious thing that Lachlan gave to me was his love of Bruce Lee and kung fu movies. When I was, like, eleven, I can remember on Saturday afternoons, right after "Soul Train," spending the next two hours watching "Kung Fu Theater" with him. Chance was there also, he was just too little to appreciate the art.

I remember watching with amazement as Bruce Lee fought with flawless precision his attackers, shamelessly defeating them with carefully staged choreographed moves that kept me on the edge of my seat. The way he fought made him seem from another world. It was obvious from his movies that he was invincible.

He became my hero. There was nothing and no one better. He was the first man I ever fell in love with. Because of him, I grew up and became a woman drawn to men who were fearless, whom I perceived as capable of defending my honor and my life. The guy didn't have to be a football player or cop. He just had to have a certain fire in his eye, a certain edge to his demeanor, and an intimidating voice. I measured the worth of a man by his willingness and ability to protect me. If I felt he couldn't, he would not hold my respect. He could have my love, but he would never have my respect.

I studied Bruce Lee's kung fu moves, trying to slow them down in my head with my eyes, picturing myself as the one delivering each punishing blow to the evil ones who challenged him. I secretly wanted to someday learn how to move like he did. He stood for all that was righteous and good. He was confident, not cocky. He was the first symbol of greatness on television that I ever believed in.

And when my brother broke the news to me, after one Saturday afternoon, that Bruce Lee was dead, I instinctively refused to entertain for even one minute the thought that it could be true. Bruce Lee, dead? My ass Bruce Lee is dead. There's no force on this earth that could ever stop him, I believed. No, he's doing secret martial arts training somewhere on the outskirts of the Chinese countryside, preparing to defeat the sinister forces that continue to lurk amongst us, I reasoned.

And I still somewhat believed in that when, after moving to Bayside, I passed by a small kung fu studio on the corner of Manchester Boulevard. I would have driven past, but when I reached a stoplight, I turned my head to the right, just slightly, and the banner on the front of the studio that read Far-East Kung-Fu caught my attention. This was my chance, I thought. Something magical is going to happen to me inside those four walls, I believed, something life-altering. I was too shy and too unfamiliar with the area to go in, so when I got home, I told Jack about it, told him I would like to take kung-fu lessons. He signed us both up the next day.

"I want you to meet my wife, Sydney," I heard Jack say from around the corner of a wall, a few feet from where I had been silently, anxiously waiting on a bench inside the studio for our first lesson together to begin with Mr. Randal, one of the instructors at the school. I hadn't known what to expect, but as soon as I heard Jack's voice, I sat up straight and tall and smoothed my hair. I cleared my throat in order to speak fluidly and without hesitation. I wanted to be taken seriously. I wanted the instructor to think maybe I would be a fast, eager learner, possibly one of his best.

The look that changed on Mr. Randal's face when he had come around the corner and saw me told me he had not been expecting me to be black. I stood up, and I put my hand in his, shaking it firmly, looking directly into his eyes. My body temperature rose slightly after seeing the easy smile form on his face as he said hello in a deep, gruff voice that caught me by surprise. It didn't match his face. Not James Earl Jones deep, which is extremely deep, but more like the smooth richness of something like Alec Baldwin's.

His eyes were like the blue waters surrounding the Hawaiian Islands I'd seen in vacation brochures. His face couldn't have lit up more if it had been struck by the sun, and there was something I can't find the words for that was set off between us when he first came around that corner, when our eyes met, when his face told me everything that his mouth didn't have to, that he was going to enjoy being my teacher and I his student.

Mr. Randal was the first short guy I was ever attracted to. He stood somewhere between five-seven or eight. His thighs were strong and thick, his lips thin, and his nose pointy. His skin was a milky white color, but it was the base in his voice, the firmness and self-assuredness of it that was truly turning me on. Jack, of course, was standing there oblivious to it all. He had traditionally underestimated me, and he couldn't have been more clueless of the strong attraction this testosterone-filled, overly muscular, kung fu guy was having for his wife and she for him.

Our lesson together that day began with Mr. Randal showing us some basic kung fu moves, like front punches and front kicks. The three of us were inside one of the four tiny, roofless private rooms that lined one wall of the studio. Our bare feet stood on a cushy mat. I felt, after doing my first front punch, that I had mimicked Mr. Randal perfectly.

"That was great, Ms. Cassavan!" Mr. Randal said excitedly.

"Yeah, if you don't mind looking like a dope," Jack said. I glared at him and whispered to him a few seconds later to shut up.

"Mr. Randal, please call me Sydney," I requested.

"We only use last names here, Ms. Cassavan. Sorry," he replied strictly.

"Well, duh," Jack said.

"Okay. Now, Mr. Cassavan, I want you to do the front kick I just showed you. Then Ms. Cassavan will do it for me."

Jack attempted to perform the simple front kick we'd just been shown and fell to the side, almost crashing into the sliding paper door that gave our room privacy. He clearly had a problem with balance. It probably had something to do with his weight, his flabby stomach hanging over, or maybe he just had bad knees from carrying all those pounds around. Could have been a combination of them all. I wasn't sure. But I, for the first time, was embarrassed to be his wife. I looked over at him, wondering why I was even with him. But I wasn't ready to address that question. I did, however, wonder what Mr. Randal thought about when he looked at me, if he was wondering the same thing.

He remained a professional, a gentleman, and my attraction to him I would keep a heavily guarded secret. I resigned myself to the fact that he would only be a fantasy I would dream about, an unresolved desire, something I could never have. And all of that was fine, since I, after all, did belong to Jack. And he made fun of every kung-fu move I made. I couldn't tell if it was out of spite, or envy, or if he was just being an asshole. But I could see Mr. Randal felt sorry for me, that he felt I could do better without Jack, that he was perplexed by the nature of our relationship.

After our third or fourth private lesson, in which Jack, while trying to execute a front kick then follow it up with a back kick, crashed to the ground, falling hard, he told me on our way home in the car that he couldn't take kung fu with me anymore because his job hours were changing. I knew his excuse was a lie, and I didn't try to think of a way we could work around his schedule.

The following week, I sat on a bench in my kung-fu uniform, long-sleeved white top and white pants, all pulled together and cinched with an orange cloth belt that let everyone know I had only just begun my long quest to get my black belt. I waited for Mr. Randal to come around the corner to get me.

"So your husband's dropped out," Mr. Randal said, standing before me with his hands on his hips. "Well, it's better to teach one-on-one. You'll learn faster now. There won't be any more stopping and waiting for the other person. We only have a half hour anyway. Well, are you ready to get started?"

"Absolutely," I said, as I caught a whiff of his cologne. Having my lesson alone, without Jack, was like being a kid and suddenly not having to share your room with your pesky brother anymore. I came alive. I didn't have to worry about what I looked like, if somebody was going to think I looked stupid. I was just doing my thing, being and learning who I was as a martial arts student.

Mr. Randal watched me perform the moves he showed me with a piercing seriousness to his face, like he was breaking down every inch of me. At times, for me, it could be erotic, especially when his eyes were fixated on me or when he would come up behind me and place my arms or body where they or it needed to be.

"No, like this," he would say, putting his hands on my elbows, or sometimes it would be my wrists that weren't right, or my waist.

"You mean, like this?" I would ask, adjusting myself.

"Yeah, that's perfect," he would say.

"You know, you're doing really well, Ms. Cassavan."

"Thank you, Mr. Randal."

"I look forward to our next lesson, and don't forget to go to at least two group lessons a week," he said.

I had to know his first name. It was driving me crazy and messing with my fantasy. I went to the group lesson that started every day of the week at 7:00 p.m., which consisted of about forty or fifty men, women, and children standing in at least five rows, simultaneously going through the same called-out routine.

"Front kick!" Mr. Randal commanded. And we all kicked hard and with everything we had, like we were fending off an attacker.

"Kick!"

We all kicked.

"And kick!"

Then we moved on to punches.

"Right punch!" Fifty arms flung out into the air.

"Left punch!" Sweat began to trickle down my face, and my thighs began to burn with heat, but I loved the rush I got from this. When the class was over, I felt like I could run around the block five times. So I went home and pounced on Jack like a tiger. I mauled him over and over again until I was satisfied. And when I was done and sweating on top of him and looking down at him, it was Mr. Randal's face I saw.

I discovered I was not alone in my erotic fantasies starring Mr. Randal. He had a sizeable following. In the women's locker room after classes, talk of Mr. Randal flowed over the other women's mouths like warm lip gloss. Silently I listened.

"No, he doesn't date his students. It's against the rules. The owner of the school won't let him. He says it has something to do with favoritism," one student stated. She was taking off a purple belt that had three stripes on it that let me know she'd been taking lessons at the school for at least a year.

"And, no, he doesn't ever break that rule."

"Well, he's gonna break it for me. I can get him," a pretty, tall blonde declared, tossing her hair back over her shoulders.

I turned to the wall, bending over to strap on my sandals, wondering how much more they would say.

"He's so damn cute. And muscular. Does he have a girlfriend?"

"No. He used to, though. She broke up with him because he didn't make enough money."

"Yeah, so don't waste your time. Mr. Randal likes those girls who need rescuing. It's like he has this need to be the knight in shining armor. His girlfriends are usually all screwed up in the head. I know this, I've been here for five years," a lady about fifty said.

I was about to leave the locker room content with the new information I'd just obtained, but became even more surprised when someone still inside the sweaty crowd of women asked, "Hey, what's Mr. Randal's first name?"

"Scott," someone said.

Scott Randal. So his full name was Scott Randal. Finding that out didn't keep me from asking him his first name at our next private lesson, even though I already knew it. I had been working hard, going through my many different punches and kicks, and during a break I asked him what his first name was. I just wanted to hear him say it, wanted to be able to see the way it looked coming out of his mouth, see the way his lips would part and change when he said it.

"It's Scott," he said softly, tilting his head slightly as if he were flattered by my asking.

"That name has always been one of my favorites," I said. And that's how the ice was broken, or shattered, or better yet, blown to bits, because after that, our lessons became more lively, less awkward but more mentally intense, and he set us on a road of discovery with every question he decided to ask me.

"Do you like martial art films, Ms. Cassavan?"

"Yeah. Bruce Lee is my hero," I said enthusiastically.

"Are you the middle child?"

"Yeah, I am. How'd you guess that?" I asked.

"You're strong-willed," he said.

"And how would you know that? Were you a psychology major?" I asked. He became a little nervous before he told me,

"Well, no, I.... well, see.... I've never been to college. I never even finished high school. But I have my GED. I got, like, one of the highest scores they'd ever seen before," he said. I was astonished at his honesty, and my eyes could not leave his face.

"But I read a lot, so I know a lot of things," he said. I was beginning to see the guy behind the kung-fu outfit, behind the muscle and the brawn and the voice, the person behind the teacher, and without him realizing, his weaknesses. They were becoming more apparent. Up until then, I didn't think he had any.

Over the course of the next year, he and I formed a silent bond that neither of us would admit to or acknowledge. I was falling in love with my kung-fu lessons and with him in a way that kept itself contained in a boundary that would not cause me to leave my happy home, since I knew I could not have him in the way I wanted. In the back of my mind, I knew some day, just maybe, I would. But I chose to focus on the one day a week I was alone with him and half my lesson was spent by him talking to me about my life. He was vicariously reaching into me, my world, my desires through my words. He listened to me. His eyes danced around the stories I told him about my life with Jack and with Aden.

He told me he came from an extremely dysfunctional family, made up of his morbidly obese mother, his mentally disabled youngest brother and fractured relationships with his five bothers and sisters, who were living scattered throughout the country. He said he had grown up plotting the death of his stepfather who had verbally and physically abused the family. Kung-fu was his escape, and he started taking lessons when he was fourteen. Eventually his mother divorced his stepfather, and life became better, easier.

He said he was an atheist and didn't believe in God. That was the most shocking of everything he said. How could this be? This meant, to me, he had a dark soul. People who don't believe in God have no faith, they've been so hurt, so let down, that they are unable to believe that there is a higher power up there somewhere answering prayers and saving people. So I would save him. I just had to save myself first.

I told him I married Jack when I was nineteen, mainly because I was young and stupid. I knew he was wondering. I told him I was not working at a full-time job. I was trying to figure out what I wanted to do with my life, and Jack made enough money anyway. I told him the biggest influence in my life was my father, and the relationship I had with my mother was strained, that I had one brother pass away on me, another still alive for me to adore, and a sister I could otherwise forget existed.

Mr. Randal never judged me and what I said. He could relate in most instances to the stunted relationships within my family. He and I could have been defined as just friends, but under the surface was a longing found only in a look, a glance, an innocent touch, a tone of voice. So he knew, I knew, we knew, someday we would speak of it, as well as act upon it, because it was one of those things that just had to be done.

25

The only reason I agreed to move in with Gloria after we lost our house in Montara Valley was because she too was losing her home after Sal left and moved to Florida, and I was promised to by her and Jack that my name would be put on the house if I moved there. Jack and I were supposed to take over the payments and both our names were going to go on the title to Gloria's house. That didn't happen.

After we had moved in, after I had painted the whole inside of the house, scrubbed the bathrooms and the kitchen to get them to my level of cleanliness, did I find out that my name had not been put on the title, but that Aden's name and Jack's name were the only two names on the title of the house.

Of course I was angry, but what could I do? And it wouldn't have been the first time Jack had betrayed me. Never again, I told myself. How could he allow his mother to do that to me? Or was he the one that decided I would be left off the title to the house? I just knew I resented them both. I was regretting all the time I'd spent with Gloria, helping her through her problems with Sal. She and I were a war about to begin.

Everything went along smoothly at first, but like the shifting winds of winter, things began to blow. Before Jack came home in the evening, his pattern was to call me at home, see what was up for dinner, give his estimated time of arrival. I began to notice, just after we'd hang up, his mother's private phone line would then ring. Then I'd see Gloria go into the bathroom, fix her hair, and then come into the den as if she were waiting for something, for someone. My husband, as if he were her own, is what I realized she was waiting for. I resented his calling her just after calling me, as if he had more than one wife. The way she waited for him, my husband, caused me to feel as if we were sharing him, we were in competition for the title of Lady of the House.

She became the third party in our marriage as Jack made her a part of our private world of husband and wife. All that he needed to do was fuck her and she'd be me. He would complain about my money management and secretly give money out of our account for his mother to hold, as if I were incapable of handling the finances. If I bought Aden an extra outfit, or toy, or spent the day sleeping, she reported it all back to Jack. Gloria spoke Spanish to Jack in front of me, which was infuriating to me. I felt left out of their world, while she was able to be a part of mine. She was allowed to shut me out when she chose to. She had her son all to herself when she felt like it, excluding me, excluding the daughter-in-law she never wanted. Gloria's husband had run off and left her, so Jack became his replacement.

So where did that leave me? But Jack was more to blame for this more than she. I despised Gloria so deeply for this that I envisioned her slipping on the kitchen floor or falling in the foyer on one of Aden's toys, requiring her to be in the hospital for a year. She undermined my judgment by running to Jack with everything I did. She and I argued over anything and everything, from Jack's attention to who left a crumb on the kitchen counter, to her speaking Spanish while I was in the room.

When I couldn't take it anymore, which took a few months, I decided not to speak English or anything at all while she was in the room. Jack's questions and statements to me went unanswered and unnoticed as long as his mother was within earshot. He'd become enraged and try to intimidate me into speaking, but my lips would not part. This was my way of protesting his treatment towards me regarding his mother. She came first, and I ran a distant second or even third or fourth, because much of Jack's job consumed him, as well as whatever it was that he was doing that

I didn't know about. Aden was not even closely part of the equation. She was my sole responsibility.

One day, while sitting alone in the house, after I had unsuccessfully tried to locate Draper on the Internet, I opened up a phone book on the desk and saw an advertisement for court reporting. The ad said I could be a court reporter, working in court, in as little as two years, making a lot of money. The idea of making a lot of money was the motivating factor for why I called the number that day. With that thoughtless turn of pages through the phone book, I would forever change my life.

"Mr. Randal, I've been thinking about going to court reporting school," I said to him before the start of my lesson. I couldn't wait to tell him, to tell somebody. I didn't know when I'd tell Jack.

"Well, that's great, Ms. Cassavan," Mr. Randal said.

"I'm not sure if I'd be any good at it, but I need to do something with my life, you know. Jack makes all this money, and...."

"Ms. Cassavan," Mr. Randal began earnestly and softly, as he moved in closer to me, close enough to almost kiss me, lowering his voice to a whisper, to where I had to compensate by reading his lips to make sure I got what he was saying.

"You can do anything you set your mind upon. Don't you know that? I mean, from what you've shown me here as a student, I know you will go far. And you're so pretty, you could have any man you wanted," he said gently.

I just stood there looking at Mr. Randal, hoping the pain searing my eyes at the truth in what he was saying wasn't showing that I was trying my best to hide. He was making me realize things I'd never contemplated before. He was saying things, at the time, that I couldn't believe but so needed to hear someone say. This man I was trying to hide from, with my facade of a smile, with my manufactured enthusiasm, hadn't been fooled at all. And I was getting attached. Although I had taken many lovers, none had survived Jack. Each affair had served its purpose for the limited time it lasted, only to have me fade back into the darkness of what was my life with Jack. I truly did not think I would be able to find better than Jack because I simply was not better. If I did, I believed it would be a miracle hand-delivered from God.

Now, standing before me was a man filling my head with compliments I wasn't receiving at home. He was seducing me with his words, killing me softly, drawing me in. I wondered if this wasn't just some method of foreplay for him and if there were others he was doing this to.

His appetite for sex, judging by the way he handled me, had to be abundantly large, as large as the swelling bulge in his pants that every time we met, my eyes somehow found. With each private lesson he gave me, I felt as if I were inching my way closer to him, closer to crossing the line. Where did he actually draw it, and how could I get him to stand on the other side of it? On the other side of my fascination with Mr. Randal, there was court reporting school and all it would change in me and my life.

My happiest day came when Gloria got on a plane bound for Argentina, not to return for a whole year.

"Adios, motherfucker," I said to her picture sitting on the mantle above the fireplace, right before I tossed it into a small box I was holding underneath my arm that was balancing on my hip. I enjoyed the rattle and clank it made as it crashed into the other five pictures I was carrying in the box that had her same annoying image on them. I thought of Lachlan and wondered how it was that the evil people are allowed to live on and on and on, to cause pain and misery, while the good ones God takes always too soon. Surely Gloria by now had lived long enough, I reasoned. I cleared her things out and put everything belonging to her in the garage to collect the dust of someone, of something unwanted, ridding my mind of her. The other woman was gone now. And I, dammit, was still here.

26

I walked into the Court Reporting School of California not knowing what to expect, and I was late. The night before, I had fought a small garage fire that started from lint that had built up at the bottom of the dryer. The flames raging from the dryer had singed a crop of Jack's ties that were hanging above it. He, of course, was nowhere around, working late, miles away, and I was home alone with Aden. I was in the garage, attempting to put out the flames when I was told to move aside by some men passing by. My husband should have been home, here saving my life, not these men I didn't even know and had never seen. I was embarrassed by needing their help, but I thanked them for putting the fire out, and they continued on their way.

I didn't bother to call Jack. What would have been the point anyway? He wasn't what I wanted anymore, and wanting to get the hell away from him was the reason why I was standing in the main entrance of the court reporting school, nervously giving an excuse for being late on my very first day. The receptionist showed me to my class that had already begun and filled with anxious girls. I took a seat in the front row, and from that moment on, I never looked back, not at my unhappy marriage, not at my unhappy self, not at all my many mistakes. Nope, I was at the school for me, and nothing and no one was going to stand in my way. I clung to becoming a court reporter as if it were my last crumb of bread and I had been starving.

That night when Jack got home at eleven, not even trying to explain why he was so late, I didn't ask him where he'd been. I looked over at him from the other side of the bed, thinking he could go ahead and sleep, softly and soundly, because in two short years, I was going to leave him for good. He wasn't going to know what hit him. So I began to plot, knowing I would need to be patient. I didn't know how much I could endure, but I was determined to become a court reporter before I turned thirty.

Court reporters write everything that is said in court on a small machine that sits on a stand positioned between their legs. They mostly write phonetically, sounding out words in their head, with three or four strokes from their fingers on the steno machine. Court reporters also use briefs to write words, which is a shorter version of any particular word. It would take me six months to learn how to write the complete alphabet, as well as anything a person could possibly say on my steno machine. I loved it. For example, pressing a T and a P together made an F or the F sound, and pressing just the letter T on my machine made the word "it." It was rather confusing at first, but I was intrigued.

At home, Jack didn't want to talk about what I was learning in court reporting school. He was resentful that I was going to school full time and not working. But I didn't care. In two and a half years, I would be gone. I fantasized about meeting and marrying an attorney. Jack grew less attractive, and my kung-fu relationship with Mr. Randal deepened.

My lessons with him lasted well over the half hour they were scheduled, because Mr. Randal deliberately left the slot after me open so we could chat. We talked about court reporting school and politics. I couldn't be sure how he felt about me, but I had a feeling he felt the same way. I told Mr. Randal how unhappy I was with Jack, and he encouraged me to end it. But I couldn't end it just yet, not before I finished school.

Going to court reporting school kept me energized and motivated. I ate, slept, and dreamed court reporting. When I was in the grocery store, briefs for words were turning over in my mind. I wrote every word I heard in my head. Even when I left the school I was still there, because it never left me. I couldn't wait for someone to say to me, "What do you do for a living?" And I would be able to say, "I'm a court reporter." At that time, I could think of nothing better, and that was what was going to keep me going, but it also made me a very competitive student. I wanted to be the best student there, finish the course in the shortest amount of time ever, and have everyone know who I was.

There were girls enrolled in the school of all ages and of all walks of life. The two girls in my class that were, like, around twenty, I wrote off right away. I figured girls that young didn't have a clue about striving and working hard and would probably drop out before the end of the week. The older women I felt wouldn't have the stamina to keep up with the pace I was going to set for myself. But there were at least four other girls who were around my age of twenty-seven that I couldn't size up. So I would have to wait to see who my real competition was. But I knew if I wasn't number one, I'd be in the top three.

During our first week, our instructor, Sabrina, had us go around the room and do the typical who are you and why are you here kind of stuff.

"Okay. Starting with you on the right. State your name, and tell us a little about yourself and why you're here," Sabrina said, pointing to a slightly overweight, short-haired blonde with bright-red lipstick smeared over her lips that were almost bigger than mine.

"Hi, my name is Diane. I'm thirty-four, and I have three kids. I used to do real estate, but I don't anymore. And I'm here because I need a new career. My husband cheated on me with another woman, and now we're getting divorced. And so, you know, I can't let him destroy me, you know." All that drama, I thought. What a pathetic whiner. I was instantly annoyed and decided she was someone to avoid.

"Hi, my name is Terri. I'm twenty-eight, and I had my daughter really young, so I'm getting into a career kind of late. I thought court reporting would be a good thing to do. I live up in Arrowhead with my parents, and I'm here because I want to change my life." She was a tall, skinny girl with a hardened edge to her. She had badly permed hair that frizzed at the ends. There was a pack of Marlboros and a lighter resting on her desk, and she was reminding me of Casey.

"Hi, my name is Rainbow." I wondered if I'd heard that right. Did she say her name was Rainbow? Okay. Whatever. She was short, light-skinned, and obviously racially mixed with something, I just couldn't guess what.

"I'm from Hawaii," she said.

"Rainbow, are you pregnant?" Sabrina asked, like she was curiously surprised.

"Yeah, five months, by my boyfriend. And I have a two-year-old son at home being watched by his mother, because his father won't help me, so I may be going back to Hawaii in a few weeks." I wanted to ask her what the hell she was doing here, then. And just when I started to believe I was surrounded by a pack of losers....

"Hi, my name is Marissa. I'm married, with one son. I'm ready to work hard to become the best court reporter I can be." Oh, is that right, I thought. Well, not before I do. Marissa was slim and pretty, with dark, medium-length hair that matched her dark eyes. She was the one whose life most resembled mine, and I was intimidated.

So when Sabrina got to me, after having suffered through all of that other bullshit, I decided to just keep it real. I sat up straight and tall in my chair and said, "Hi, my name is Sydney, and I'm here basically for the money I've been told I'll make."

Everyone turned and looked at me as if I'd just claimed to be Dorothy from the Wizard of Oz. But I was able to still make a few friends. Getting a group of women together brings out the best and worse in them all, and when Sabrina left the room, and when we were all alone, some of the women told their deepest, darkest secrets, aspirations and hurts. It was rather entertaining at first. I gave the persona that my life was great with my husband, I lived in a big house, had a great little girl, and did kung-fu in my free time. I also drove a sports utility vehicle that the girls envied and wondered how I could afford. I told them my husband made a lot of money.

But I wasn't there to make friends and to foster friendships. I was there to make money, my own money, to be able to leave my disgusting husband, to be able to travel the world and buy nice things, to be able to say fuck you to whoever I pleased. I didn't join a clique or make lunch buddies. The girls that I occasionally did go to lunch with, our interaction stopped once we got back to school, because then I became a ruthless bitch who couldn't be bothered. I was determined to blow through school as fast as possible, to prove to myself and everyone else watching that I was the best.

There was just one problem, I wasn't the best. That title had gone to Marissa, and I disliked her for it. She was near perfect in her proofreading skills. I wasn't quite as good because I was impatient. If it hadn't been for her, I would have been number one in my class. Still, we became friends because we fed off of each other's determination, and drive and sheer talent for court reporting. There were no other girls like us in our starting class. Neither of us held a job while we were in school. She had the talent, and I had the drive and determination. There was a silent competition between us that we knew existed that we never talked about but was apparent to everyone else.

Learning how to write in steno was one thing, and gaining the speed to be able to write the spoken word at 200 words per minute was another. Once we learned everything we needed to know to be able to write in steno, we entered into speed classes. The first was 60/80, and we had to get up to that speed in order to pass out of that class and progress all the way up to 200 by passing in each class one literary test, one jury charge, and two testimony tests. My first day in 60/80, I was already writing at that speed.

Having played piano since I was ten, my fingers were limber and my speed was there from the very beginning. So I just knew I would pass the first literary test that was given. 60/80 was taught by Trish, a softly beautiful girl, who was an ex-student, with long, brown, wavy hair. 60/80 was read at a very slow pace, slower than the speed at which normal people talk, but with an untrained brain and fingers it seemed like lightning speed. The literary test was made up of words that you would typically find in a fictional book. The jury charge is a test made up of words that are actually out of a real court case in which a judge has given instructions to a jury before they deliberate, and the testimony test is taken from real trials; civil, criminal, whatever.

I was going along, easily and carefully, taking down the words that Trish was saying for our first literary test, when my nerves hit me. I wanted to pass my first test so badly that my fingers stiffened up, and my writing faltered, and I began to miss words and then fall behind. Marissa was sitting two rows ahead of me, and I knew she possessed nerves of steel, and I didn't want to blow it, but I had.

Seven days later when our tests were handed back, Marissa was the only one who passed. I envied the amazement the girls showed towards her. I couldn't bring myself to be congratulatory. And I grew annoyed and angry when she pretended to be shocked herself that she passed. I missed passing my test by two mistakes. I figured she must have been practicing for hours the night before to be able to pull that off.

I had never been so completely jealous of anyone in all my life. I blamed myself and the self-created competition I had going with her for the reason why my nerves were so bad. Why did I care who was better? Where did this competitive need to be number one come from anyway? It was making my life at school hell. I was putting undue pressure on myself. The one good thing that was to come out of my competition with Marissa was the fact that I did study harder because of her, and although I set unrealistic goals for myself, I was still blowing through school, just not as fast as Marissa. Most people would have been fine with being number two in the class, but it felt like number two hundred to me, because for me there really was no other number but one. Anything else meant I was a failure and had failed.

"Daddy, I'll never get out of 60/80," I said, sniffling, because I was almost near tears.

"Yes, you will, Sydney."

"Nope. I suck."

"Don't say that, Sydney."

"Daddy," I began, like the next thing he could say would solve everything, "tell me I'm going to be a good court reporter, that I'm not just wasting time."

"Sydney, you will be an excellent court reporter, and you will get out of 60/80 probably next week."

"Thanks, Dad."

"Now, can I go to sleep, Sydney? It's almost midnight."

"Oh, yeah, sure. Sorry, Dad."

I would make a hundred or so of the same phone calls to my father before it was over. He was my cheerleader, my sponsor, my rock, and I couldn't get out of court reporting school without him and his reassurance. Without it, I would fail and then die. No, really, I would die. I was afraid of failure more than anything else, because I knew it would kill me. I had so much to prove to myself, to my family, to Jack, to the world, and I carried that weight around with me everywhere I went.

The following week, as my father predicted, I got out of 60/80. I only took a moment to revel in it. Then I prepared myself for the next speed that I would be going to the very next day, which was 100s. 100s was a whole new thing. It was, of course, spoken faster, and there were more girls in the class, with some of them starting months before I had.

The animosity in the room was palpable when I took a seat in the front row. They'd heard about me, been told that I was blowing through school, was a good writer destined to get out before they would. But Marissa had already come and gone out of that class, leaving them behind, and here I was poised to do the same thing.

I couldn't blame them for being annoyed with me. My presence and my talent was a constant reminder of their failure the same way Marissa was a reminder to me of mine. The whole school for that matter was made up of nothing but disappointment and failure. I would fail many more tests than I would pass, and the pain at times from not passing a test was excruciating, the pain of wanting something so badly and not getting it was unbearable.

I would go home and study my fingers off, go back to school, sit for a test, and wait one to two weeks to find out if I'd passed it or not. Tests were normally handed back on Fridays, and we would sit in our chairs, with the anticipation so thick you could reach out and touch it, waiting for the teacher to arrive, to know if we had succeeded or failed. If we got a test handed back, it meant we failed it, because tests that were passes were announced by the teacher at the front of the room.

"Sydney has passed her first literary test in 100s!" the teacher, announced. The girls clapped as I rose to accept my test. I smiled widely as I basked in the perfect sun of my moment.

"Congratulations, Sydney," the teacher said. Those were my favorite words. I brought the test back to my seat, and after looking it over a few minutes, I handed it back and felt like a million bucks for the rest of the day. I'd been in 100s a week and had already passed a test. There were girls in there for over six months who hadn't passed anything. I was the shit. But then there was Marissa. How was I ever going to catch her? She was already in 120s and causing a stir. She passed the first three tests she took and only needed one last testimony test to advance to 140s.

"Stop telling her your secrets if you're mad she's getting out of classes before you," my dad scolded. And he was right. I'd shared my studying technique with Marissa early on, my ego being the size of Texas, and she used it to her advantage. But I was convinced Marissa was studying an extra two hours longer than I was at night.

Marissa was a quiet competitor, whereas it showed all over my face. She always seemed surprised when she passed a test, like she had no clue how it happened. This pissed me off even more. She knew what she was doing, knew she probably wasn't even bathing at night she was studying so hard. I, however, accepted my passes with pride, like I deserved them. Marissa tempered her success with being nice, and she made a lot of friends using this strategy.

While walking out of the school bathroom, which I rarely used because I despised using public rest rooms and made a point to avoid them whenever possible, a lowly student accosted me.

"I just felt like I should tell you there are girls here that don't really like you and think you're a bitch." I'd seen this girl before, a portly blonde, kind of cute. I remembered her name as being strange for a person, like Rainbow or Echo. No, her name was Brownie, I thought. She was one of the students I liked to refer to as a lifer, meaning she would spend the rest of her life trying to get out of court reporting school. She was still in

60/80 class after a year, and why she thought I should care about anything she had to say was a mystery to me. Still, I decided to humor her by giving the conversation my undivided attention.

"Oh, really. So there are girls here who actually don't like me?" I said raising my eyebrows, folding my arms, and looking her directly in the eyes.

"Yeah, you never say hi to anyone. You're always just flying down the halls with this nasty look on your face like you're mad or something. I just thought you'd want to know. I would want someone to tell me," she said.

"Well, Brownie," I began.

"It's Ambrosia."

"Oh, sorry. Well, Ambrosia, you go back and tell those girls that I'm not here to make friends. I'm here to make money. And every single day that I'm still here, I'm kept from doing that. So I couldn't care less what they or anyone else thinks about me, because I'm not going to be here long enough to. Now, is there anything else I can do for you? I mean, would you like some tips on improving your speed?" I asked.

The horrified look on her face told me no. There was a twang that went off inside me at the thought of being disliked. I worried about it for about two seconds before I walked slowly to my next class.

At home, Jack and I continued to function in our underdeveloped marriage. It was early May, and school and Aden all but consumed me. Jack had befriended an unmarried couple, Ramond and Cinnamon, and I didn't care for either one. Ramond had four kids from a previous marriage, ranging in age from three to eleven, and Cinnamon wasn't old enough to have been the mother of any one of them. She and I didn't hit it off very well, but that didn't stop Jack from suggesting that we go to Las Vegas for the weekend. Cinnamon was petite, with sandy blonde hair. I resented how cute she was, wished her nose wasn't so perfectly set between her pretty blue eyes. She was what Jack thought was attractive, and I hated how she subtly flirted with him. I'd been putting up with it since January, when I started court reporting school.

We were on our way to Vegas, while Ramond and Cinnamon and the kids had already made it there. Ramond had booked the rooms and told us he was gambling downstairs and to get our key from Cinnamon, who was in the hotel room with the kids. Jack, Aden, and I made our way to the hotel room and knocked on the door. I stood off to the side while Jack spoke to Cinnamon, who was leaning against the door as if to conceal the rest of her body. I figured we'd caught her at a bad time, and she wasn't able to get properly dressed.

She had a conversation with Jack that began to last a little too long for me, and I grew frustrated and glared at Cinnamon from behind Jack. All we wanted was our key, and all she needed to do was give it to Jack so we could leave. The kids began to congregate in the doorway around her feet, when suddenly one ran out.

"Hey, get back here," Cinnamon called.

"I'll get him," Jack said. As Jack turned to grab the little boy, Cinnamon stepped out from behind the door, revealing the bright-red, lace teddy she was wearing as she came out into the hall. My body boiled with anger at the nerve she had wearing that in front of my husband. The other three kids followed behind her, closing their room door, and it locked behind them. Jack, Aden, the four kids and I, and the trashy slut I wanted to beat down to the ground, all stood in the hallway.

I could see amusement in Jack's face. He was thoroughly enjoying the moment. We all ended up in our hotel room. I didn't bother tying to hide my anger as I looked her up and down, knowing full well what she was trying to do. Jack said he would go down to the casino floor to get another room key from Ramond. I left the room and followed after him into the hallway.

"Hurry up and get that key because I want this tramp out of my room now!" I called after him.

"What is your problem?" Jack said as if he were oblivious as to why I would be so upset. That, and his continued friendship with Ramond and Cinnamon is the reason why I moved out of our home and got an apartment. I told myself that I was on my way to becoming a court reporter, no longer needed Jack, and I could go it alone.

So I filed for divorce, seeking child support and alimony. I was initially awarded four thousand dollars a month. Jack walked out of the courthouse next to me, telling me I'd better watch my back. I thought maybe he really hated me now, and I was glad. I felt vindicated. Bastard, didn't he suspect he'd driven me to it, I thought. Now he was mad because he had to pay up? What a jerk. I don't think I even cried. I was still married to court reporting school anyway, and I couldn't divorce that.

Back at school, I told no one that I was getting divorced and had moved out of my house. I couldn't bear the embarrassment after I had painted such a rosy picture of my home life. I didn't want the minor setback to interfere with my pursuit of becoming a court reporter in the shortest amount of time. Getting a divorce was not going to be some monumental thing with me, it was but a mere speed bump in my life, and when I stood in my brand-new apartment, that is when I was finally able to cry. I was so incredibly thankful to be alive, to have a dream, to be me, to be rid of him that I fell to the empty floor of my living room and thanked God for second chances.

27

And then there was Jade Greene, the queen of second chances, always coming close to ruining your life, and then all of a sudden wanting to be forgiven with her tears, wanting you to give her another chance after she'd just rocked you to the core. Yeah, she was still around. And soon after leaving Jack, I stood at the top of the stairs in her house, listening to her shrill voice. She was arguing with my father. Her tone of voice was enough to make me wish I was someplace else. After a few more minutes of waiting for her to stop yelling, I wanted out of there before I reverted back to arguing with her myself. I hadn't argued with her in a few years, and I didn't think I had it in me after the stress from leaving Jack and being in school. She and I still didn't get along, and I despised the majority of her personality.

I was standing there fixated on a memory from when I was a little girl and I found out my father had high blood pressure. I'd overheard him and my mother talking about it, and I'd watched a TV show where a guy who had high blood pressure got really angry, had a heart attack, and died. So I'd grown up believing whenever they fought there was a chance I could lose my father, because my mom couldn't stop being her awful self for even just one moment.

She will never change, I told myself, standing at the top of the steps, listening to what was going on downstairs. But I didn't live there anymore.

I'm not getting involved. It's time for me to get Aden and go. Yeah, we'll go before I say something she'll regret. Turns out some things don't always go as planned or intended.

"Seneca, get off the phone. I asked you for help fifteen minutes ago. I need you to help me. If you don't get off that phone, I'll..."

My mother was not a person to be kept waiting. My father was on the phone long-distance with a friend, but that didn't stop her.

The eleven steps it would take to get to the bottom seemed like eleven hundred. Each step I took was full of dread. Each word she spoke penetrated my skull, hitting me like an angel dust flashback from my past, and I started to give in to my hallucination. My head pounded and throbbed. I wondered when was there ever a time when she didn't need help? I was remembering how since I was a kid, she'd always needed someone's help, or she was sick, or always talking about how awful her mother was, how mean she had been.

There had always been something wrong with Jade, and I was numb to her problems, her pain, her needs. She was like the boy who cried wolf, and I just couldn't conjure up the energy needed to care anymore. I despised her the most when she needed help. With her perpetual hypochondria, psychiatry appointments, bad-mother stories, to me, she was happiest when simmering in her unhappiness. I wished for once she would just leave my father alone.

When I'd made it to the bottom of the last step, I called for Aden. We were leaving. I didn't want to go into the kitchen where my mother was sparring with my father. I didn't want to see her. I just wanted to grab my keys, grab my kid and go. I remembered just then that minutes before I'd gone upstairs that I'd asked my mother to baby-sit Aden, and I hoped my attempt to take her and leave would go unnoticed. No such luck.

"Aden? Why are you taking Aden?" she screeched, unseen from around the corner just inside the kitchen.

"Mom, because I'm just gonna go. I'm just gonna go," I offered, fraily, picking up my keys, hoping nothing more would come of it.

"You asked me to take care of her, and I'm going to take care of her." By this time, she was in the foyer, in my face, and I couldn't stop the words from coming out of my mouth. They took on a life of their own. Maybe it was years of listening to her yelling and not being able to say exactly enough, always holding back. I'd always gone up to the finish line, but I'd never crossed it. Would I go ahead and cross over the finish line this time? If I did, what would I win? Let the games begin.

"Well, you're in there foaming at the mouth, and I don't want Aden to be a part of it. I waited for you to stop, but you just kept going on and on and on," I fumed.

"Oh, I'm not doing anything. You always take your father's side."

"I'm not taking anyone's side. You're always yelling at him, and maybe he feels like he has to sit here and take it and listen to you, but I don't," I said bitterly.

My mother looked outraged at my disrespect for just a moment before she lunged toward me, grabbing at my shoulders. She spun me around towards the front door. Caught off guard, my body was easy to manipulate. With one hand she opened the door, and used the other hand to shove me out of it.

"Go, then. Just go. Fine. You want to go, go," she said with her teeth clinched as she slammed the door behind me. I turned to face the door, and I stood there for what seemed like eternity, looking at it, noticing the dust build up around the four-square pattern. It had been so long since she'd touched me that she felt like a stranger, and I didn't recognize the hands she used to turn me around and shove me out of the door. They felt like round little sausages pressing into my skin, not the one I'd remembered. Through the force of her grab and shove, I could feel just how angry she really was when she touched me. I was perplexed by her strength.

I could hear nothing as I stood alone out on the porch in front of the door as dust swirled slowly, coming to rest around my ankles. Did she really just shove me out of the door? It was as if I'd just been pushed into Siberia. There was a haunting stillness to my present situation. There weren't any birds singing in the trees. No cars were driving past to make me turn in fear of being seen. There were no children playing, skipping, roller-skating by. The wind seemed to have stopped blowing. Everything was quiet, like in a ghost town.

Time had stood still for me, waiting for me to catch up. Everything looked kaleidoscopic. I felt tears start to fill the bottom crevices of my eyes. They twitched from the saltiness as I blinked them back. A lump welled up in my throat with a burning sensation, and I had trouble swallowing.

In an effort to regain my composure, I took two deep breaths, moved two steps, and reached for the door, not knowing what I'd be encountering. I didn't want her to be there, but I figured she would be. She had successfully intimidated me, and I was afraid of her now. I reached for the doorknob and twisted. I knew, no matter what, I could never strike my own mother.

"I will never come back here again," I announced once inside. My voice quivered, though I was trying to be loud enough for my father, who was still in the kitchen, to hear. As I said it, I'd meant every word. A promise that was made even easier to keep after my mother said, on her way back to the kitchen, that she didn't care whether I came back or not.

By that time Aden was sullenly standing at the door. She followed behind me like a good little soldier. I packed her in the car, kissed her forehead, fastened her seatbelt, and drove off. The houses through my rearview mirror grew smaller and smaller as I got farther and farther away. I took one last look as I rounded the corner. My grasp of the steering wheel was weakened by the flood of tears streaming uncontrollably down my face, as the events that had taken place spun around and around. I suddenly felt tired.

I waited all night for my father to call. He never did. I fell asleep with tears in my eyes, thinking I'd finally crossed over the finish line only to lose to myself. His not calling allowed me to realize for the first time that he wasn't to be the object of something I could win by defending, never should have been, and never will be again.

The next morning I stood in front of my bathroom mirror, smarting over my puffy red eyes. My vanity was unmistakable as I fumed, allowing the anger at my appearance to get the best of me. The irony of yesterday's episode was that today was Mother's Day.

"Mother's Day my ass," I said, frowning at my reflection. "I'm not about to call Jade, and she'd better not call me," I said aloud to my reflection. Just then I felt a burst of wind pass across my calves. Hurricane Aden.

"Happy Mother's Day, Mommy," Aden exclaimed, waving a card she'd made especially for me towards the ceiling. That was enough to instantly transform my scowl into a smile and turn my salty tears to sweet ones, as I pulled Aden into my side.

Later that morning, Jade Greene, who never ceased to amaze me, did have the audacity to call me to say the proverbial Happy Mother's Day. It was not accepted. I showed her just how happy I was by slamming the phone down as if she had been an obscene caller who had just asked me what color panties I was wearing. My day was instantly ruined.

I decided maybe some fresh air would do Aden and me some good, so we left. As we stood in the produce section of the market, squeezing tomatoes, Aden decided to ask a question.

"You don't like your mommy, do you?" Aden asked.

Damn, does it show that much? I was stunned. That was something that I never wanted her to become aware of. My relationship with Aden would be, and was, different. I held Aden tight in my arms and kissed her often, just so she would never question my love. Even at Aden's tender age of seven, I could tell somewhere along the line we had formed a bond, built a connection as mother and daughter.

"No, Mommy does like her," I lied.

"Hey, which of the seven dwarfs do you think is Snow White's favorite and why?" I asked Aden, trying to change the subject.

"Um, I think she just really wants to find her prince," she said.

I glanced down at Aden and smiled. My beautiful child was a realist. So I went about the rest of my afternoon trying to find the reality and the beauty in the things around me. I began to loose the energy to be cynical. I bought chocolate from a couple of raggedy-looking kids standing outside of the grocery store, claiming to be using the proceeds for some summer camp I hadn't heard of. I never even let it enter my mind that it was probably bullshit. I took my cart all the way back to the designated area, something I don't do, and told myself to be thankful for the carts since they probably didn't even have them in places like Beirut. On my way back to the car, I raised my head towards the sunlit sky and let the glow from the sun penetrate my face, nourishing my still recovering eyes. Thank you, sun. Thank you, sky.

The reality of the day was that, for whatever reason, the sun had chosen to shine brightly and reward everyone who ventured out in it with a quiet, unselfish warmth that laid everything beneath it bare. Out in it, I could not cover my scarred heart with a heavy coat or conceal my throbbing head with a beanie. And even though I could not run from yesterday, I could choose to be happy, or I could choose to be sad. It was my choice to make.

Driving beneath a sky so perfectly blue made it easy to choose to be happy. I was fresh out of anger. I didn't have any more tears, and I was mentally exhausted. But I was still hurting from my father's seemingly lack of interest in my state of mind. My heart felt like it had just been through major surgery, had gone into cardiac arrest, been revived, and was now in intensive care. I used the beauty of the day as a painkiller and decided never to underestimate the power of the sun.

The tomatoes were for tacos, which I quickly began to prepare once we got home. As Aden took her last bite, the doorbell rang, followed by a couple knocks on the door. I looked at the door and instinctively knew my father stood on the other side of it. I raised myself from the table without apprehension and walked over to the door, opening it softly, without intention or pride. I told him to come in, using a tone so even he could not place it. He walked through the door and sat on the couch. He did not speak, so I said nothing, forcing him to speak first. And I didn't have to. He had come to me.

"You know you have to go back there," he said, finally.

"Oh, no, I don't," I said as evenly as before.

"Then you won't be able to see me anymore," he said.

"You mean you wouldn't come here to see me, if I don't go there to see you?" I said.

He didn't answer. He sat there staring into my eyes.

"She's my wife," he said after awhile.

"So."

"She gets mad sometimes. You both do. You two always want to put me in the middle," he said.

"You're always in the middle because you refuse to choose a side."

"And what side should that be? Yours?"

"No, that should be the side that is right, whoever that happens to be."

"Look, you have to go back there, and that's all there is to it," he said standing up, walking towards me, wrapping his arms around me, collapsing me into his chest, breaking my will to resist what he wanted.

He still had a power over me. He would wear me down. I knew he would not call or come by. He would wait me out, and he would win. I hated how much I still needed him. His eyes and embrace told me I had his love, but she had his devotion. I couldn't decide which meant more. In his and my relationship he was the strongest, but I knew it wouldn't be long before I was. And one day I wouldn't have to wait a whole day for him to come running. I would make his very survival, his happiness wrapped around mine, and I would use my mother and her craziness to do it. She may have won the battle, but she would not win the war. I wanted every time she looked at him, looking at me, she would know that she may be his wife, but his heart belonged to me.

Two weeks later I walked through the same door I said I never would walk through again, acutely aware that nothing had changed, not her, not him, not me. It had been easier than I thought it would be to go back. After all, my father was there waiting for me. I stepped in, greeted her kindly, and saw my father. Although she remained in the room with us, her presence soon faded from my view and my memory. As fast as the breeze that had been caught behind the door disappeared after it was closed, she just wasn't there anymore.

28

Mr. Randal and I walked out onto the large mat of the studio with the white glow of the sun softly cascading down from the skylights above, the room so quiet we could hear each other breathing. Facing each other, we did the customary bow. I immediately went into my fighting stance, but Mr. Randal had something else in mind.

"Ms. Cassavan, how's school?"

"It's great. I've only got a year to go," I said, standing up straight, bringing my fists to my sides, realizing he wanted to talk.

"I'm so proud of you."

"Thanks," I said.

"You know, you've been working really hard on your belt, and your improvements really show," he said. I'd been taking kung-fu now for almost three years, and we had finally achieved a comfortableness with each other that made us more than teacher and student. We were friends, good friends.

"I'd really like to show you something, but I'm not sure if you can keep a secret."

"Who, me? My middle name is secret. Yeah, I can keep a secret." I was coming out of my skin wondering what it was he was about to share with me.

"Well, I'd like to show you a video of myself when I tested for my brown belt."

"Okay," I said with my heart beginning to beat faster.

"But there's just one thing, the place where I would have to show you."

"That's fine. Where?" I would have followed him up Mount Everest, at that point, I was so enamored.

"My loft."

"Your loft?" I said as if I didn't understand.

"Well, I'll just show you."

I followed Mr. Randal to the back of the studio, past the bench where we'd first met, to an area in front of the ladies' changing room. He took a long stick and poked a square hole in the ceiling that I would have otherwise mistaken for an attic. Then he grabbed a ladder that was resting on a wall nearby and positioned it inside the uncovered hole in the ceiling. I followed him up the ladder, into what I thought would be a dusty old attic. I stood in a room the size of a studio apartment. There was a raised area where a bed was, a couch and television, and a kitchen. I did a few turns around the room and asked him to please explain.

"This is where I lived for a long time, up here, without anyone knowing but me and the owner of the studio."

"Are you kidding me?" I said amazed.

"Sydney, you can't tell anybody. I was never supposed to make this or live here, like this, in this building. We could get shut down if anybody found out," he said.

"No, of course I won't tell anybody," I said plopping myself down on the couch. For the first time he had called me by my first name. And I was trying to ignore it, but I felt as if this was a form of foreplay he was creating with me, and I began to realize the fact that this man really wanted me. Looking around, I could see that he had running water, had laid tile on the floor and counters.

"You did all this yourself?" I asked.

"Yep, I did," he said. He was reminding me of my father, and I began to see another side to him that made him even more attractive. He put in the videotape of his brown belt test, and we watched it together. I was impressed with his performance. He was aggressively strong, talented, and intense. I was convinced he was born to be a kung-fu master, but I knew I hadn't been brought up there just for that. Mr. Randal was sitting next to me, and when the video was over, he turned to me, brought his hand up to my face, and began caressing my cheek. I allowed my head to lean into it, and just as my eyes were falling shut, the phone rang in the studio downstairs. Mr. Randal got up and climbed down the ladder to get it.

I drove home, telling myself someday we would lie next to each other naked, looking deep into each others' eyes. I thought about marrying him and living happily ever after.

I had been separated from Jack for over three months, and we were getting to the point where we were able to carry on a normal conversation. Through it all, through the eight years that had passed, I thought about how we had always been able to laugh together. I couldn't deny that we'd had some good days, and at times we had been able to truly enjoy each others' company.

Jack came into my apartment, and I could tell he was impressed. He never thought I would do anything without him. The look on his face told me he had once again underestimated me. I had dropped ten pounds and was wearing cutoff jeans that highlighted my svelte figure. Out of the corner of my eye, I caught him noticing me. I told myself I obviously was still a weakness, that he had probably been missing the days of touching me, the taste and smoothness of my skin, the curves of my body, the way I made love.

"Would you like to come and get some dinner with me and Aden?"

"No, Jack. But thanks," I told him. Not even if Jesus said it was okay, I thought.

"Oh, come on," Jack pleaded. But I wasn't about to fall into that trap again, wasn't about to sooth my loneliness by becoming dependant upon him, even though I couldn't remember the last time I'd actually had sex.

"Okay. Well, at least will you come with me to take Aden to Disneyland for her birthday?" Jack asked from the window of his brand-new BMW.

"I'll think about it, Jack," I said as I waved good-bye to Aden. We had a court date coming up that very week, and I was growing anxious and worried. My neighbor, who had been through a divorce herself, told me that the money I was getting now would probably be drastically reduced by the time we got back into court and settled things permanently. This sent a shock wave of fear through me, and I panicked. I was counting on living off of my spousal support until the day I got out of court reporting school. I was spoiled, and I didn't want to have to get a job, so I went to Disneyland.

That night Jack and I were making love on the king-size bed in my apartment.

"See, this is why you've always gotten away with everything," Jack groaned into my ear, as he was holding me, while running his hands all over my back, covering my neck with kisses. I was on top of him, moving my hips sensually, in a way I knew would please him the most. My thighs squeezed him tighter and tighter until he screamed. Smiling down at him, I got up and blew him a kiss. Then I turned and couldn't wait to be on the other side of the bathroom door, where I sat on the stool in the dark, quivering, breathing heavy, with my hand covering my mouth to muffle the freakish sound that wanted to pour out of it. I couldn't believe what I'd just done. Until that moment, the moment of our shirts coming off and our bare skin touching, of my lips meeting his, and him being inside me, I had felt far removed from Jack and our so-over-with marriage. Since I'd filed for divorce, his hold over me had diminished, and my desire to be with him had completely vanished.

I couldn't believe we'd just had sex, and I wanted to throw up. I felt dirty, like I had just raped myself, and I hated him. But I hated myself more, because I had just slept with the enemy and taken a million steps backward. It was so wrong I felt like a criminal. My weakness and fear, the fear of not having enough money to get through school, and the thought of my dream disappearing, caused me to run back to him. I was about to graduate from the school of mistakes never learned, and I was at the top of the class. We were back together, but I insisted he not spend the night.

I couldn't bring myself to tell Mr. Randal that I was seeing my soon-to-be ex-husband again. I was afraid he would have us go back to a platonic teacher-and-student relationship. Only when he thought Jack was gone for good had he allowed his feelings for me to become apparent and materialize. I couldn't let us go back to the way we were. I didn't mean to have them both, it just ended up that way. Jack and I agreed to allow the divorce to go through, and we reached a settlement where I would receive three thousand dollars a month total. He had some ridiculous idea of us getting married again, the right way, as he put it, once I finished school, and I said okay, but I still knew where I was headed.

Jack was making more money than ever working for Eastwood Financial, and we found a house we wanted to buy, and waited for it to be built, a thirty-two-hundred-square-foot dream home. There was a winding staircase, office downstairs with a bonus room upstairs, a master suite, with a walk-in closet big enough to be a bedroom, an oval tub and glass shower. There was an extended sitting room inside the master bedroom and a gourmet kitchen. I was in heaven, and I felt like a princess. All I had to do was go to school. What could be simpler?

Jack had convinced me that my credit was too bad and that he would have to buy the house himself and put my name on the title once we were moved in. Still looking up to him, believing he was smarter and knew what was best, and not wanting to have anything go wrong with the purchase of our new house, I let it happen without finding out for myself if what he said was true. Jack bought a house that I was moving into that he would solely own.

29

It was January, and I was in 200s, the qualifying class, the last class that I needed to get out of before I could sit for the state exam, to be a certified shorthand reporter, able to work in court. I had been trying to qualify for the state exam since early December. I set the goal of qualifying on the first test I was given in that class, and I was devastated when it didn't happen. I had only two chances a week to qualify for the state exam, once at noon on Tuesdays and once on Thursdays at five o'clock in the evening. I tried like hell to pass it, but my nerves continued to get in the way. I continued to take kung-fu, beginning my fourth year. It was a good way to blow off steam.

"Sydney, do you want to meet somewhere this weekend?"

I'd been waiting for this day to come, so I answered without hesitation.

"Yeah, where did you have in mind?"

"I don't know. What do you like?"

"I like book stores," I said.

"Okay. Which one?"

"How about the book store on 5th in Ontario?"

"That sounds good. What time?"

"How about six o'clock?" I offered.

"Now, remember, I'm not supposed to be with you, enjoying your company, but I'll meet you here at the studio, and I'll drive us to the book store. Then what do you say we come back here?"

"Great."

I drove home, trying to think up a lie to tell to Jack, to explain my absence on a Sunday evening. A baby shower at a friend's house is what I told him. He didn't have any trouble believing me. I marveled at how easy it was to lie to him now, how easy it was for him to believe me. He didn't question it. And why would he? I'd never lied to him before. I never gave him a reason to believe I ever had cheated or ever would cheat on him. All the way up until the time when I was pulling out of the driveway, I never once felt worry or guilt. And then at the first major stoplight intersection, it hit me that I could actually get caught. I quickly shook it off and decided it was, no, Scott was worth the risk.

I was tired of being good, of being truthful, of being the good wife, of constantly being the one to do the right thing, of always making Jack feel secure. Where had it ever gotten me anyway? He had lied to me over and over, time after time, throughout the years. I wondered why it was that just this once I couldn't completely deceive him, crawl into bed next to him and sleep like a baby. How many times had he done that to me? Was I really someone who could cheat on the man I lived with, that I was divorced from but still mentally married to? Yes, I thought I could.

Scott and I browsed around the bookstore, walking through separate aisles, careful for it not to appear that we were there together. It was funny how even though we were trying to avoid it, we kept bumping into each other. I got a sexual charge each time we met down the same aisle. But we both knew what we wanted, so after about fifteen minutes of the silly charade, we got back into his car and headed for the studio, up the ladder, into the loft.

My hair was long then, reaching to almost the middle of my back. As we relaxed on his bed, Scott pulled off my shirt and moved my hair, putting it to rest to one side over my shoulder. His hands trembled, and he seemed afraid to touch me, like he thought I would break. After he moved my hair, with his hands resting warmly on my shoulders, he leaned forward and left a long, lingering kiss on the nape of my neck that gave me shivers.

"Take off your clothes," I said to him over my shoulder. He complied, removing his shirt, revealing his muscular upper body. I quickly pushed off my pants, and he was, by that time, already out of his. I moved myself in front of him and kissed his chest and moved my hands up and down over his torso, feeling the ripples of his stomach. And then I let myself fall backwards onto the bed and waited for him to enter me, and as he did, it felt as if he were filling my whole body. My face tensed up, my back arched and lifted off the bed, as he pulled me up onto him. My body opened as wide as it could to receive him.

The feeling was exhilarating. I'd never had anything as large inside me, and I was not prepared for what I was getting. His thrusts were amazing, and I could feel his strength penetrate my body. I was startled by how strong he was. This man could break me in two if he wanted. I was so overwhelmed by the size of his penis that I couldn't climax, but I didn't care, he was sending pulsating tingles throughout my body that felt just as good as any orgasm I'd ever had before.

"Oh, my god, you are driving me crazy," I said out of breath. My hands were clawing at the sheets, and I was trying my best to take what he was giving.

"You're driving me crazy, too. I want to come so bad," he said. And I believed him. I must have felt extremely tight he was so large. He came and the whole place shook. He laid beside me for a while, with our chests both heaving up and down simultaneously. He touched my hand, and we looked into each others' eyes as we savored the moment of finally sleeping together. He kissed me outside in the alley where I'd parked my car, and then I left.

I drove home and began to smell the scent of him all over me. I began to shake at the thought of getting caught. Could Jack have totally believed my lie, completely believe at the sight of me that I was coming home from a baby shower and not the fuck of my life?

I pulled into the parking lot of a supermarket a half mile away from home to fix myself up. It was nine o'clock. My hair was a wild, wavy, tangled mess. My body, my clothes, my hair, everything smelled of Scott. His scent was rising up from every pore of my body. I rolled down the window. Then I took out a rag I had stashed in the glove box and tried to wipe the smell away. I pulled into the garage. Jack was downstairs watching TV. I called to him, telling him I was back, and rushed upstairs, turned on the shower, waited for the steam to rise and jumped in.

I couldn't get to the soap fast enough to wash away the unmistakable smell of another man and sex before Jack was in there with me, pushing me forward towards the shower wall, cupping my breasts, and shoving himself inside me from behind. Somehow the feeling just wasn't the same. He was fucking an empty shell. He left the shower within ten minutes and disappeared back downstairs. I felt like the star in someone else's movie. Jack obviously had no idea where I'd been, and it was perfectly apparent I had actually gotten away with cheating on him.

Still, when his hands were firmly latched onto my hips, and he inside me, with every push of his pelvis, it seemed as if he was trying to tell me something, wanted something to remain in the air between us long after he was gone, silently telling me no matter what, I was still his; that he owned me, could plunge himself into me whenever he liked. Deep down I think he must have known, or at least suspected, I had been with another man he came so forceful and fast, like he had something to prove. Maybe he wouldn't allow himself to know.

I let the hot water run over my body for a long time, turning in my head over and over again the events of the evening. I didn't know who I was anymore. Yet the lack of guilt I felt let me know I would never be the same. I could allow myself to lie, to cheat, to be selfish, doing it all without remorse. Was it revenge that I had really been after? Now, was I no better, not different from Jack? I had always thought of myself in the most simplistic of ways, as just a nice girl. I wondered how God was going to make me pay.

30

I woke up one morning in April and I was twenty-nine, realizing that if I were going to reach my goal of becoming a court reporter by the time I was thirty, I would have to get myself in gear and finally pass the qualifier, so I could go to the state exam. I had until June to qualify for the November exam, given in San Francisco. If I didn't pass the qualifier by then, I would have to wait until the following year in May to take it in Los Angeles. I would be thirty-one.

Marissa had already passed the qualifier and was eligible to sit for the exam given in May, which was only one month away. I had watched my chance of qualifying to go to Los Angeles with her evaporate back in December, when I missed the cutoff and did not pass the last qualifier. I blamed it on my being ill, and I had been. Still, the devastation and shame I felt stayed with me. I was forced to watch Marissa live out the life I wanted, as she went to the preparation classes given specifically for the girls going to the State exam. I read the flyers handed out to celebrate her graduating class. The school was giving them a pizza party celebration that I was going to avoid like the plague.

Marissa and I had barely spoken since she qualified. I turned her into just another student that I didn't care to know. And at that point I had wished I'd never known her, never been aware of just how awesome she was. But I would have given a kidney to be standing in her shoes or at least beside her. I couldn't wait for her to be gone, and then I started to think maybe she wouldn't pass the state exam on her first try, maybe she'd be right back at school, with me, waiting another six months to take it again, having to admit to herself that she wasn't that great, not the best, wasn't as good after all.

No, Marissa would pass on her first try. I knew this. She'd gone too far too fast not to. It was written in the stars, her success, so I didn't feel the need to congratulate her when it was announced that she would be going to the state exam. I looked the other way, couldn't congratulate her. My writing faltered, and words jumbled in my head and were unable to flow freely from my brain to my fingertips, my mind clouded with envious thoughts of Marissa.

My mind was finally set free when three months later it was announced that Marissa had passed the state exam. I would never have to see her again, could forget about her, our competition. I was on top now. I felt with Marissa gone I had evolved and was now competing with myself. So when I was approached to put my picture on a board, along with all of the other girls in the qualifying class for the state exam, I readily de-clined. The qualifying class had girls in it who had been trying to qualify for the state exam all year, some even for two and three years. To me, that was not something to be celebrated, something to be excited about. Qualifying for the state exam was not easy, and putting my picture on the wall, letting everyone know that I was trying to qualify was not something I wanted to advertise.

Most of the girls felt it was their rite of passage to finally get their pictures up on that board. Being in the qualifying class for the state exam was just another obstacle in front of me. I was not happy to be in that class. It was something else holding me back. My picture being on that board meant nothing to me, because I was still there, in school, not work-ing in court. I still had work to do. I had to go to the state exam, pass it, and find a job. There my work would end. Where was their picture board for that?

I was told by one of the girls that people thought I felt I was too good to put my picture on the board. I'd said that wasn't true, but it was. It had been true. I did feel I was better than the girls in qualifying, too good to be in the class with all of those girls who couldn't pass out of it.

Those were dark days for me, struggling to go to the state exam, to prove I had what it took to be a real court reporter. Darker still was my relationship with Jack, our many ups and downs, the roller coaster existence we'd led for eight years. I wondered when it all would end. But I didn't have to wonder for too long.

We continued to argue, and he continued to come home late. I displayed my anger by locking the bedroom door when he came home. He'd bang on it, demand that I let him in, but I had left a comforter and his pillow in front of the door. He took to sleeping in the guest bedroom. And one day he came home and told me he was leaving, and I let him.

Then one quiet Thursday night, I passed the qualifier. I typed it up with my hands shaking, because I knew I held in my hand my ticket out. I turned it in and could barely speak I was so choked up, but I would have to wait until the next day, after school, and after I'd already been home to have the final result. I sat on the couch waiting for the call to come through. If I'd passed, the qualifying teacher and the main person I'd offended by declining to have my picture on the board, would be calling me. I jumped when the phone rang.

"Hello," I said steadily.

"Sydney, you passed. You're going to the state exam."

"Thank you," I said and hung up. I immediately called my father.

"Daddy," I gasped, the words weren't quite there I was so overcome with emotion.

"You passed out of qualifying, didn't you?"

"Yeah, I did."

"I knew it," he exclaimed. "Last night at 9:00 I looked at the clock, and I wrote on a piece of paper that you had passed your qualifier and showed it to your mother as proof," he said.

"I finished typing it up at 9:00. Then I turned it in and went home and fell asleep, but I didn't actually find out until just now. And you already knew I'd passed?"

"Yes, I did. Congratulations, sweetie."

"Thank you, Daddy."

And then it hit me, what should have been one of the best moments of my life turned into a sad version of something I wish the impact of I could forget, the feeling I could lose, could shake and remove its indelible memory forever from my brain. But the truth, the reality was inescapable. I was alone, alone in the house after I hung up the phone, surrounded by the emptiness of the air I was struggling to take in. Jack was long gone, moved out, and Aden was spending time with him. I wasn't seeing any other man. I had stopped taking kung-fu lessons, dumping Mr. Randal and kung-fu to concentrate completely on making it to the state exam, had alienated all my friends, consumed with my quest, with my offensive determination and my I-don't-need-anybody attitude.

I sat at the top of the steps, which seemed like the top of a dreary mountain, at the time. I felt queasy staring at the stair steps winding their way down to the bottom. The cordless phone I'd just used to call my dad was still gripped tightly in my hand. If I let it go, my link to the outside world, my father and his words, would be gone. So I sat there for what must have been an hour as the sun went down. And then I was sitting in the dark. The quietness of the house broke my strength and caused my tears to fall, and I, for the first time in a long time, was truly regretful and sorrowful.

I thought about how overrated success is, or maybe I hadn't succeeded at all. All I knew was I felt alone, and it didn't matter that I was done with that school, had overcome all the curves it could throw at me, could finally go to that goddamn state exam. What did it all mean when there wasn't anyone, or even a man, I truly loved there with me to share my success? Jack had been gone for two months, and I'd hardly missed him the first week. It was as if he'd never been there, had never been my lover, never been my friend, never really known me at all, since I was now and had become court reporting. After all, I still had the house, or so I thought.

Two weeks later I got a call from Irma. She worked with Jack, and in the past we'd gone out as couples with her and her boyfriend and some other people. We were only the slightest of friends, but I liked her.

It was early evening, June, in fact, and I was studying for my state exam in November. I would have to learn three hundred vocabulary words, study extensive medical, legal, and English. In addition to that, I would have to keep my writing speed up, 200 words per minute. Every day after school I studied until nine at night. Usually I sat on the steps of the front porch, enjoying the pleasantly warm summer evening and the serenity of my neighborhood and read, while Aden roller-skated in the driveway. She was nine years old, smart, feisty, and determined. It got late, so we headed inside, and that's when the phone rang. I picked it up from inside my bedroom.

"Sydney, this is Irma. Are you sitting down?"

"No," I said, "Should I be?"

"Yes, you should sit down. This is about Jack." There was an urgency in her voice that scared me, a this-is-going-to-be-bad tone that made me think the worst.

"Okay. I'm sitting down on my bed." My heart was pounding in my chest, making a thud that was almost painful. At first I thought Jack was hurt. No, he was dead on the highway. He had always been a speed demon, constantly disregarding the rules of the road. For years I had predicted his death that way. Yeah, he was dead. Oh, no, my God, Jack was dead, I fretted.

"Sydney, Jack got married yesterday," she said. And then I couldn't take another breath. I slid off my bed and slunk down the side of it, my head becoming too heavy for my body to hold up, with the gravity of her words weighing it down.

"Sydney, are you there?" No, I wasn't there. I could only listen as Irma told me Jack had married a freckled-faced blonde woman named Sarah, who worked at Eastwood with her and Jack. They had been carrying on for months, even before Jack had moved out. She said she didn't like Sarah, because she was snobby and wore heavy makeup and JCPenney suits. I pictured this Sarah in my mind, Jack holding her hand, him making love to her. I wondered if she was good in bed, what she thought of his size.

Irma said their Vegas marriage had been announced at the Friday morning meeting. She said there had been a few chuckles that the dubious couple chose to ignore. Everybody at their job knew they must have only known each other for three months and doubted it would last. I was in disbelief. Jack had certainly outdone himself this time. Or had he? After all, I had only known Jack for six months when I married him and in Vegas style also. But that was the capricious mistake of a nineteen-year-old, not something I'd do now at twenty-nine. This woman was twenty-six. What was her excuse?

I phoned my father. He said he'd heard it all now. He was thoroughly amazed. But before we hung up, he assured me, as always, that I would be okay. And then I began to breathe, the first breaths were forced, then easier, and then I could start to figure out what it all was going to mean for me.

I was living in a house Jack was paying for. He was now married to someone else. I had roughly six more months before I would be a real court reporter. Would he continue to pay the mortgage? Would I be forced out, forced to move, to relocate, when I needed to be studying? The exam, my chance, my dream, my way out, I was not going to sit back and watch it all go up in smoke, evaporate. I'd come too far. I couldn't know what Jack had in store for me, but I knew what I had in store for him.

After I was done feeling hurt and betrayed, I got determined. I would not leave that house until I was finished with school. I would watch it burn to the ground first.

"I heard you got married last weekend, Jack," I said coolly when he finally got up the nerve to call.

"Who told you that?" Jack asked, sounding surprised, like I wasn't supposed to find out. "That's not true. I didn't get married."

"Oh, yeah, right. Whatever. Like hell you didn't. Just stop lying, okay? Why have you always been such a fucking liar?"

"Stop cussing at me."

"Go to hell," I said. At that point, I felt as if I could and was ready to say anything to him. "You're so stupid. I mean, how long have you two even known each other, like five minutes?"

"No, we've known each other for three months," he said, like that was some monumental duration of time.

"Well, I understand you wanna be out here marrying anything that moves, and I don't know what you're thinking, but I'm not leaving from this house."

"Then you had better be prepared to pay to stay there."

"No, you listen to me, you sonofabitch, I'm not paying for anything. You are the one who decided to leave, you are the one who decided to marry someone else, and you are the one who is going to fix this. I hope you don't think that I'm going to stand by and watch you move yourself and that sloppy bitch into my house and have me and my child move out. The hell that's going to happen. Sorry."

"Quit screaming at me."

"I'll scream if I want."

"Well, we'll just see then, Syd. Don't push me. Your name isn't exactly on the house, now, is it?" Jack said, making a strong comeback. And he was right. He was the sole owner of the house. I had no rights to it, just the right to live there for the time being only because I was in possession of it.

"The right thing for you to do would be to help pay the mortgage until I get out of school and can pay for it myself," I said.

"But I'm not exactly into doing the right thing, now am I, Syd?"

"Hey, listen, good luck getting me out of here," I said before I slammed the phone down.

The next day while Aden and I were gone, Jack put an eviction notice on the front door. I pulled it off before Aden could read it. I told myself if he wanted a war, I was going to give him one. My anger rose at the thought that Aden could have read the notice, could have found out her own father was trying to kick us out. I called my dad to come over and change the locks. Then I went to see a lawyer.

The lawyer took one look at the notice and said it was invalid since I was not a renter and we had no rental agreement, and we'd been living there as a family. He said Jack could not just decide he wanted me to leave. It was a family law matter. The attorney also said it would take Jack at least six months to get me out, and that was all the time I needed. I smiled broadly and went home, satisfied that I was covered. I couldn't wait for Jack to call again so I could tell him the good news.

"Um, I'm sorry to tell you this, but you know your little eviction notice? Yeah, well, it's not worth the paper it's printed on. Nice try, though. You'll never get me out of here. Never," I said smugly. "You see, Jack, I just became a woman with nothing to lose, and this house will go into foreclosure before you get me out of here."

"Oh, yes, I will get you out of there," Jack said like he already had a plan.

Jack had moved to Rockford Beach with his new bride, into an apartment that was only three hundred dollars less than the mortgage on the house. I didn't think he could afford both places. One, two, three months went by, and he hadn't paid a cent on the mortgage.

I went about my business of studying for the state exam, and when October came, I filed papers to modify the child and spousal support, and I asked for sole use of the house. My attorney told me I would probably win, but that eventually I would probably have to pay the mortgage, which was fine with me. I had fallen in love with the house, and I didn't want to move.

I was in the upstairs den studying when I heard my garage door open. I ran down the stairs to the garage just in time to catch a glimpse of Sarah, Jack's wife, backing out of the driveway with her new SUV. I panicked and almost called the police, but I called my attorney instead. I frantically told him that Jack was trying to take possession of the house, that his wife had opened my garage door with Jack's old garage door opener, and when she found my car inside, she tried to back out of the garage before I could see her. He told me that what Jack was trying to do was illegal and not to worry.

But I did worry. I knew Jack must have been trying to take the house back. I remembered a conversation we'd had the previous week in which he kept asking me when I would be going to the state exam. I lied and said I would be leaving Wednesday, which just so happened to be today. A light came on in my head, and I realized Jack thought I was in San Francisco, and he thought he would seize the opportunity to reclaim the house.

My attorney and I went to court in the afternoon and tried to get a temporary restraining order that would keep Jack away from the property until I could come back from San Francisco. We failed. The judge would not grant the restraining order. And I told everyone who would listen about my fears of Jack's plot to take over the house while I was in San Francisco. All my pleading fell on deaf ears. No one believed he could be that evil, that fucked up, that vile. But I believed, and I knew. Thursday evening before I got on my plane, I asked my mother and father to watch the house for me, that I figured Jack would try to take the house back that Saturday.

Friday afternoon was the day for academic testing at the state exam. I whizzed through English and felt confident that I had passed my test until I walked through the double doors and saw all the long faces, girls rolling on the ground in agony, others being held up by walls and other people while they cried. I wondered how it was that I could feel like I'd passed the test with flying colors when other girls were clearly distraught and felt they had miserably failed. Just before I began to believe I must be crazy, someone saw me and came to my rescue.

"Sydney," Sally began, the one I had offended the most by not wanting my picture on that damn qualifying board said, softly touching my arm, "How did you feel when you first came through those doors?"

"I felt good," I said.

"Then keep that feeling with you," she said.

I went upstairs to my hotel room, threw myself on my queen-sized bed, rolled over, grabbed the phone off the nightstand, wrapping my body in the cord, called room service and ordered myself a great big heaping hot fudge sundae. When it came, the chocolate was oozing out over the dish. I was on cloud nine. I sat in my room, going over flash cards and mentally preparing myself for the next leg of the exam, which covered medical and legal.

I came out of the testing room feeling pretty much the same as I had the first time. I retired upstairs to my room to practice on my machine. Saturday morning at eight a.m. I would take the machine portion of the test, and I fell asleep, exhausted from the stress, around seven p.m. But my dreams were haunted with dark images of things I could not make out enough to describe. I blamed it on the rain pounding against my fourteenth-floor window and the planes overhead, the hotel being situated so close to the airport.

I finally awoke a little after nine p.m., the darkness of the room so dense I almost forgot where I was. I called home, to Montara Valley, to my parents', who were taking care of Aden.

"How is she?" I asked.

"Aden? She's fine. Are you done with your testing?" my mother asked.

"No, Mom, Saturday is the last day. I'll be done sometime in the afternoon, and I'll be back Sunday morning." My mother sounded reserved, careful, like she was avoiding something. I couldn't place her mood.

"You just do your best, honey, and call me when you're done with your test."

"Okay, Mom." I hung up and felt more at ease, like it was okay to finally fall asleep until morning.

I stood in line with about twenty other girls to take the last portion of the test, the machine portion of the state exam. I was mentally kicking myself because I hadn't thought to bring gloves to lock in the heat for my fingers. I told myself I would have to overcome cold fingers; there was no time to worry about what I should have done and hadn't. At that point, I was going to pass that test even if my fingers burst into flames.

We pulled numbers, and my number matched a chair in the middle of the third row. Perfect, I thought. We sat on a platform that allowed us to see over each others' heads with a four-person panel seated directly in front of us. I would have to take down all four voices and be ready when each person spoke. I was intimidated by the faces I had never seen and had no idea how their voices would sound, the rhythm they would carry, the tone, the enunciation.

My machine tumbled to the floor during the five-minute warm-up, and I wanted to die, but it happened so fast I didn't have time to think. I was just happy my paper tray hadn't broken. I picked my machine back up and proceeded to write. It never entered my mind that it could possibly fall again during the actual exam.

The test started. I got nervous for about ten seconds and then a calm glow came over me that felt like a soft-flowing current. I reasoned later it must have been Lachlan and his grace from heaven, reaching out to me, cradling me, helping my fingers glide across the keys, and I wrote smoothly, without hesitation, without concern or worry. I seemed outside myself, like I was somewhere else.

And after taking down the test for five minutes, all that was left was for me to type it up in the typing room filled with a sea of typewriters. The noise in the room from the other girls typing was like a million rattles shaking in my ear. My hands were shaking, too, and I wrinkled my first sheet of typing paper trying to maneuver it into position. I had to pull it out, then a second, then a third after it became unusable from the sweat of my palms.

I knew I had come to the end of the road. I told myself it was important that I calm down. I was not going to lose and be defeated by the test in the typing room. The test could have been lost to me when my paper tray fell, if that was going to happen. I just had to find a way to block out the noise around me and type the sonofabitch up, turn it in, go back to my room, wait for tomorrow to come, go home, and wait another four weeks for my results. I wasn't sure if my effort had been enough to pass, if I hadn't made any major mistakes. I took one last look at my finished test and then down at the typewriter. Touching the keys one last time, I figured they must have been dampened by a thousand tears from girls who knew while typing up the test that they had failed.

I was done around 1:00 in the afternoon, having begun my ordeal at 6:00 a.m. Back in my hotel room, I remembered what my mother had asked me to do when I was all done, so I called her.

"Are you all done?" she asked.

"Yes, Mom, I'm all done."

"Syd, I'm so sorry, but that bastard.... he....."

"Mom, what is it?" I was growing concerned, extremely concerned, because my mother was now beginning to cry, then sob as if someone had been run over by a truck. She couldn't get the words out. I didn't know what to think, so I asked her again,

"Mom, what is it? What's wrong? What happened? Mother, please tell me what happened." And she began to explain to me what had happened while she cried.

"That bastard, he went into the house and he threw out everything that belonged to you and Aden. Aden's toys... I don't know how he could do it, Syd. He even threw Aden's toys out, and some of them are broken. Your pictures were everywhere, some of them are ripped or bent, and he put everything into trash bags. And your poor father, he and Uncle Bunchy had to rent a truck, go over there, and get your things. They worked all night. Jack would only let you have some of your furniture. Your father and Jack almost got into a fistfight in the middle of the street."

I stood in the middle of my hotel room pacing back and forth, listening. I finally screamed into the phone.

"How could you guys let this happen? I told you he was going to do it. I told you. Oh, my God, I told everybody. Nobody would believe me. Nobody would listen. Oh, my God."

"I know, and we are sorry, but I had a doctor's appointment," she pleaded. "We're sorry, but by the time we got to the house, he had a locksmith there. He had a paper showing that he was the sole owner of the house. There was nothing we could do. He got into the house and started bagging up yours and Aden's things. His wife and his mother were all there. He also had two other guys there helping him move out the furniture. I can't believe his mother helped him throw her own grandchild's things out like that. Your father and Uncle Bunchy worked all night collecting your things. They're in storage now. But don't worry, you can stay here. He has moved himself and his wife into the house now."

The horror of what had happened was beginning to sink in. I wanted to believe I was in the middle of a bad dream. I fell to the floor and cried because I knew I would never step foot in my home again, would never walk up the spiral steps I so adored, never cook in the kitchen, or soak in the oval-shaped bathtub. It was over for me. That life was gone. My greatest fear had come true, I was forced to move back home to my mother's, and Jack knew the hell and humiliation he was sending me to when he was thinking up his diabolical plan. I could see his smug smile in my eyes, hear his robust, triumphant laugh in my ear. I hated him now more than ever.

"Mom, how is Aden? Does she know?"

"Yes, she knows what happened, but she's fine. She just wants to see you."

I called the airline and told them I had an emergency, and they allowed me to take the next Saturday evening flight home without an extra fees. It was leaving in an hour. I sat in the back of the plane, losing my battle to keep from crying in front of the few people awake on the flight. It was raining, and the plane was shaking from turbulence. I couldn't control my fear. I kept thinking the plane was going to crash. The turbulence, the swaying movement, was unsettling. When the turbulence stopped, it seemed like the plane was speeding up, then slowing down, then speeding up again. I couldn't take the sensation. I was convinced we were in trouble and about to crash, so I called to the flight attendant.

"Um, Miss, please, is everything all right with the plane?"

"Yes, everything is all right," she responded carefully.

"Yes, but are you sure? I mean, it feels so weird, like we're not flying right."

"Yes, I can assure you that everything is all right, okay. Try to relax. We'll be there soon." But that wasn't enough for me, so I pleaded again.

"Ma'am, are you sure? I think something's wrong."

"Everything is all right, really." But I wasn't all right. I was about to have a nervous breakdown. I needed some proof, not some blow-me-off response, not the worthless words I was getting. I was afraid I was beginning to look unstable to some of the people on the plane. I worried that if I kept it up and asked again, a couple of flight attendants would dart back to where I was, and while one held me down the other would stick a needle in my arm, filling my veins with some strange liquid, placing me in a twilight sleep, having me wake up in some padded cell. So I decided to pray to God for the plane to stop making me crazy and for a safe landing. I got both.

For days all I could do was visualize Jack, and his wife, and his mother, and two men I did not know and their hands touching personal items that belonged to me. I wondered what his wife, who I'd heard was a bit chunky and had a fat butt thought when she took my size fours down from the rack in my walk-in closet, when she saw my huge box of sexy lingerie that was obviously bought for Jack, when she noticed from my shopping bags that I went to only the expensive stores. I hoped she had been overcome with jealousy. And then I envisioned her callously stuffing it all into garbage bags.

And Jack's mother, how pleased she must have been with it all. One day she'd come by the house not long after Jack had moved out. She was so envious that I lived there she could hardly breath, couldn't even say something nice, couldn't even bring herself to look around upstairs. She left after only seeing the living and dining rooms. And I'd said to myself, can't be happy for me, well, then bye, bitch, and slammed the door behind her. What, I didn't deserve to live in a nice home? I had certainly paid my dues, had fucked her son for nine long years, delivered a beautiful grandchild for her to love that she had now betrayed. Hell, I deserved it all after everything I'd endured.

But there I was on the floor of a room that had gone through as many changes as I had, first belonging to me, then transformed into a den, then becoming my nephew's room, and finally serving as a guest bedroom that I now called home, and I couldn't move myself to get off its floor. The only time I left the sanctuary of the room was to take Aden to and from school. All day long I sat there staring at the sports-theme wallpaper my mother had placed on two of the four walls, counting the footballs, soccer balls, and baseballs, bats, and jerseys. I couldn't eat, couldn't sleep, couldn't function. I wallowed in self-pity, feeling sorry for myself, grieving for what I no longer had.

Most days the pain was almost too much for me to bear. I cried all the time, feeling defeated, so low and humiliated, embarrassed living at my parents' house while I was approaching, no, speeding towards turning 30. The worse was wanting revenge with no way to get it. I thought of Jack and his wife often and told myself they would get theirs. His mother too. But believing that wasn't making me feel any better. The three of them tied together, roasting on a stake would have worked. A week went by, and one day my father burst into the room, looked down at me and said,

"Enough already. Your mother and I know you're sad, but you've got to get up, get out of this room, and get going again. Now, you've grieved long enough. It's time to get on with things. You have to believe you'll get your life back again."

I did not respond, did not look his way, my eyes were dry but almost swollen shut, itchy and aching from when I had been crying. My father's words could not reach me; my grief was too dense and had taken ahold of me and wasn't letting go. I wondered what right he had telling me I'd been sad long enough, when half my shit was still sitting in heavy-duty garbage bags and the other half in one of his friend's garages, collecting dust and bugs. I sat on the floor pissed off at him the rest of the day.

When I finally ventured downstairs that evening to the kitchen for some water, my father was cooking his signature creation, pasta and chicken with a secret white sauce he thought up. Its aroma was intoxicating.

"Come here," my father began, turning away from the stove, "I want to talk to you." I put my hip against the counter to hold myself up and folded my arms across my chest. This time my wounded brown eyes met his.

"This too shall pass," he said softly. "You will get over this and be okay. You are a strong girl who has been hit with a devastating blow, but you can't let Jack knock you out and keep you down. You staying down is exactly what he wants. Then he'll feel like he's won, and you can't let him win. It's time to get up, Sydney. Sweetheart.... baby, get up."

Looking into my father's eyes, I knew why I had avoided them before. They always had the power to make me believe. I stood there crying in front of him as his Rocky speech breathed new life into my slumped, defeated body, knowing every bit of what he'd said to be true. I stood up straighter, felt better, and prepared to fight back.

And then a letter was delivered into my parents' mailbox from the California Board of Court Reporters, deep into December, just a couple days before Christmas. They had impeccable timing. I was out hunting for an apartment, and my father called me on my cell phone.

"Your letter just came," he said.

"What!" I said, swerving in my lane, unable to keep my car steady. "Oh, my God. Okay. Dad, just put the letter on my dresser, and I'll open it when I get there. No, I can't do that, because what if I didn't pass? It will ruin my Christmas. I'll wait until after Christmas to open it."

"Sydney, you passed."

"You don't know that for sure."

"Yes, I do. I opened the letter, and it said you passed, you know, congratulations, you have passed the state exam, blah, blah, blah."

"You mean, you opened it already? Dad, how could you do that to me?" I said growing annoyed. "I can't believe you deprived me of my moment. It wasn't yours to open. How could you...."

"Are you kidding me? Not mine to open? Do you remember all the whining you did, all those middle-of-the-night phone calls, the worrying you did, all the, 'Dad, I can't get out of this class. Dad, I can't get out of that class?' Well, I may not have enrolled in that school, but I should have been, because I sure was there. And you were not going to sit this piece of paper on your dresser and drive me crazy until after Christmas whining, 'Dad, do you think I passed? Dad, should I open it?' So I opened it. And I don't care."

And all at once memories of those days came flooding back to my mind. What a wonderful, loving, caring father I had, couldn't have asked for better. He had been there with me, for three years, every day, believing in me. His spirit had gone with me to the test in San Francisco. His words, "Just remember that it's not over until it's over," were burned on my brain while I took my tests, keeping me from getting too cocky. The way he'd raised me, telling me I could be anything I wanted, because I was just as good as anyone else, never give up, to have pride and dignity, to know what I'm worth, were there too. I owed everything to him.

"You're right, Dad. And I'm sorry. But what in the world would you have done if I hadn't passed? How were you going to tell me?"

"There was never a doubt in my mind that you weren't going to pass that test."

My father's never-ending belief, his faith in me, I would live on it forever. It gave me the strength to carry on, to believe I could do anything because I was Seneca's kid. But I was Jade's kid too, and for many years I failed to acknowledge that. I had used my dad as a father and a mother, telling myself he could be both, always leaning on him for support. None of my desperate calls had ever been placed to my mother. She had been reserved, put on ice for nothing, to be used never.

But she had insisted on being the one to break the awful news to me in San Francisco, had cried for me, had been angered and devastated as if it had been she who had been wronged, and that fact was hard to ignore. Still, when I would gaze upon her from afar, unable to recognize who she truly was, she continued to remind me of what it was like to walk into a fog. No matter how hard I tried, I just couldn't see her. And during the solitary nights when I couldn't sleep, in the quietness from the stillness of it being 3:00 in the morning, she was what haunted me and haunted my thoughts. Our past, the years she'd done so much damage, it was still there, still a wound left unhealed, lying underneath a Band-Aid.

I wondered if she deserved my forgiveness, my trust and ultimately my love. I figured, if anything, maybe she deserved another chance, even though history had proved she probably would screw it up. But I decided to accept the truth, setting myself free of it, and resign myself to the fact that sometimes I don't love my mother, and my marred relationship with her was something that would probably never change, would continue to ebb and flow like the tide. I just knew it would no longer consume me, I would no longer allow it to define who I was, and I would move past it.

But I couldn't move past hating Jack. I still longed for revenge. I shocked myself with the evil things I sometimes wished would happen to him. Every day I thought about how much I wanted to make him pay for what he'd done to me and my child.

I picked Aden up from school and told her the good news, that her mommy was now a real court reporter, that our life was about to get better. It was amazing to me how resilient she was, how quickly she'd gotten over all the bad stuff with me and her father, how fast she'd adapted to our new life. I wondered if one day she wouldn't have a story to tell, an ax to grind, a grievance to share, a wound I gave that never healed, what story I had given to her.

One night my father told me that all the hate I had bottled up inside me for Jack would kill me if I didn't let go of it.

"But I don't know what else to do. I don't know how to stop, and I despise him so much," I pleaded.

"But remember what God said, 'Vengeance is mine.'"

A year later I was on the freeway, flying through the desert towards a sun so brilliantly bright it made half the sky look like it set on fire, on my way to Palm Springs, with the radio blasting, my body swishing and swaying to the sounds of the smooth jazz I was listening to. I was working in superior court. My parents had moved out of their house, into something bigger and brand-new, and I was now renting their old house, the house I once ran from so many years before that now served as my refuge. I was healthy, happy. Aden was healthy, happy, thriving, and our life was good.

I had heard through the grapevine that the house Jack threw me out of had been repossessed, that his second wife had left him; he was unemployed and being sued by Eastwood, accused of stealing some software program they had invented. He was now driving a funky old, beat-up Chevy, living in a small rented house with his mother in a rundown area of Bayside. I chuckled when I heard the story, because once again my father had been right. All the time I'd spent wishing Jack harm, what a waste. Funny thing was it seemed as if it had all happened many light-years ago. I thought about how far I'd come after being so far away and behind and how none of it mattered anymore because I couldn't remember anything before that very moment.

Soon after, someone at work asked me one of those trivia questions we all love, "If you could change anything at all about your life what would it be?" My reply was unequivocal.

"I wouldn't change a thing."

But deep within myself it was Lachlan's death I would indeed change, if I could. The pieces of his life I remember, of not understanding his death and why, are like torn apart, fading photographs floating around in my mind. Watching him taught me how so completely thrilled with myself I should be, and so to this day I am. I'm living the life of two people, with glory, with guts, with gusto!

www.ingramcontent.com/pod-product-compliance
Lightning Source LLC
Chambersburg PA
CBHW070603130626
46556CB00001B/264